PRAISE FOR

"Curran's debut is a fast and funny mind-bending trip. The potentially confusing concept of shifting is nicely handled, and the mystery's reveal is tantalizing. Realistic British teens and a couple of completely creepy villains make this sci-fi thriller a must for genre fans."
Kirkus Reviews

"Well constructed, sharply written and full of surprises."
SFX

"I loved the main character and the ideas behind the book and am thoroughly hoping that I won't have to wait too long for another instalment of what promises to be a fab series."
The Overflowing Library

"*Shift* is the type of debut that Curran should be exceedingly proud of."
Iceberg Ink

"*Shift* is ingenious: what if every decision was malleable, every regret an opportunity? In her debut novel, Kim Curran handles these mind-bending concepts with a deft hand, showing us she is truly a bold new talent to watch"
Adam Christopher, author of Empire State

"It's slick and quick with just the right amount of squick, and the central premise unfolds satisfyingly."
Tom Pollock, author of The City's Son

"Shift is exciting, funny, clever, scary, captivating, and – most importantly – really, really awesome."
James Smythe, author of The Testimony *and* The Explorer

KIM CURRAN

CONTROL

STRANGE CHEMISTRY

An Angry Robot imprint
and a member of the Osprey Group

Lace Market House	4301 21st St, Ste 220B,
54-56 High Pavement	Long Island City
Nottingham NG1 1HW	NY 11101
UK	USA

www.strangechemistrybooks.com
Strange Chemistry #13

A Strange Chemistry paperback original 2013

ISBN 978 1 90884 416 3
Ebook ISBN 978 1 90884 417 0

For Mum and Dad,
who taught me to never give up
on a dream.

CHAPTER ONE

Another heavy drop of rain fell down the back of my neck and dribbled all the way down my spine. I zipped my hoodie up and shrugged, trying to keep the wet out. I don't know why I was bothering. I was already soaked through and shivering. It was two in the morning. I'd been standing here, leaning up against a grubby wall, watching the rear exit of a seedy bar somewhere in Manchester for an hour. And it had been raining hard for the last twenty minutes.

The bar door opened and I leaned forward to try and see who was coming. A bearded man staggered out as if he was walking on the deck of a ship at sea, bouncing from the doorway to the bins. He propped himself up against the wall and promptly threw up into the gutter. He wiped his beard with the back of his hand and wove his way back into the bar.

"He's not coming. Can we just go?" I moaned.

"Not yet," said Aubrey, for what was probably the tenth time. She was huddled under a small outcrop of concrete and seemed to be avoiding the rain all together.

Her hair was still perfectly dishevelled and her dark make-up untouched. I watched her watch the door and smiled. I still couldn't believe that this girl, the Girl, Aubrey Jones, was my girlfriend, even after six months of getting to know me.

A crack of light appeared in the door way and I tore my eyes away from Aubrey to look back at the bar. Maybe this time.

The door took the longest time to open as if whoever was behind it was teasing us. Eventually, a heavy-set man wearing a pale blue T-shirt emerged. He pulled out a cigarette and tried three times to light it with a glinting zippo. It caught on the fourth attempt. He inhaled a lungful of smoke, sneered up at the grey sky and suddenly he was wearing a black bomber jacket.

He'd Shifted.

"Got 'im," Aubrey said.

Adults weren't meant to be able to Shift – to undo their decisions. It was supposed to be a power that only kids like Aubrey and I possessed; a weird ability that allowed us to go back over our choices and take alternative paths. I'd only learned I was a Shifter a year ago, when Aubrey found me lying at the bottom of an electricity pylon, looking pathetic and confused. Instead of arresting me for Shifting without a licence, she'd taken pity on me and explained the whole crazy thing. After that, my life got increasingly complicated. I killed my little sister, brought her back again, joined a top secret government division, almost got eaten – twice – and finally, uncovered the evil plans of a mad scientist to give the Shifting power back to a handful of adults. Project Ganymede.

There had been side effects. Going insane and trying to kill people was one of them. Not something ARES – the Agency for the Regulation and Evaluation of Shifters – approved of when the Shifters were children. And something they were especially not keen on when the Shifters were adults who'd been the result of a top-secret experiment ARES was doing its best to cover up. "Containment" had become the word of the hour.

Which is why Aubrey and I had been ordered to track these adult Shifters down and bring them in. Dead or alive, it didn't matter to the new boss. Whatever it took to stop the word getting out.

The man we were watching would be number seven. If our information was right, he was up to his thick neck in underground cage fighting.

"Shall we take him down now?" I said.

"No. Let him lead us to the fight. See if there are any other rogue Shifters involved," Aubrey said.

Number seven – whose real name was Jack Glenn – finished his cigarette and stubbed it out on the wall. He immediately lit up a fresh one and stepped out into the rain. We waited for a few moments, then followed.

Glenn led us down increasingly tight and more pungent alleyways, his cigarette smoke leaving an easy trail to follow. Aubrey sniffed at it, like a cartoon character following the smell of roast chicken.

"What are you doing?" I hissed.

"I haven't had a cigarette in three weeks, thanks to you!" she hissed back.

"Watch out!"

I pulled us both behind a black crate. But it was too late.

"Oi!" Glenn shouted out. I heard his footsteps stop and head towards us.

"Do you want to do the honours?" Aubrey asked.

I closed my eyes, focusing on the decision I'd made thirty seconds. I'd deliberately considered waiting a little longer before following him down the alleyway. And now I was about to make that choice a reality with a simple Shift. My stomach lurched slightly and Aubrey and I were still crouching at the mouth of the alley, while Glenn strode out the other end, oblivious to our presence once again.

He led us to the canal that cut through the east of the City, which had once, according to a tourist leaflet I'd picked up because it came with a map, been the industrial heart of Manchester. Now, it had been transformed into yet another place hoping to attract bright young business executives. Glass and chrome blocks of flats stood dark and empty, and large, plastic signs offering penthouse accommodation for reasonable prices flapped in the wind. The place was deserted.

Up ahead, on the other side of the canal, a glow of light came from an abandoned boatyard. A trickle of burly men was making their way inside. Glenn was heading that way too.

"Looks like we've found tonight's fight."

"Just don't let there be dogs," Aubrey said, chewing on her bottom lip.

We'd seen some unlicensed Shifter fighting last month when we'd raided a gypsy camp on a tip that number four was hiding out there. Turns out he wasn't. But we did find kids as young as ten being forced to go up against each other while adults looked on and placed bets. One boy we took in had been put in a ring with a pit bull. It hadn't been pretty. Aubrey had suggested we give the men a taste of their own medicine, although she'd said it wouldn't have been fair on the dogs. No animal should be forced to eat anything as foul as them.

We'd brought some cadets along on the raid for training. Including CP Finn, my old ARES classmate. That had turned out to be a very bad idea. Being from a gypsy family herself, CP had not taken the whole set-up well. In fact, she'd gone crazy and knocked out three of the men. She kept screaming about family and how these people weren't true gypsies. That true gypsies would never hurt their own. I'd had to throw her over my shoulder and carry her back to the van before she could hurt anyone else. For a tiny thing, CP sure could cause a lot of damage.

Glenn crossed over the bridge and entered the yard, pausing to talk to the huge man on the door. The two were in deep conversation. Now was our chance.

I looked left and right, checking that no one was coming, then darted out from the alleyway and towards the water's edge.

As we approached, I saw the bridge was just planks of wood hammered together to form a temporary crossing. I hesitantly placed a foot on the plank and tested the weight. The wood creaked.

"Come on," Aubrey said, simply running across without worrying.

I followed her with less enthusiasm, slipping on one of the planks and almost ending up in the canal. As I gratefully jumped off the bridge and onto the safety of the concrete on the other side, I saw two men walking towards us. The first had a shaved head that revealed intricate tattoos inked onto his skull. The other was small, slim and wore a tatty suit jacket that might have once been expensive. I gasped and looked around for a hiding place. I was about to Shift when Aubrey grabbed me by my collar and pushed me up against the boat yard wall. I banged my head and was about to complain when her lips silenced me.

I still hadn't got used to kissing Aubrey Jones. Even though we'd been doing it a lot lately. Each time her lips pressed against mine, I felt my heart pound and my stomach do weird things. It felt a bit like Shifting. And once, I'd got so confused, I Shifted and I found myself back in my bedroom.

"My money is on the Beast tonight," I just about heard one man say as they passed us.

"Nah, no one's beat Bonecrusher yet. I'm putting a monkey on him," another voice said. And I wondered, dumbly, if monkeys were fighting too.

Aubrey broke away and looked up at me, her expression soft and slightly dazed. I loved this moment. The seconds between the kiss and when Aubrey's defences went back up, when I got to see the real her.

"Hello, you," I said.

"Hello, yourself," she said back.

There was a loud bang from our left and the moment was gone. Aubrey was back on the job.

"So, standard procedure?" she said, leaning around the edge of the wall to watch the two men approach the bouncer.

"You mean start with Plan A and work our way through to Z?"

"One of them's bound to work," Aubrey said. She turned to me and smiled. The smile she knew meant I would do absolutely anything she said.

We headed for the large doors, trying to blend in with the straggle of men milling about the entrance. Some glanced at us through tight eyes. Most simply ignored us. We were just another couple of feral kids come to see the fun after all. I could already hear cheering and chanting coming from inside.

Just as we were about to enter, a large hand landed on my shoulder.

"Where do you think you're going, sonny Jim?"

I looked up at the bouncer. And up. He was at least six foot eight and built like a truck. I mumbled, trying to think of something to say.

That was Plan A – just walk in – down. Time for Plan B.

"We're here to see our dad fight," Aubrey said, in her best little-girl voice.

"Oh yeah? And what's your daddy's name, sweetheart?"

"The Beast," she said.

The huge man hesitated for a moment. "The Beast doesn't have any kids."

"None that he told you about," I said, trying to shake off his grip.

"Well, I think he'd tell me that kind of thing," he said. "He's my boyfriend, after all."

Well Plan B was a dead end too. I looked at Aubrey, but she didn't need telling. She Shifted.

This time she had slipped her jacket off her shoulder and told him she was here as "the entertainment". The guy was still laughing.

I rolled my eyes. Aubrey's Lolita shtick wasn't going to work on this guy. Not when he went for muscle-bound men called the Beast. This was the problem with Aubrey forgetting previous realities so quickly and the problem with Shifting in general. It's not time travel. You couldn't just pop back, tap your past self on the shoulder and say: "Hey, you know what you need to do to get around this guy?" You didn't find yourself back in the situation suddenly armed with everything you know from the future. I wish. It was so much trickier than that. You could only ever change a genuine choice, a real decision you had seriously considered at that time. That's if you could remember it. And once the change was made, Shifters forgot there had ever been an alternative. Most Shifters anyway.

At this rate we could be here all night. I decided to take charge.

I Shifted and instead of bothering with sneaking or lying our way in, I went for the direct approach: punching him in his face. He was now on his knees holding a bloody nose.

"I'm here to fight," I said.

The bouncer looked up at me. I thought he was about to return the blow. A couple of men behind us had laughed when he'd gone down so easily and his face was burning more with embarrassment than pain. Then he seemed to change his mind. He got to his feet slowly and looked me up and down.

"We'll give you a fight," he said, his numb nose muffling his words. "Joey," he called through the doors, not taking his eyes off me.

A moment later a slim, blonde woman, dressed in a

leather jacket and leopard print leggings, came out. "What now, Dave?"

"This kid wants a fight. Put him in with Bonecrusher," the bouncer called Dave said.

The woman laughed and then noticed Dave's broken nose. She turned back to me. "You did that, kid?"

"Like I said," I said. "I'm here to fight."

She looked from me to Dave and then laughed again: a hoarse, dirty laugh. "You got balls, boy. I'll give you that." She slapped her hand on my back and grabbed a fist full of my jacket. "Whether you still have them by the end of the fight, well, that remains to be seen."

She pushed me ahead of her through the doors.

"You should have let me try my Lolita routine," Aubrey said, as we entered the darkened warehouse.

"You did. It didn't work."

Aubrey looked offended for a second and then was distracted by a loud roar from inside.

A crowd of men was gathered around what I assumed was a boxing ring, although it looked more like a cage. A scrawny man clung to the chain-link fence, blood flowing freely from his mouth. He slowly slid down the fence and collapsed in an unconscious heap on the floor. A bell sounded and the crowd cheered as he was dragged out by one leg.

The man standing in the ring, his fists raised, drinking in the applause, was none other than Jack Glenn. Bonecrusher himself.

It made me sick looking at him, bouncing up and down as the crowd cheered his name. Sure he was huge and had fists bigger than most men's heads. But that wasn't why he was winning all these fights. He was winning them because he was cheating. And he was able to cheat because a Shifter kid somewhere had had their brain sliced open as a part of Project Ganymede. And I was about to put an end to it.

Joey dragged us through the crowd and towards the ring. She stopped in front of a man so short he had to stand on a tea crate to be eye height with the rest of the spectators. He wore a tiny, brown hat perched on the side of his head and was smoking a cigar so massive it looked ridiculous in his tiny hands. Joey spoke in the dwarf's ear and pointed at us. He had pretty much the same reaction as Joey. He threw his head back and laughed. Then Joey pointed to the exit where Dave was standing, his arms firmly crossed. His nose was swollen and purple already. The dwarf laughed even harder this time. So hard that I thought he was going to fall off his crate.

"Are you sure about this?" Aubrey said, looking up at Glenn, who was now doing chin ups from a bar running across the top of the cage. She looked cute when she was concerned, with that small wrinkle between her eyebrows I'd come to adore.

"I'm never sure about anything, Aubrey."

The dwarf calmed down enough to beckon me over.

"What's your name, kid?" he shouted.

"Scott. Scott Tyler."

"Oh, dear, no. That will never do. We can't have you going up against Bonecrusher with a weak name like that."

"His friends call him the Pylon," Aubrey chipped in.

"The Pylon, hey?" He looked me up and down. "You are kinda lanky. OK, the Pylon it is." He cleared his throat and reached for a microphone hanging over his head. "And next into the ring," his voice boomed over the sound

of the crowd, "to face the invincible, thirty-six-time unde-
feated Bonecrusher, a newcomer who has everything to
prove and a long way to climb. It's… the Pylon."

The crowd booed and jeered at my name. Some of
them threw half-full cans at the cage, drenching me in
warm beer. At least, I hoped it was beer.

"Well, go on kid, get in the ring," the dwarf said. "We
don't have all night."

I clambered up the stacked boxes that served as steps,
ignoring the pool of blood from the previous contender.
The booing turned into laughter when I entered the
ring. I slipped off my jacket, pulled my T-shirt over my
head and threw them to Aubrey.

"Go get 'em, Pylon," she said and winked. The cage
door was shut behind me.

I looked out at the crowd. They were already betting
furiously on just how quickly I would go down.

I faced Bonecrusher for the first time. Up close he was
even more terrifying. His hair was shaved close to his
scalp, revealing a crisscross of white scars. But the scar
on his forehead was the deepest of all. The scar that
gave him away as a beneficiary of Ganymede.

He looked me up and down, as if wondering whether
I was going to be worth his while. Then shrugged and
stretched his neck. It cracked loudly.

"I don't know what you got to prove, boyo," he said,
spitting on the floor of the cage. "But I'll try and make
this as quick as possible."

I just smiled.

The dwarf rang his bell and the fight began.

CHAPTER TWO

Glenn strode towards me, not even bothering to put his fists up, and lazily aimed a punch for my head.

I waited till the very last second and then side stepped it with ease. The momentum sent him staggering forward a few steps. He righted himself and looked a little shaken.

And that's when the real fun and games began.

He half closed his eyes and dropped his head back, as if enjoying the feeling of a gentle breeze on his face. Everyone had a different way of bringing on a Shift. Some squinted. Others stared into the distance. This was his way.

I started to count down from ten.

Eight. He opened his eyes and looked around, startled. Then shook his head and tried again.

Six. This time, he scrunched his face up in concentration so much his eyes disappeared beneath his Neanderthal brow. He was starting to look constipated.

Three. His eyes snapped open and he staggered back, looking shocked and, I was pleased to notice, a little scared.

One.

"What the...?"

"Scott Tyler, Fixer, Third Class, *boyo*," I said. "Which means: you're Fixed."

I wish I'd had a camera to take a picture of the expression on his face. It was priceless. It went from fear to confusion, to shock, to fear again and then settled on anger. He looked as if he was having a fit. All because I was stopping him from undoing his decisions. Fixing was a power only a few Shifters had. It meant we could stop other Shifters from undoing their decisions, because our willpower was stronger. I didn't usually like using the power, because it made me feel like a kind of psychic bully. But today, looking at Glenn's face, it was worth it.

He went bright red and breathed out of his nostrils, like a bull ready to attack. This was not the fight he had been expecting.

"Jack Glenn, as empowered by ARES I hereby charge you with–" He didn't let me finish.

He charged, clearing the space between us in two long strides. He was so fast I had to Shift in order to flip over his back and out of the way, and he went crashing into the fence behind me.

The crowd booed their dissatisfaction. They'd paid to see men beat each other into a bloody pulp, not jump around.

Glenn pushed himself away from the fence and roared at the crowd to shut up, before turning back to me.

Now he knew what he was up against, he was going to be more cautious. He raised both fists under his chin and came at me, bouncing left and right, his head twitching as he watched for any coming attacks.

He faked low and punched high. I blocked the blow aimed for my left cheek and countered with a punch to his throat. I was a good Shifter. Maybe a great one, if the rumours I heard at ARES were to believed. But I was also a bit handy when it came to martial arts. A black belt in kickboxing, not to mention a year of training at ARES. Bonecrusher was finally going to get a fair fight.

Glenn choked, unable to breathe, yet still managed to flail at me, trying to grapple me around the head. I easily spun out of the way and finished with a back kick to his thigh that drove him down onto one knee. He must have become so used to going up against drunks and washed-up fighters he'd forgotten the basics. Well, I was about to give him a refresher course.

He stood up, clutching at his throat and dragging his back foot slightly. I saw him clench his jaw trying to fight back the pain. I'd give him one thing: he wasn't a quitter.

Glenn came at me again, throwing out rapid-fire jabs. I only just managed to dodge the blows as his anvil fists brushed the hair on the side of my head.

I didn't see the sidekick and for a moment all I knew was white-hot pain exploding from my knee. I managed to focus enough to Shift and the pain vanished. This time I managed to grab his foot before it connected. I held it as Glenn and I looked at each other. His eyes begged me to let him go. But the echo of the pain tingled like an image afterburn and I wasn't in a forgiving mood. I twisted his foot. He went spinning around and landed heavily on the floor.

"Just give up," I said. "This is one fight you're not going to win."

The crowd started to cheer again, but I couldn't work

out what they were saying. Even if I managed to persuade Glenn to come with me, I might have them to contend with. I looked out of the cage, trying to find Aubrey to check she was OK. I found her jumping up and down, shadow boxing and looking like she was having a great time. Alright for some, I thought.

I didn't see Glenn get to his feet and before I knew it, he'd grabbed me in a headlock and was squeezing hard. I thought about Shifting, then decided I wanted to settle this the old-fashioned way. I pressed against his face with my left hand, while punching his knee with my right. Sergeant Cain had called that move the "back breaker". Glenn cried out and let go. He staggered back, gasping for breath, his face now the colour of beetroot. Time to end this. I aimed a punch straight for his groin. I wasn't that old-fashioned.

He doubled over, making little gurgling noises. I spun on my back heel, flipping my foot around in a roundhouse, which connected with his jaw. Spittle and blood sprayed across the floor of the cage as Bonecrusher toppled.

The crowd went suddenly silent. Men who had bet sure money on me going down in five seconds now stared open mouthed, dirty bank notes clutched in their hands. I wondered if they would all turn on me, pissed that I'd lost them money. But slowly they started to clap and then cheer and finally whoop.

The dwarf reached for his microphone again. "Unbelievable! A first time contender takes down Bonecrusher in..." he checked his watch. "In one minute and thirty six seconds. Let's hear it for the electrifying... Pylon!"

The cheers grew louder and a chanted started up.

"Pylon. Pylon. Pylon."

I raised my hands in victory and turned in circles.

"Hey, Rocky," Aubrey shouted up. I snapped out of my reverie to see her pointing behind me. I turned to see Glenn making a swift exit out of the cage and through the crowd.

I chased after him, but my way was blocked by people patting me on the back and trying to shake my hand.

"You got something, kid. You could make some big money. Stick with me and I'll see you right," the dwarf shouted, his cigar bouncing around between his clenched teeth.

"Where did he go?" I said, trying to see over the press of people.

"What? Bonecrusher? Forget about him. You're my new kid now."

I pushed the dwarf away so hard he went toppling off his crate and into the crowd below. I shouted at people to get out of my way and elbowed them aside. When I finally broke free of the audience, I saw the back door swing closed.

I slammed the doors open and looked left and right. I just caught sight of Glenn cutting down an alleyway that ran from the canal back towards the city centre. I chased after him, instantly feeling the cold night air on my bare chest.

I turned into the alley and was hit in the face with a green wheelie bin. I staggered back, unable to see for the pinpoints of lights dancing before my eyes. I shook my head.

Glenn slammed the bin at me a second time, knocking me off my feet. He turned and leaped to grab hold of a wall at the end of the alley. He chin-lifted himself over it effortlessly.

I clambered back onto my feet and shoved the bin out of the way with a growl. Glenn was going to pay for that. I raced at the wall and seconds before slamming into it, I leapt, planting one foot on the wall to the left, springing off it, and grabbing hold of the wall in front of me. It was a neat free-running move I'd been practising for months and this was the first time I'd pulled it off without needing to Shift my way out of head-butting brick. It still needed work though. I had the most tenuous of grips on the wall and had to scrabble with my feet to get purchase. Finally, I managed to pull myself up, and swung over.

I landed heavily on the other side, the shock sending tingles of pain up my shins. Glenn was waiting. He smiled as if he was actually impressed.

"Well, well, looks like you're one of ARES' finest. I'm honoured. But what does the old agency want with me now?"

"You know full well what they want," I said, straightening up. "We're shutting down Project Ganymede, once and for all."

Glenn nodded as if that was a perfectly reasonable request. Then he got that glazed expression I knew only too well. He was trying to Shift: trying to change some choice he'd made along the way that brought him here, change the reality he found himself in by undoing his choices. Only that wasn't going to happen.

I sighed before I said it. It was becoming a bit of a cliché. "Are you going to come quietly?"

He looked to his left where the road led to a busy street and then to his right where it led to a warren of council flats. He was breathing hard, whereas I had hardly built up a sweat. He knew he couldn't outrun me. There was only one thing for it. He was going to fight.

He reached down, hiked up his trouser leg, and pulled out a large, jagged knife from a calf sheath: all black blade and holes bored out for extra lightness. Military issue, I knew. I'd come up against one of these three months ago when we were tracking down number five. That guy had not gone quietly at all. In fact, he'd gone very loudly. And I had a nasty scar on my upper arm to prove it. It could have been worse. It had been worse. In another version of reality number five stabbed me in the stomach. I still remember looking down to see my intestines falling out of the gash in my stomach, before I Shifted to safety.

But this time I was ready.

Glenn flipped his knife around in his left hand so it still pointed forwards as he raised his fists. He slid one foot behind him and bent his legs.

"Oh, come on!" I said. "Do we really have to go through with this? You know you can't win."

"I'm not going down to a jumped up little runt like you," Glenn panted. He jabbed out with the knife. I stepped back and watched it slice past my chest.

It was a clumsy move, made by a man who'd become so reliant on his Shifting power that he probably didn't even bother trying any more. Whereas I tried not to take it for granted. I knew the power would fade in a matter of years when entropy set in. It's why I trained so damn hard.

I stopped the blade as it came in for a second swipe with an upward block, then punched with my left, sending Glenn's head snapping back. Like the blades of scissors I caught his arm between mine and twisted. There was a satisfying crunch and he screamed, dropping his knife to the floor. I kicked out, the side of my foot connecting just below his knee, and it bent back on itself at an unnatural angle. Dislocated but not broken, I reckoned. I swiped his other foot away and he crumpled to the floor like a coal stack being demolished. He rocked on the floor, sobbing and cradling his arm, but I didn't have much sympathy.

"I'm cold and tired and you made me wait for hours in the rain," I said, as much to myself as him, as I knelt down and rolled him on to his side and into a puddle. "And you had to go and pull a knife, didn't you?" He groaned as I pulled his injured arm back, pinning his two wrists together. "Why didn't you just come quietly? Number four did."

The hunt for the remaining adult Shifters hadn't let up in months, with the new boss breathing down our necks demanding results – and giving us a good shouting even when we'd got them – and the Government breathing down his neck and watching every little thing that went on at the agency. It was exhausting. So when I found number four and he invited me in for a cup of tea before coming into ARES without a fight, it had made a refreshing change.

"Why can't you all be like number four?" I said.

Aubrey appeared around the corner.

"About time!" I said, pressing my knee further into Glenn's back. He made a gurgling noise as his mouth was pushed deeper into the puddle.

"I couldn't find a way around. Besides, I knew you'd

be OK on your own."

She clearly hadn't seen me being smacked in the face
by the bin. But she was right. I had managed on my
own. The first few times I'd gone up against an adult
Shifter had not gone this smoothly. I'd still been a bit of
a mess after what had happened at Greyfield's; haunted
by what had been done to me and what I'd done in
return. Aubrey had told me to try and forget it and
throw myself into the job. It had worked. I'd managed
to go a whole week without having a flashback from
that night. I was still having nightmares though. They
weren't going anywhere.

Aubrey passed me her cuffs and together we slapped
them on Glenn's wrists.

He struggled for a moment, spitting swearwords and
insults in our direction, then went loose and stopped
struggling. I rolled him onto his back and he smiled up
at the grey clouds overhead.

The cuffs were designed to stop anyone from Shifting, by sending a disruptive current through the body
and stopping the brain from focusing. Only we'd mod-
ified them a little in our hunt for the members of the
project. Now they also made the wearer a bit more
compliant.

Aubrey looked down at his twisted leg. "Did you
have to?"

"He had a knife, Aubrey. A really big knife."

She rolled her eyes at me, threw me my clothes, and
knelt down next to him. As I pulled my T-shirt and
jacket back on, Aubrey rested one hand on his calf and
the other behind his knee. There was a loud, comic pop,
like someone pulling their finger out of their mouth, and

his leg was straight again.

He let out a muffled cry, like someone being woken from a dream, then returned to staring dully ahead.

Between us, we hauled him to his feet and pushed him forward.

"Come on, Pylon. Let's get him in the van."

"About this nickname," I said as we half-carried, half-dragged Glenn down the street. "I'm not sure I like it. I mean, other people call each other Bunnykins or Peanut or Studmuffin. But the Pylon?"

"Well, look at you. You're tall and all spiky. I think the Pylon is perfect."

We directed Glenn all the way back along the canal, past the boat yard, and to the pub where we'd found him.

The ARES van was still waiting for us. Only someone had taken the time to scratch their name into the black paintwork with a key. Brilliant. Just what I needed. The Regulators would go mental when they saw that.

I kicked the bumper in frustration and it fell off.

"Why don't we get special issue vehicles? You know, with titanium armour and run on flat tyres. All that fancy military spec stuff?"

"With ejector seats and smoke bombs?" Aubrey said.

"Sure, why not? We're spies, aren't we?"

"We are most definitely not spies, Scott."

"Well, secret agents then. No arguing on that. So, where are all our cool toys?"

Aubrey smiled and shook her head. "Budget cuts."

"Budget cuts?"

"Yeah, and when you don't officially have a budget, because you don't officially exist, then it makes it harder to complain. What do you want us to do? Go on strike?"

Aubrey slid open the door and we bundled Glenn inside. He curled up in a corner and started to snore happily. We slammed the door closed.

"So that's seven down," Aubrey said, with a happy sigh. "And only one left to go."

I hoped number eight wouldn't give us any trouble.

CHAPTER THREE

"I'm driving!" Aubrey shouted, grinning at me.

"Oh, come on!" I moaned, opening the passenger door. "You drove on the way here."

"And wasn't it a lovely drive?"

"You almost got us killed. Three times." I held up three fingers to emphasise my point.

"Stop complaining and get in."

I hopped up onto the seat as Aubrey fired up the engine. She'd stepped on the pedal before I'd even shut the door.

Aubrey drove like a lunatic, cutting between lanes like a skier doing the slalom. After all, if anything went wrong – and it did, all the time – she'd just Shift. I think she did it in part just to scare me and in part because it was one of the few times now that she didn't have to obey anyone's rules. Everything had changed at ARES in the past few months. After everything went down at Greyfield's, the Government had been informed and now the agency reported directly to the Ministry of Defence. Everything we did was watched, monitored, measured.

One toe out of line and the new boss came down on us hard. There were security systems as backup to the security systems and more paperwork than ever before. Aubrey threatened to quit on an almost daily basis. But the truth was, it was even worse for Shifters not in the Agency. Now, anytime someone wanted to Shift, they had to apply, in person, and provide evidence of why their Shift would lead to a better world. *Ad verum via*, as the motto stitched in gold thread on our new, too-stiff uniforms said. Towards the true way.

That had been Mr Abbott's dream too. A man I once believed was my friend. But who I learned was nothing but a power-crazed maniac who was willing to do anything to bring about his vision of the true way. Six months ago, I'd stood outside a burning hospital watching his dreams turn to dust while he was trapped inside screaming my name.

I shuddered at the memory.

"Please slow down!" I shouted over the sound of a car blaring its horn.

"We're still miles away and I'm hungry," she said, changing into fifth gear. "And once we get this guy back, we still have to type everything up."

"If we get this guy back," I said, closing my eyes as Aubrey squeezed between two trucks.

I knew there was nothing to worry about. Not really. Aubrey was one of the best Shifters in the Agency and we were in no real danger. But every time I heard the screech of brakes from a truck next to us, it brought back a memory I'd been trying to forget for almost a year: the night I'd got my little sister killed in a car crash. I'd managed to Shift to a new reality where she was alive again. But the image of her crushed body was yet another of the images that came back to haunt me at nights.

"Please, Aubrey. Just a little slower," I said, resting my hand over hers on the gear stick.

She side-eyed me, as if working out if I was joking or not, and then let up on the accelerator pedal.

"Besides," I said. "I'm in no rush to get back to HQ. Not with everyone panicking about the big visit tomorrow."

"Gee, I can hardly wait," Aubrey said. "The Prime Minister coming to have a good old nose about the place. Just to make sure we're all behaving. Gah, that place!" Aubrey slammed the steering wheel with the palms of her hands, causing the van to swerve wildly. "Once we bring in the last of the Ganymede guys, I swear, I'm quitting."

"You said that after number two," I said.

Number two was a quietly spoken man who'd sobbed after we told him how he'd been given his power back, and then tried to strangle Aubrey.

"Yeah, and after number three," Aubrey said.

Number three worked on the trading floor of the London Stock Exchange, where he'd been using his power to play the market and make a packet. He'd not come quietly either. Number four was the only one who had. A lovely guy, working as a caretaker in a graveyard. He'd said being around the dead made him feel safe. *"They were dead when I got here. So there's absolutely nothing I can do to change that."*

It was number four who'd given us the names of the remaining members of the project. And we'd tracked them all down apart from the very last one. So far, we knew absolutely nothing about him apart from his name: Frank Anderson.

"But this time I mean it, Scott. I'm quitting. If only to see the look on Sir Richard's face."

Sir Richard Morgan. Our new boss and, as Aubrey liked to put it, asshat of the highest order. Sir Richard had taken over from his son as head of ARES after it became all to clear that Morgan Junior didn't have a clue about what was really going on at the agency. Since starting, Sir Richard had been busy trying to make up for his son's lack of control. Our first day back at work after Greyfield's, he'd pulled us in to his office and screamed and shouted at us for a full hour. He'd known Aubrey had been there, because her name had been found on a scrap of paper recovered from the wreckage. And he had his suspicions about my involvement.

"I hate to say this," Aubrey said, checking her rear view mirror. "But I almost miss Dick."

"Yeah, I guess," I said, remembering when Richard Morgan Junior had been in charge. Morgan was a jumped-up prat, but he'd been a harmless jumped-up prat. And at least, as a Shifter himself, he'd had a vague idea of what we were up against. Something Sir Richard had clearly forgotten long ago.

The lights of the oncoming traffic streaked across the damp windowpane leaving glowing trails. I turned away and tried to hide my yawn.

"Tired?" Aubrey asked.

"I guess. It's been a pretty full-on day."

Aubrey glanced towards me and then back at the road. There was no point in trying to hide anything from her. She could see through me better than anyone else. "You still having the nightmares?" she said.

Ever since that night, I'd not slept well. Images of that night kept haunting me. Sergeant Cain, my old instructor, lying in a pool of blood. Abbott's face contorted in pain. Benjo Greene, the grossly fat cannibal, crunching through metal tools, blood pouring from between his sharp teeth. Worst of all were the things I'd seen when I was hooked up to Abbott's simulator. The things I'd done.

"They weren't real, you know?" Aubrey said, taking her hand off the wheel and laying it on my knee. "The simulator."

Like I said, she could see straight through me. I'd told her all about what Abbott had done to me and what I'd done while hooked up to his machine. The simulators had been designed for training Shifters: a tool to help them experience different choices and see how the consequences could possibly play out, without actually affecting reality. Only Abbott's version had been different. His simulator made you experience your very worst choices. But they were still your choices. Even though I was now in a reality where none of those terrible things had happened, I had done them. Given the right circumstances, some potential version of me was capable of doing it all again, inflicting all that pain. I shuddered, despite the heating being on max.

Aubrey had told me time and time again that I hadn't done those things. That they weren't real. And I tried to believe her.

But I hadn't told her everything. Maybe now was the time I did.

"There's something I haven't told you… about that night," I said, picking at a loose thread on my cuff.

"What?" she said.

This would be the third time I'd told her the truth. The truth about what had really happened at Grey-field's and how we'd escaped. The last two times, she'd looked at me with so much fear I'd chickened out and Shifted my decision to tell her. As I tried to force the words out of my mouth, I wondered if this time would be any different.

"That night, I did something…"

"Scott, how many times do I have to tell you?" she said.

"No, not the simulators," I said hurriedly, worried that if she interrupted I'd never get it out. "Something else."

"Scott, you're scaring me," she said.

"I'm scaring myself," I said.

She glanced over at me. My expression must have really worried her because she steered the van across the lanes of traffic and pulled up in the lay-by. A truck speeding past made the van shake almost as much as I was.

"Scott, you can tell me. You can tell me anything," she said, taking my quaking hand in hers.

"I don't know if you'll believe me. I don't know if I believe it myself."

She just nodded encouragingly.

"That night, when I died on the table, when I begged Benjo to kill me to stop the images…"

Aubrey closed her eyes in anger and muttered Benjo's name.

"After I came back…"

"After the hypnic jerk brought you back?" she said.

The hypnic jerk. The Shifter's ultimate defence mechanism. For normal people it was a weird jolt experienced when falling asleep: the brain's way of making sure the body was still alive. Only with Shifters it kicked in when we really were in trouble. A desperate Shifting of all choices to avoid dying.

"Yeah, well, I didn't overpower Abbott. I just told him to take my place."

"What do you mean?" she said, her eyes tightening.

"I just told him. And he obeyed. Benjo too, I told him to eat start eating all his blades and he did. Just crunched them down like they were popcorn."

She slipped her hand away from mine, the fear appearing in her eyes. "What are you saying, Scott?"

"I'm saying I could force them to do what I want. And not just them. Everyone. All the guards, they just lay down when I told them too."

"But... But that's not possible," Aubrey said.

This was going exactly as it had the last two times. She was freaked out by me, and why not. I was a freak.

"And changing reality is?" I said, with a sigh.

"That's different."

"Is it? That's what Shifting is about, isn't it? Being able to make the reality you want. Well, I wanted Abbott and Benjo dead. So that's what happened. And I wanted you..."

"Me? Are you saying you forced me as well? Scott, look at me."

I couldn't bear to. Couldn't bear to see the terror in her eyes as she wondered exactly what I'd been wondering for the last six months. Was Aubrey really with me because she'd made the choice? Or because I had?

I forced myself to meet her gaze. "I don't know."

She leaned back and took a deep breath. Then something changed. The fear left her eyes, leaving only a light, like sunshine catching on a wave. "Scott, I don't know what happened for sure. But I know one thing. You're not making me do anything I don't want to do."

"But how can you be sure?"

In answer, she leant forward and kissed me. Harder, more desperate than earlier. I pulled her closer, pouring all of my own fear and doubt into that kiss. It was the realest thing I'd ever felt.

When we finally broke free, Aubrey cupped my face in her hands. "Doubt anything, Scott. But don't doubt this," she said. "Don't doubt me."

I nodded and wiped a tear away from my cheek, hoping she hadn't seen it. Maybe I wouldn't need to Shift this time. Maybe she could finally accept me and what I'd done. But I kept the decision to tell her clear in my mind, just in case.

She settled back into the driver's seat and started up the engine again. "We'll talk more about this when we get back to HQ. It's a few hours yet," Aubrey said. "Why don't you try and get some sleep?"

"OK," I said, coughing to clear my throat. "But wake me if you want me to take over. Or if we crash."

I pulled off my jacket, glad to be free of it, crumpled it up into a ball and put it between my head and the window. The gentle vibrations of the van shook through my cheek, making me feel as if I was wearing a pair of the cuffs. There was something soothing about it and before I knew it, I'd fallen asleep.

• • • •

We pulled up at around the back of ARES HQ just as the sun was rising, turning the white building the colour of sand.

"Oh, no," Aubrey said, when she saw who was waiting at the back doors.

Lottie and Lane, our two least favourite Regulators, met us with matching scowls. They were stood, arms folded, in front of five NSOs. Non-Shifting Officers.

Apparently, the MOD had decided the security of ARES could not be left in the hands of a bunch of kids. So a team of ex-military specialists had been brought in to keep us in check. I'm not sure even Sir Richard, with all his rules and bluster, was happy about them stalking the halls. The Regulators had been most offended though; keeping non-Shifters in check was supposed to be their role. And at least they understood what it was like to have been Shifters once. The majority of them refused to work with the NSOs. But not Lottie and Lane. They'd taken to the NSOs like a starving man to steak. They loved having their orders backed up by men with guns.

Lottie was tall and broad with dark, greasy hair that she kept tied back in a tight bun. Lane was smaller, with mousy brown hair in a short bob. And yet I still managed to get the two of them mixed up. Lane had been a Fixer, like me, and had spent the last year in Africa working on some project over there. Lottie never made it above Second Class and had a chip on her shoulder the size of Cleopatra's needle. They'd both lost their Shifting powers recently, entropy catching up with them within a few weeks of each other and they were still pissed off about it. I guess I didn't blame them.

I often wondered how I would deal when entropy came for me. It couldn't be long before I lost my powers, a couple of years, maybe three, or four if I was really lucky. Sometimes, I looked forward to it. Being rid of the constant buzz in my head and having to worry about every single choice. Other times, I knew that once the power was gone, I'd be a nobody again. A nobody with absolutely no skills to get by in the real world. Joining The Regulators was the only thing I'd be cut out for. Just like Lottie and Lane.

"Howdy, girls," Aubrey said, jumping down from the driver's seat. "Got another one for you."

"State your name, rank and purpose here," Lottie shouted.

"Come off it, Lottie," I said. "It's us."

"Name. Rank. Purpose," Lane, repeated as a couple of NSOs raised their guns and pointed them at us.

I looked at the guns and blinked. If we really wanted to get past, there was nothing they could do about it, they had to know that. A gun up against a Shifter was pointless. But I was too tired for a fight.

"Tyler. Fixer, Third Class. Transporting a prisoner."

I looked at Aubrey, hoping she'd just follow my example and we could get this all over and done with. She was staring at Lottie.

"Jones. Spotter, *Third* Class." She put an unnecessary emphasis on her rank, just to get at Lottie, I was sure. "And my purpose is to do my actual job, so if you would get out of my face..."

Aubrey's head only came up to Lottie's shoulder. The two of them stared at each other, waiting to see which one would back down first. It was Lottie.

She sniffed and stepped out of Aubrey's way. "Bring him in then," she said, affecting nonchalance.

But I could tell by the way she kept clenching and unclenching her hand the confrontation had unnerved her. Maybe it was the knowledge that without her power to Shift she'd have had no chance against Aubrey. Or that even when she was at the height of her powers she still wouldn't have had a chance. Not many people could beat Aubrey, Shifter or non-Shifter.

The NSOs lowered their guns and went back to radiating menace.

I slid the door of the van open and the smell of urine burnt my nose. Lottie and Lane recoiled in disgust. "Yeah, sorry about that," I said. "The cuffs have that effect, you know?"

The girls clicked their fingers in unison and two of the NSOs stepped forward to pull the dozy Glenn out of the van.

"Be careful," I said. "He's tricky."

Lottie and Lane looked at Glenn's drooling expression and laughed.

"Yeah, Tyler. He looks like a real hellraiser," Lottie said.

"Laugh it up guys," I said. "Just don't take the cuffs off till we've had a chance to question him."

Lane tilted her chin at me. "We'll be doing the questioning, Tyler. But maybe we'll let you have a word. When we're done."

She spun around and followed Lottie and the NSOs back inside. I rolled my eyes.

"I swear, Scott," Aubrey said, coming to stand by my side. "I'm quitting."

I felt the warmth of her next to me and wanted to reach out and hold her. But I resisted. There were rules about ARES members fraternising. Sure, there was little they could do to stop a bunch of hormone-crazed teenagers hooking up, but they could stop us working together as partners. And neither of us wanted that. So we kept our relationship secret. Kept it ours.

There was something thrilling in that. In the secret smiles, the stolen kisses. Sometimes, I worried if that's what Aubrey liked most about it. That it was a sort of "screw you ARES". I also worried it was because she was embarrassed to be seen with me. I'd look at her and then look at me and wonder how the hell I ever got so lucky.

I reached for her hand and caught her little finger in mine. It was enough, that tiny physical connection that said I'm here, I've got you. I'm not going anywhere. It was like an anchor in a storm.

She stroked the back of my hand with her thumb and it sent little shivers up my arm.

"Come on," she said. "I need some caffeine."

CHAPTER FOUR

NSOs guarded the doors to the cafeteria, checking the ID of everyone going in and out. Kids, who used to charge around this place, their trainers squeaking on the marble floors, now walked quietly in single file. The cadets no longer wore T-shirts with "Fresh Meat" on the back as they had when I was training. Instead, they were in full, official uniform and looked as unhappy about it as I was.

As Aubrey and I walked in, showing our ID to the grim-faced NSO, we saw CP, my old classmate, being shooed off to her class by one of the new teachers. Lessons started at 6.30am sharp, now. I would never have made it out of basic training had that been the case a year ago.

CP waved in our direction, then quickly slapped her hand back down to her side when she saw the teacher looking over. I waved a weak greeting in return, not raising my hand higher than my hip as I didn't want to get her in trouble.

CP and I had been cadets together when I'd joined ARES. She was a tiny thing, who spent most of her time peering out at the world from behind a too-long fringe. But I knew that she was not a kid to be messed with. Like Aubrey, she too had been kidnapped by Abbott and would have ended up as a vegetable if Sergeant Cain and I hadn't turned up. Now, I felt responsible for her. There was no one else at ARES to look out for her – not that she couldn't take care of herself. But I worried. If one of the teachers saw her waving at me, it might mean detention or worse. It was bad enough I'd got Jake, another of my ex-classmates, in so much trouble he'd been put in solitary for a week. His sister, Rosalie, had pulled him out of the agency after and I'd not had a chance to see him since. I don't know who missed him more, me or CP.

CP and the rest of her class disappeared out of the room, the slam of the door behind them ringing in the now empty hall.

Aubrey grabbed two cokes from the surly dinner lady and threw me one. I fumbled the catch, but managed to pin it against my chest. It opened with a loud hiss and sprayed cola fizz all over Aubrey.

She gasped, and wiped her face, flicking the liquid off her hand. I tried not to laugh. I tried really hard. But when a drip fell off her nose I lost it.

In revenge, Aubrey shook up her can, and opened it right into my face. I squealed, actually squealed, and ran away as the spray exploded over my back. Aubrey raced after me, laughing hard, and soon we were chasing each other between the long tables of the cafeteria. I caught up with her, grabbed her in a bear hug, pinning her arms to her side, and lifted her off her feet so her face was level with mine. She licked a droplet of coke off her lip.

I held her there, our faces moving closer, millimetre by millimetre.

"What is going on here?" a voice boomed, the last syllable echoing around the hall.

I dropped Aubrey to the floor so quickly she nearly fell over. Sir Richard stood in the doorway, moustache twitching, his already red cheeks even redder. Lottie and Lane stood behind him, grinning.

"We were... We were..." I babbled.

"We were nothing," Aubrey finished, giving me a shove that hurt my ego more than anything else. "Sir," she added, seeing Sir Richard's expression darken.

"We cannot have this sort of... horseplay going on around here. What if I'd been the Prime Minister?"

"But the Prime Minister isn't coming till tomorrow, sir," I said, straightening my uniform.

"And a good thing too." He let out a snort of impatient breath that made his nostrils flare. "Well then. Don't you have a job to be doing?"

"We've already finished interviewing Glenn and he's in the cells," Lane said, stepping forward. "If Tyler and Jones aren't too busy doing... nothing." She gave us a dirty look.

"Well, get to it then," Sir Richard said, spinning on his heel.

We waited till the sounds of his heavy feet faded away. Then walked out of the hall.

"I'm serious, Scott–"

"I know," I said, interrupting Aubrey. "You're quitting."

Aubrey and I took the lifts all the way down to the basement level – to the cells. This is where they kept Shifters who'd broken the rules while waiting for processing. It was also where they locked up serious offenders until entropy kicked in. I'd never been down here before. And as soon as I stepped out, I knew I never wanted to again. The corridor ahead smelt of bleach but not enough to cover up the stink of stale urine.

"Name, rank and purpose!"

I sighed as I saw two NSOs standing guard.

"Scott Tyler, Third Class and…"

"You again," one of the NSOs said, looking at Aubrey. "Back to see Black?"

I looked at Aubrey, wondering what he meant. Then remembered who else was down here. None other than Isaac Black. Ex-leader of the Shifter Liberation Front and my nemesis.

Zac had trained with Aubrey and had been one of ARES' finest Mappers – Shifters who are able to plot out events and their consequences. But he came to believe the agency was lying to us all and had gone rogue, plotting to bring the whole organisation down. He'd been caught a few weeks ago by the Regulators and given a choice. Go legit or end up here. He'd chosen the cell.

While I'd not been down to see him, it was clear from the guard's reaction that Aubrey was a regular visitor down here. A bubble of jealousy fizzed in my stomach.

"We're here to interview Glenn," Aubrey said, glaring at the man.

He considered her, looking her up and down, then turned to his fellow guard. "What do you think, Ben? Shall we let her through?"

"Remember what happened last time you tried to stop me?" Aubrey said, sounding bored. "How's the knee?"

I saw the colour rise in the NSO's cheeks. The other NSO, the one called Ben, was fighting to hold back a snigger. It looked as if Aubrey had already made quite the impression on these two.

"Cell 8," he grunted and waved us along.

Aubrey pulled off a mock curtsey and when we were out of their eye-line, flicked her finger in their direction. "They are such tools," she said.

We walked past the cells and their inhabitants. Most were bored-looking teenagers, lying on the metal beds just waiting to be released. In for small crimes, like cheating on exams or stuff like that. But a couple looked more serious. The guy in Cell 3's face was covered in blue tattoos, including one on his forehead that read FATE. He snarled at us as we passed.

I heard a rhythmic grunting noise before I reached Cell 5. Zac had his bed turned on its side and was busy doing chin-ups. Stripped to the waist, the sweat glistening on his bare chest.

"Hey, Brey," he said, finishing one last chin-up and lowering himself to the floor. "And if it isn't Scott Tyler himself. Long time no see, Scott. How's tricks?"

"Um… tricks are good, I guess," I said, looking uncomfortably at the floor. "How are you hanging?" I winced at the unintentional pun.

Zac just laughed. "Oh, just counting down the days till I get out of here."

"No sign of entropy then?" Aubrey said.

"If entropy even exists," Zac said. "You know how I feel about it."

"Well, that means you could be in here for years. Why don't you just accept the offer and–"

"And what? Sell out on everything? Drink their Kool Aid?" he said, pointing at the ceiling. "Can't you see what's going on here, Brey? It's worse than ever, with the Prime Minister getting his mucky paws all over this place. They want to control us. Crush us."

"They want to protect us," I said, annoyed at Zac's conspiracy crap. Clearly being locked up hadn't changed him.

He snorted. "Sure, if you want to believe that, go ahead."

"What would it take to change your mind?" Aubrey said, holding on to one of the bars. "I hate to see you in there."

The fizzing jealousy was dialled up a notch.

"If they just promised to leave me alone," Zac said, holding the bar an inch above Aubrey's hand.

Aubrey stepped back and shook her head. "Maybe one day, Zac. But not today."

She turned to go and Zac called out after her. "You'll come and see me again, won't you? You too, Scott. Any time. I'm not going anywhere." There was a desperation in his voice that sounded so very un-Zac. Aubrey scrunched her eyes, blocking out his pleas, as we walked on to Cell 8.

Glenn was sitting quietly on his metal bed, squinting in the bright light, his hands still in cuffs.

I tutted. "Lane should have taken them off him. He'll be no use if he's still fogged up."

"Mr Glenn," Aubrey said. "Could you stand up and walk over here?"

Glenn obeyed, but he moved sluggishly, as if he was drunk. He approached the bars and leant his head against them, propping himself up.

"Turn around," Aubrey said, and again, he did what she said.

I reached in and unlocked the cuffs. He staggered back, blinking and looking around as if he was only just waking up.

Aubrey pulled out her tablet and brought up Glenn's file. "OK, Mr Glenn," Aubrey said. "As our colleagues have no doubt already explained, you're being charged with Shifting without a licence and using your power for monetary gain. But I'd like to talk to you about a certain matter of being in possession of stolen goods, too."

Glenn looked confused. "Stolen goods?"

I tapped my forehead. "That bit of brain you have implanted in there, the bit that gave you your powers; yeah, well, it doesn't belong to you."

"What are you on about?"

"Come on, Jack," Aubrey said. "Don't pretend you don't know what went on at Project Ganymede. Don't tell me you didn't know about what they were doing to the kids."

Glenn took a few steps back and sat down on the bed. "Sure, I was part of Project Ganymede. But I don't know anything about any kids."

Aubrey looked at him, feigning disbelief. But the truth was, none of the volunteers had really known what had been involved. They'd been taken in for an operation, woken up with their Shifting power returned to them, and been sent back to work, no questions asked.

Aubrey sighed. We both hated this bit. "The only reason you're able to still Shift today is because the part of the brain responsible for the power was cut out of a kid's head and implanted into yours."

"And that child was left in a vegetative state," I said.

"What? I... I don't know..."

"A vegetable, Mr Glenn," Aubrey said. "A child was turned into a vegetable, just so you could have your power back."

Glenn leant back on the bed, blinking even more. "I didn't know anything about that. If I'd known, I would have never... never..." He covered his face with one huge hand. "Take it back," he said. "I don't want it anymore."

"It's too late for that, I'm afraid," I said, almost feeling sorry for him.

"Then what do you want with me?" Tears leaked from the corners of his eyes.

I stepped forward, my face an inch away from the bars. "We want to keep you under observation, Mr Glenn. Other members of Project Ganymede have experienced, shall we say, side effects? We wanted to know if you've been having any trouble?"

"Trouble? No, no trouble."

"No fits of rage? Delusions of grandeur?" Aubrey said, tapping at a report on her screen. "What about this incident last month when you broke a man's nose for standing too close?"

"He was asking for it, he was."

"Exactly how was he asking for it, Mr Glenn? Was he breathing too loudly for you?" I said.

"I was trying to have a quiet drink, right? And this guy comes up to me and challenges me to a fight. There and then. He thought he was a big shot. But I knew that he was just a nobody. They're all nobodies."

Aubrey and I exchanged a look.

Not all of the Ganymede men showed signs of the psychosis or whatever the hell it was that turned them into lunatics. So far, out of the six we'd brought in, only three had been on the brink of total bonkerdom. This guy looked as if he wasn't far behind.

I saw Aubrey type a note on Glenn's file. "Psych Eval Needed."

"There's also the small matter of a bomb in your frontal cortex," she said, without taking her eyes off the screen.

"My what?" he said, standing up.

"In your brain," Aubrey said, looking up at him. "Dr Lawrence placed a small bomb in the brain of some of his subjects so that he could do away with them if he wanted. All it needs is a signal sent from a mobile phone and boom. You're dead."

Glenn started scratching furiously at his scar. "Get it out. Get it out!"

"We will. But only if you cooperate with us," I said, swallowing down my discomfort. I'd seen one of these cortex bombs blow up at close quarters and it was not something I ever wanted to see again.

Glenn moved his hand away from his head and stood very still, as if worried that the smallest movement might set the bomb off.

"What do you want to know?" he said.

"Frank Anderson. Where do we find him?"

Glenn sniffed and his eyes twitched. "What do you want with Frankie?"

"We just want to speak to him. Just like you."

Frank "Frankie" Anderson was the final name on our

list. And so far the one we'd had the least luck in locating. Absolutely nothing came up on ARES' database when we did the search, which either meant he was an unregistered Shifter or, the idea that really intrigued us, he'd not been a Shifter at all. What we all wanted to know was: could you make someone into a Shifter who'd never been one before?

Glenn let out a controlled breath, like someone about to jump off a diving board. "I've not seen Captain Anderson in over fifteen years. So, I don't think I can help you. And even if I could, I wouldn't. The Captain saved my life."

"You're willing to risk that bomb going off just to protect this Anderson, is that what you're telling us?" Aubrey said.

Glenn nodded, stiffly, making the smallest movement possible.

"Well, if you're quite certain, Mr Glenn. I hope you enjoy the rest of your stay with us. You don't mind needles, do you?"

I heard a cough from behind us. The two NSOs were now flanking a man in a white lab coat, here to take Glenn away for further evaluation. I'd heard whispered rumours about what went on during "evaluation". About how they tried to find out as much about the men who'd gone through the process as possible. About the secret operations taking place in the agency labs. But this place was filled with rumours.

I nodded at the doc as we passed. "He's all yours," I said.

I heard a crash. It sounded as if Glenn was putting up a fight again.

"Captain?" Aubrey said as we headed for the lifts, ignoring the ruckus coming from the interview room. Lane and Lottie could handle it themselves. They'd been through the same training we all had, after all. And they had the NCOs for back up if needed.

"Yeah," I said. "That's the first we've heard Anderson called that. Do you think he was their leader?"

"Maybe. It might explain why none of them seem willing to give him up," Aubrey said.

"Yep, another dead end. So what do we do?" I said. "Apart from working our way through all the Frank Andersons in the country?"

"I don't know," Aubrey said, pressing the call button. "But I know one thing."

"Which is?"

"When today is over, I need a drink."

CHAPTER FIVE

Bailey's Bar, formally known as Copenhagen's Gambling Club, had a queue twenty people long. It had taken Sir Richard a while to work out what was really going on at Copenhagen's – the Shifter controlled gambling, the blind eye turned to a "misappropriation" of Shifters' skills – but once he had, the place had been shut down.

Rosalie had been a croupier at the club – when she wasn't hanging out with revolutionary organisations. And when it closed she found herself out of a job. And with entropy on its way, she knew she'd have to get a proper job. So she decided to open up a bar in the same place. The previous owner just handed her the keys and went off to live in Malaga with his ageing mum. Within a few weeks Bailey's Bar had become one of London's coolest hotspots, filled each night with office workers and students desperate to dance away another boring day. Other people from ARES still came to hang out when off duty. But no one was allowed to Shift once inside the doors. Bailey's rather miserable doorman made sure of that.

"Dick!" Aubrey said as we approached. "How's life?"

Richard Morgan junior, son of Sir Richard, formerly our commandant, was now working at Bailey's using his fading powers to stop Shifter kids from changing decisions, like which drink to have or who to ask to dance. It would be depressing if he hadn't been such a massive arse.

Morgan closed his eyes and dropped his head to the floor as we approached. "Yes, yes, come to have a good old laugh, have we?"

"No," Aubrey said, patting him on the arm. "Good to see you, Richard. Honestly."

Morgan, who was never very good at resisting Aubrey's charms, brightened. "How are things at ARES?" he asked.

"Well, not as much fun as when you were in charge," I said.

"Yeah, your dad's a real ball breaker. I wish you were back at the helm."

"Well, he's under a lot of pressure," Morgan said. "According to Mother – I've not spoken to him in months." He rubbed a drop of rain off his black bomber jacket. "Anyway, you didn't come here to chat with me, clearly. Go on." He stepped aside, lifting the red rope that blocked the door, and let us pass, ignoring the moans from those still in the queue.

I turned back to offer a grin of apology and saw a man standing at the back of the queue who was so out of place I was surprised Morgan hadn't already told him to push off. He had mats of dark hair and a thick, wiry beard. Not the kind of beard you saw on hipsters. The kind you saw on homeless people. And I guessed that's what he was. Perhaps hoping to come inside just to keep warm. I hoped Morgan wasn't too rough on him. He didn't look as if he'd had an easy time of it. His grey eyes, peering out from the nest of hair, were filled with sadness.

"I actually feel sorry for him," Aubrey said once we were inside.

"Huh?" I said, thinking she meant the tramp.

"Morgan. It must be hard having fallen so low. It's almost Shakespearean," Aubrey said.

"Yeah, I guess."

As soon as Aubrey pulled open the doors the music hit me. Beyond, the room was packed with people jumping in time to a pounding beat. They were pushed up against each other, arms raised, as if they were showering in the sound. I pulled off my jacket and threw it over my shoulder. I was off duty now. Finally.

Bailey's was done out like a circus, with red and white striped material hanging from the ceiling and strings of lights wrapped around long red poles. Instead of stools, the bar had trapeze bars hanging on golden ropes for the clientele to swing on as they drank. The bar staff wore sexy versions of clown outfits. It was all an homage to Rosalie's past as part of the famous Bailey's Circus. There was even a statue of an elephant stuck in the middle of the dance floor. I patted it as I passed, remembering the night Aubrey, Rosalie and I had stolen it from the street around the corner.

I pushed through the crowd, making way for Aubrey behind me, waving at a few familiar faces as I passed, before finally reaching the bar.

Rosalie was on duty, wearing her tight ringmaster's

outfit, complete with small top hat and fishnet stockings. She was holding her hand up to her ear to listen to orders being shouted at her. I waved and caught her eye.

"Hey, guys," she said, hopping up on the bar to give Aubrey and then me a kiss on the cheek. "Two cokes, right?" she said pointing at us.

"Actually, I think I need something a bit stronger," I said, rubbing at the sticky wetness her kiss had left behind.

"You got any ID?" she asked.

"Oh, come on, Rosalie. Don't be like that. It's us," Aubrey said.

"And I'm eighteen in a few months," I said.

"Besides, we really need it."

"Crappy day?" Rosalie asked.

"You have no idea," Aubrey said.

"And I don't ever want to," she said, holding her hand up. "Every time I think about the stuff they put Jakey through... I'm just glad I pulled him out."

"Shame Jake wasn't so pleased," I said, under my breath, assuming she wouldn't hear me over the noise of the bar. I was wrong.

Rosalie scowled and threw a soggy beer mat at me. "Don't you start! You're the one who got him put into solitary with that stunt you pulled at the horse races."

We'd found number two working at a horse track, gaming the betters and scamming the trainers. Jake and I had come up with a plan to catch him out, which included Jake posing as a jockey.

"I had no idea he'd actually end up winning the race," I said. "Or that Sir Richard would be in the royal box with the Prince and the Prime Minister."

Rosalie made a dismissive snorting noise and grabbed a bottle and two shot glasses from the bar. She hovered the bottle over the glass. "This could cost me my licence, you know? But you get one shot, OK? Just one. As long as you promise never to try and drag Jake back into the agency."

I reluctantly nodded my agreement and Aubrey and I threw back the shots. The heat of the alcohol burned my throat and settled in my stomach. I shuddered.

"Just tell Jake that CP says hi. And she misses him."

"Maybe." Rosalie joined us in downing a shot, then returned the bottle to the shelf before heading off to go and serve her customers.

Aubrey and I headed for the stairs to the mezzanine level that looked down on the dance floor. It was where the clubbers came to get a break from the noise, but mostly to get off with each other. We found ourselves a place in the corner and sat down. Aubrey leant her head against my shoulder and we stayed like that for a bit, just watching the legs of people moving around us.

I buried my nose in her tangle of blonde hair and breathed in the smell of vanilla and the apple tang of her new shampoo.

"I know I keep saying this," she said. "But I'm serious about after we find Anderson."

"What do you mean?" I asked, lifting my head to look at her.

"Quitting ARES. I want a life, Scott. A real life. And maybe some fun before entropy kicks in." She took my hand between hers, and started drawing patterns on my palm.

"So, why wait? Why not quit now?" I asked.

"I don't know. Unfinished business, I guess."

I'd been so caught up in my own need for closure I'd hardly stopped to think about everything Aubrey had been through. Being drugged and kidnapped by Abbott, nearly being lobotomised. What kind of boyfriend was I?

"I'm so sorry, Aubrey," I said, holding her hand tightly. "I keep thinking back, wondering if there was a way I could have stopped it all from happening. A Shift I could make."

"But if you did that, we'd never have found out what they were up to. Plus, maybe you and I would never have been." She raised my hand to her lips and kissed each of my knuckles in turn. "It worked out for the best. It always does."

"For us, anyway," I said, thumbing her cheek. "Not so much for Zac."

Aubrey stiffened and pulled her hand away. "Zac has only himself to blame. He had a choice: go straight or…"

"Go straight to prison, do not pass go," I said.

She shrugged. "Something like that."

That bubble of jealousy made a full comeback. "About you and Zac?"

Aubrey rolled her eyes. "I was wondering when we'd get to this."

"Oh, come on," I said. "Just tell me. Were you and him… a thing?"

Aubrey leant back. "Are you asking me if I ever slept with Zac?"

I coughed. "Well, not exactly. But did you?"

Aubrey gasped, her mouth making a perfect "O". "Of course not."

"Oh, good. So, what did you do then?"

"Stop it, Scott. You don't want to know."

I really did want to know. "You can tell me. I'll be OK with it." I wrapped my arm around her shoulder, trying to reassure her that whatever she had to say would be OK. Even though I was dreading the answer.

"Nothing ever happened with us. Well…"

"Well, what?" Her pause was enough to make the blood drain from my head.

"There was this night, when Zac had just got hold of the simulators and we messed around with them. We did some stuff. But it wasn't real, you know?"

That's what Aubrey kept saying about the sims. That whatever you experienced while hooked up wasn't real. But Zac had said they were as real as it gets. I twisted away from her, trying not to think about the kinds of stuff she and Zac might have got up to.

"Scott, look at me." It was a struggle but I managed to face her again.

"It was nothing. I was a stupid kid who wanted to try everything, experience everything just once. And the sims seemed a good way to do that. But it just felt… fake. What we have, Scott, you and me," she rested her hand on my chest and I could feel my heart pound beneath it, "is real. More real and more intense than anything I ever experienced while hooked up to a bunch of wires. OK?"

I placed my hand over hers, not wanting her to go anywhere. Not wanting this moment to end. "OK," I said, after a while.

She smiled at me and rested her head on my shoulder again. I reached into my pocket. There was something I'd been carrying around for weeks, waiting for the right time to give to Aubrey. I pulled my hand out. It could wait.

"Aren't you worried about people seeing us?" I said, nudging her slightly.

"Screw 'em," she said, entwining her fingers between mine.

"But I thought you were embarrassed to be seen with me?"

Aubrey laughed and looked up at me. "You're serious, aren't you?"

"I understand, honestly. I mean, *I'm* embarrassed to be seen with me most of the time."

Aubrey shook her head a little and smiled at me. "Oh, Scott. Have you seen you?"

I chewed my cheek as I looked at her. "I don't know what you mean."

"Yes," she said, leaning in for a gentle kiss. "And that's exactly how I want to keep it."

She kissed me again and the world melted away. All the worries about Project Ganymede, about the Prime Minister's visit tomorrow, all of it disappeared as I drew her into me. Nothing was too much to deal with as long as I was with Aubrey.

I felt a buzzing in my jacket and tried to ignore it. But Aubrey pushed me away gently. "It might be HQ," she said.

I checked my phone. It was a text from Katie.

MUM AND DAD ARE AT IT AGAIN. WHEN ARE YOU COMING HOME?

"Everything OK?" Aubrey asked.

"Yeah, it's just Katie. I should probably head back. Sounds like she's having a rough one."

"Your parents? Things between them still not going well?"

"Not so much. At least they spend less time shouting at each other and more time doing that frosty silence thing that's so much fun to live with. They can go for days without saying a word to each other, using Katie and me as their messengers. They're like kids. Only most kids have more sense."

"I'm sorry. It must be hard."

"I just wish they'd have the balls to get it over with and get a divorce. It's not like they love each other. They're just together out of, I don't know, fear? Habit? It sure isn't for Katie and me as we've told them enough times we'd be happier if they split up."

"You should move out. Then you wouldn't have to put up with them."

"I don't think I can leave Katie alone to deal with all that. She's still just a kid."

"A kid who can kick your arse though," Aubrey said, laughing.

Aubrey had come round to see my house and Katie had insisted on giving us a demonstration of what she'd learned at kickboxing that week. With me as the test subject. I'd ended up flat on my back and Aubrey had laughed louder and longer than I'd ever seen her laugh. Naturally she'd become Katie's instant hero.

"You know, you can always crash at mine, I mean, if you need," Aubrey said, looking down at her hands.

That was the first time Aubrey had mentioned me staying over since we'd started going out. And it was so loaded with possibilities that I felt my mouth go dry.

Before I could think of anything to say that wouldn't utterly kill the moment, my phone buzzed again.

OMG. IT'S THE XMAS PARTY THING. AGAIN. KILL ME.

"You really should go."

"Katie's a big girl. She'll be fine," I said, leaning in for a kiss. "About this crashing at yours…"

Aubrey laughed and pushed me away. "Get going. Oh and Scott," she said, as I reluctantly started to get up. "No girl would be embarrassed to be seen with you. Get it?" She pulled me in for a last, long kiss and my stomach danced faster than the people downstairs.

The first thing I heard as I let myself into my house was Katie laughing. I stopped in the hallway, without saying a word, just to listen to it. High-pitched and breathless, with a slight piggy snort, which I used to make fun of. It had been so long since I'd heard it. The rest of the house was empty and dark. So unless Katie was chatting with Mum and Dad, which was unlikely, she had a friend over.

Then I heard a second familiar laugh.

"What the…" I said, running up the stairs.

I opened the door to Katie's bedroom but it was empty. The laughter started up again. It was coming from my room.

I threw open the door to find Katie sat cross-legged on the floor, a game controller in her lap, and Hugo, my old best friend from school, sitting on my bed.

"Scotty! My man," he shouted as I stood in the doorway trying to work out what was going on. I gave up trying.

"What's going on?" I asked.

"Well, I came over here as I thought it would be harder to avoid me in person like you've been avoiding all my calls…" He looked at me over the top of his glasses, fixing me with a disapproving glance. "Only you weren't in. Surprise, surprise. I was about to walk all the way home on my own, in the dark, when Katie suggested I come in and wait, as you'd just told her you were on your way."

Katie held up her mobile phone, displaying my last text to her as proof.

"And we got to talking about her kickboxing, and while I agreed that she could easily beat me up for real…" Katie nodded at this statement, "I told her that no one could beat me on *Fists of Rage III*, the classic video game. Only it turns out I was wrong. What's the score now, Katie?"

"Two one, to me."

"Hmm, right then. Well, I went easy on you on that last round," Hugo said. "This time, prepare to reap the whirlwind."

Katie started up the game again and in seconds the two of them were bashing away on the controllers. I sat down next to Hugo on my bed, slipping off my jacket and shoes. It had been a long day. A long couple of days.

"Where are Mum and Dad?"

"Dad went to the pub. Mum's in the shed. Take that!" Katie said, not taking her eyes off the screen.

I craned my neck to see out of my window, which looked onto the garden below. The small windows of the shed were glowing and I could see Mum moving about inside. She'd be taking her frustration out on some innocent lump of clay.

"No!" roared Hugo. "You cheated. Scott, you have your controllers set up weird."

"Yeah, sure," Katie said. "Blame the controller, Hugo."

"OK, well, I was going easy on you playing as the Enforcer. But no one, no one can beat me when I play as Ra." He exited the game and flicked through the characters, stopping on a girl with black and red hair, enormous eyes and a ludicrous sexy nun's outfit. He hit "select" and she made a worrying grunting noise and punched the air.

"Get ready to be crushed," Hugo said, grabbing a fistful of air.

Katie snorted her derision. "OK, Ra. But I need a drink. You want one?" I looked at her in confusion. She'd never offered to get me a drink before and I can't remember the last time I'd seen her smiling this much.

"I'm fine," I said, smiling back.

"I'd murder a cup of tea. White with two sugars, if that's not too much trouble. And then... we fight." Hugo said.

Katie skipped off laughing.

"She's never made me a cup of tea, you know?"

"That's because you, Scotty boy, don't have my way with the ladies."

"Knock it off! That's my sister you're talking about."

Hugo shrugged, as if he was helpless to control his power. I let it slide. "It's good to see her laughing. Thanks."

"Hey, it's been fun. Looks like you could do with a few laughs yourself."

I sighed, and leaned back against my bedroom wall, the poster of a Manga robot crumpling behind my head. "I know. It's..."

"Work. I get it. You're out there in the big world, now, you don't have time for us silly school kids."

"No, Hugo. It's not like that at all." He raised a disbelieving eyebrow. "Honestly," I said. "It's just all so... real."

He fiddled with the controller for a bit.

"Did I tell you that St Francis' are letting in girls?"

"Since when?"

"Since it was announced this week. I'm hoping there will be some real hotties."

"What happened to the girl from the party?"

"Don't ask; that cow."

"Didn't end well then?"

"You didn't hear?" He turned to me and I shook my head. "She took a picture of me and put it on Facebook and emailed it to all her friends."

"Was it bad?"

"You seriously haven't seen it? Well, you must be the only person in the world who hasn't. The sodding thing went viral. I had to have a nice long chat with the headmaster. And with the school nurse."

"Why the nurse?"

Hugo flushed. "Oh, no reason. I have to say, it's nice to know someone hasn't seen my... well, seen the picture."

"I'll have to rectify that," I said, reaching for my laptop.

"Don't you dare," he said, slapping my hand away. "And don't tell your sister. She might be the only girl left I'll have any chance with. I can wait a few years."

"Seriously, dude. Stop it!" Hugo was smiling and I knew he was only winding me up. "It's nice of you to let her win," I said, softening.

"Let her? Are you kidding me? She's killing me... And here she is."

Katie came in carrying a mug of tea and a glass of orange for herself. She placed the mug on the bedside table next to Hugo and took her place back on the floor.

"How about I only play with one hand?" she said. "Maybe that will even the odds."

"Laugh it up, Tyler. Pick any character and I will destroy them. Get ready for the Wrath of Sister Ra!"

Katie picked up the controller and they were off again.

I lay back on the bed and let their banter wash over me.

I am falling. I can feel the wind whipping against my face so hard it feels as if it's trying to tear my skin off. I try to scream, to shout out for help, but the wind whips my words away. I can see the ground coming for me; racing towards me as quickly as I am falling towards it.

I clutch at passing ropes and branches that appear from nowhere, desperately trying to grab hold of something that will save me. But as soon as I touch anything it turns to dust in my hand.

Suddenly, I am yanked upwards. I am flooded with relief. I don't care about the aching pain in my wrist, only that I am no longer falling. I look to my wrist to see a black, burned hand holding mine. I follow the hand up the arm to see the face of my saviour. Only I know that whatever I am about to see will be a hundred times worse than smashing my brains on the concrete below.

The man holding me doesn't have a face. Not anymore. But I still know who he is. Or who he was.

Abbott opens a lipless mouth and speaks. "What have you done?" he says.

I scream and tear my hand out of his grip, surrendering to gravity. Death will be a relief. I feel every bone in my body shatter as I hit the ground below. And I...

I woke. Not sitting bolt upright, screaming and sweating like you see in the movies. Just one minute I was dreaming and the next I was awake. Disorientated for a moment, I tried to calm my breathing and work out where I was. I was at home. In my bedroom. And I was alone.

I checked my wrist, as I could still feel a burning pain. But there were no marks. It was only a dream.

I probed my memories, like I did every time I woke up – sensing for changes in the reality I found myself in. Sometimes, they'd just be tiny things, subtle Shifts made while I slept that altered my world. Other times, the changes could be terrifying. But tonight, it seemed everything was as it had been. I rolled over and tried to fall back asleep again. Although I already knew it wasn't likely.

CHAPTER SIX

It was Monday morning and my third attempt at getting the eye scanner on the lifts to work. It was bleeping "Individual not recognised" at me over and over. The problem with these things was if you were at all bleary-eyed in the morning they just wouldn't register you. The NSOs patrolling the entrance kept glancing my way. Any minute now, they'd have me up against the wall for a pat down.

"Still can't get them to behave, hey?" said a soft lilting voice from behind me.

I turned to see CP Finn smiling up at me.

"Stupid things," I said, punching the wall next to the scanner. "I don't know what we even need them for."

"This is the question. Are they here to keep others out?" CP said stepping next to me. "Or to keep us in?"

"Either way, they don't work," I said.

"Max says the system was ripped out of the palace of some Middle-Eastern dictator." She shrugged. "Anyway, shove over."

I stepped aside to allow CP access to the control panel. She waited till the scanner slowly tracked down to her eye level, lifted her long fringe out of her eyes, and let the criss-crossing lines of blue light scan across her face.

The machine purred happily. "Cleopatra Finn. Access granted."

CP growled at the screen and stepped in. "Now everyone knows my name," she said.

"Everyone already knew your name, Cleopatra. Because I told them."

I grinned at her and she punched me in the arm.

We stood in silence waiting for the doors to close.

"So, um, have you heard from Jake?" she said, looking down at her shoes.

"'Fraid not," I said. "I did tell Rosalie to say 'hi' though."

"Oh, yeah. No bother."

"He'll be in touch soon, I'm sure," I said, as the lift struggled to the first floor.

"Yeah, sure. Anyway, lots going on round here, right. You excited?" she asked.

"What about?"

CP turned and looked up at me, her small face wrinkled in disappointment. "The Prime Minister's visit!"

"Oh, yeah." How could I forget? It's all Sir Richard had been talking about for two weeks. "For someone who only just learned about the existence of Shifters, the PM's certainly very interested in what we're doing."

"Well, I guess when he found out that a bunch of superpowered kids were being secretly trained by the government he kinda had to do something about it."

"I heard he gave Sir Richard a right old–"

The *ping* of the lift door opening cut me off.

"Anyway," I said, stepping out. "I'm just staying out of the way. Catch you later, CP."

She waved as the doors slid closed.

I headed for my desk where Aubrey was already working, flicking through the night's reports on unregistered Shifts. The analysts had already graded which ones warranted investigation and Aubrey would be deciding which ones to follow up.

"Anything good?"

"The usual. Couple of fights in Clapham. Some kid trying to retake her exams in Isleworth. We may have to go and check out one of them in Holborn."

I heard a loud bang, and turned to see Sir Richard striding down the corridor towards us. Everyone on the floor instantly looked really busy.

"Tyler, Jones," he boomed across the room. "My office. Now."

"Yes, sir," Aubrey said, throwing him a salute. Then waited till his back was turned before throwing him an entirely different kind of hand gesture.

"What do you think he wants with us now?" I asked, pulling myself out of my chair.

"Probably just wants us out of the way so we don't upset the PM," Aubrey said glumly.

Despite knowing we were following him, Sir Richard had still chosen to close his door. I knocked on the dark wood and waited for the barked reply.

"Come!"

Sir Richard had taken over his son's office, clearing it of Morgan's old files and minimal furniture and filling it with an antique desk and an oil painting of himself. The painting wasn't a very good likeness. It showed him looking off into the distance, as if he was thinking deep, important thoughts, resting his chin on his hand. We knew that under that hand was a chin of gargantuan proportions, but the artist had wisely decided flattery was the best way to avoid incurring Sir Richard's rage.

He was scribbling into a black, leather-bound book with a gold ink pen, pressing down so hard that speckles of black now covered his face.

I coughed to hide my laugh.

Sir Richard looked up and for a second looked surprised as if he hadn't just asked us in here. "Yes, right. You two. As you all know, I'm meeting the Prime Minister today. This is huge. Huge, do you understand me?" His moustache quivered as he spoke. The big man was bricking it.

We both nodded.

"So, I'm relying on you two not to make a total mess of it all. I don't want another fiasco like the races, do you understand me?"

Asking us whether we understood was his favourite phrase. We both nodded.

"Right well. I've just been informed that the President of China, who is visiting the UK at the moment, has also shown some interest in ARES. As I'm sure you're aware relationships between the UK and China are somewhat strained at the moment."

I wasn't aware of any strained relationships between anything. But then, I got most of my news around the water cooler.

"Well, they did sell weapons to Borneo," Aubrey said, who was clearly more up on current affairs than I was.

"I don't want to hear anything about that, do you understand?" Sir Richard snapped. "That whole mess has been cleared up. Anyway, President Tsing goes everywhere with a Shifting unit called the *Banjai Gonsi*. They're his personal guard, prepared to sacrifice their lives for his. They are, I have been informed, exceptionally well trained, not to mention deadly. He wanted to come and see ARES HQ, but God knows we couldn't have had that. If he realised what a shambles this place is still, he might decide to declare war. No. We couldn't have that at all. So, Number 10 suggested that some members of ARES accompany the Prime Minister as he takes Tsing on a prescheduled tour of the Shard. Two birds. One stone, you understand? So, I want you two to go–"

"Us?" Aubrey said. "But we have more important things to do."

"More? Important? Than the Prime Minister?" Sir Richard bellowed, getting up out of his seat. "What could possibly be more important?"

"The containment of Project Ganymede personnel, sir," Aubrey spat.

"Oh, yes…" Sir Richard sat back down in his seat, his moustache twitching again. "You brought in another of Abbott's boys last night."

Sir Richard had taken to calling the members of Project Ganymede "Abbott's boys". Most likely as an attempt to distance himself from the whole mess. Despite the fact that his signature had clearly been on the documents approving the project, he still denied all knowledge. I'd yet to decide if he was actually hiding things from us. Or if he really was so big an idiot that the whole project had gone on without him knowing. Twice. First when a scientist called Dr Lawrence started it up. And second when Mr Abbott decided to try it again.

Aubrey had made her mind up the day Sir Richard walked back into ARES. She didn't trust him.

"Yes, sir. Mr Glenn has been processed, just as you required."

"Good." He regarded her with leery eyes and let the silence last for an uncomfortable length of time. It was like being with my parents again.

The lack of trust was mutual. While Aubrey was sure Sir Richard must have known about the experiments, Sir Richard believed Aubrey was hiding something about Greyfield's. I was staying well out of it. The less anyone knew about my part in the whole thing, the better. I stared up at the ceiling and made pictures out of a damp patch in the corner.

Sir Richard finally broke the silence. "And you're still not any closer to finding the mysterious Frank Anderson?" It was an inquisition, as if we weren't doing our jobs.

"We're following some leads," Aubrey said, lying fluently.

"Well, you can get back to following your leads tomorrow. Today, you're to pick a handful of reliable cadets and meet the Prime Minister and the President. It's against my better judgement, but the request has come straight from Number 10. Apparently shots of him talking with children play well with the media."

"The press will be there?" I said. "So we're going public with ARES?"

"God, no. No, the press are there because the PM needs as much positive PR as possible at the moment. So, as far as anyone without clearance is concerned, we are a military school for gifted individuals." He looked us up and down and then stroked his huge chin. "Gifted, you understand? So try and not to act like total idiots, yes? You're to smile, nod, answer any question the PM or the President might have as quickly as possible, do a bit of Shifting, and shove off. And I'll be there, so any sniff that you're not playing this by the book and you're out of ARES. Do you understand me?"

"Smile. Shift. Shove off. Got it, sir," Aubrey said through gritted teeth.

"Good. Good," he said. And then the silence again. I looked back at the damp patch. From one angle it looked like a rabbit. From another an old lady. Sir Richard hadn't had much reason to speak to me before this and I wanted to keep it that way. Keep my head down and just hope he got bored of bossing everyone around and went back to falling asleep at the House of Lords.

"So, can we go then?" Aubrey asked with more hostility in her voice than I thought was wise.

"Yes, go. And I want you both in full uniform today. So you'd better spruce yourself up. Especially you, Tyler. You look like crap."

And with that, we were dismissed.

The dress uniforms were ridiculous. Far too many buttons, stupid gold braid dangling off our shoulders and a too-tight collar. I could hardly breathe. My legs made small buzzing noises as I walked: the thighs of the nylon suit trousers rubbing against each other. But if I was uncomfortable, it was nothing compared to how Aubrey was feeling.

"A skirt," she muttered. "A bloody skirt. They have to be kidding."

"I think you look cute," I said. And then instantly regretted it when she scowled at me.

"Keep up!" I shouted at the cadets behind us, quickly changing the subject.

We'd taken the Tube and were now crossing Tower Bridge, the Shard glinting at us on the other side of the Thames. I'd wanted to walk the whole way, not being the biggest fan of the Underground network since almost being blown up on a Tube last year, but Aubrey had said it was too far for the kids. Sir Richard, meanwhile, would be arriving ahead of us by limo. Way to build morale, I thought. I'd only just stopped sweating from the unpleasant journey.

"What do you think he will be like?" CP asked, catching up with us.

We'd brought her, Max and two new cadets along.

"The Prime Minister?" Aubrey said. "I don't know. Paranoid? He sees danger everywhere, even at ARES. Someone said it's because of what happened to his daughter."

"What happened to her?" CP asked.

"She died on a school trip a few years back," Aubrey said. "Although he said her death is what drove him into politics. To try and make the country a better place in her name. So, you know…"

We stopped talking as a family of tourists passed by, snapping pictures every few steps. They pointed at us in our blue uniforms and started waving their cameras at us.

"Picture?" the mother said. "Take picture?"

Aubrey plucked the camera out of the woman's hands and threw it over the bridge, without even breaking her stride. We all gasped as it fell into the Thames below.

"Aubrey!" I said. The mother and daughter had started crying and the father looked as if he couldn't decide whether to jump in after the camera or jump on us.

"Oh, alright," she said.

A Shift later and we were posing for the tourists, unhappy grins on our faces. When they were finally satisfied we carried on walking.

"So, you two want in on the book I'm running on Sir Richard?" Max said, reaching into his jacket to pull out a small notebook.

"What's the bet this week?" Aubrey said.

"I can give you twenty to one on a stroke. Fifteen to one on a heart attack," Max said.

"Don't," CP said. "He cheats."

"I do not," Max said, aghast at the insult.

"You keep moving things in his room, just to tip him over the edge."

"Can I help it if he freaks just because his paper-weight isn't in the same place he left it and he can't work out why?" Max said, with a devilish grin. I wouldn't trust Max as far as I could throw him. And given his recent growth spurt, that wasn't very far at all.

"Well, you know what Fixers are like," said Aubrey. "Nuts the lot of em. They can't handle change."

"Oi!" I said. "I'm a Fixer."

"And your point?" Aubrey said.

The kids laughed and I was about to put them all in their place with a devastating retort when everything flipped. There was that now all too familiar feeling of being caught between two realities and suddenly we weren't walking across Tower Bridge. We were all stood in front of a huge golden pyramid. I looked around and tried to get my bearings. The Thames. St Paul's. We were still in pretty much the same location, but I didn't know this building.

It wasn't as tall as the Shard had been. But it was wider and made entirely from gold-tinted glass. I couldn't see anything inside as the glass was completely mirrored. I saw my shocked face reflected back in one of the panes.

Sir Richard was standing on my right, with Aubrey, CP and two of the other kids on my left. But Max was missing and in his place, standing with a huge grin on his face, was Jake. He was in uniform, just like the rest of us. Although it was the everyday uniform: the one without the too-tight collars and mass of gold braiding. And he was wearing trainers, something that had most definitely not been allowed under Sir Richard's titan rule.

"Jake," I said. "What are you doing here?"

"Huh?" he said, looking up at me. He'd grown a few inches since I'd last seen him, and his previously soft face was starting to develop strong cheekbones like his sister. A few more years and he'd be breaking hearts. "I'm here to meet the Prime Minister, Scott. You know? Like all of us."

I spun around and pointed at the bloody great pyramid.

"What happened to the Shard? What's that thing doing there?"

"What?" Aubrey said, looking up at me puzzled.

"The Shard. Tallest building in Europe. Great big pointy thing. It was right here!"

Aubrey looked worried. She pulled me away from Sir Richard and the rest of the group. "Scott, are you having a reality attack?"

"I don't know. I know I didn't Shift. But someone else must have."

Aubrey went to speak, but stopped as a long silver car pulled up next to us. "Just keep it together. We'll talk about it later," she said through clenched teeth.

The car doors opened and a young man, with slick brown hair and impossibly white teeth stepped out. He smiled up at the golden pyramid and gave a few waves to photographers who were standing behind cordon tape along with a crowd of people. Two men in black suits exited the car and came to stand by his side, eyes darting left and right.

Sir Richard stepped forward and stretched out a hand to welcome this man I'd never seen before. They shook hands and the man patted Sir Richard warmly on the arm. He then turned to us and smiled, his too-large teeth glinting in the sun. "And you must be the gifted children I've heard so much about," he said, putting deliberate stress on the word "gifted".

Maybe he was an advisor or something, checking us out before the Prime Minister turned up.

"Yes," Sir Richard said quickly. "Let me introduce you to the children of ARES. Children, let me introduce you to James Miller, the Prime Minister."

"Prime Minister?" I gasped looking up at the grinning buffoon. "But you're not the Prime Minister."

CHAPTER SEVEN

There was an uncomfortable silence as Sir Richard and Aubrey gawked at me. Then the man started laughing. Sir Richard picked up his cue and started laughing as well. Followed by the men in black suits.

"Children, hey?" Sir Richard said, patting me on the shoulder so hard it felt as if he was trying to crush my collarbone.

The blow actually helped a bit as the jigsaw started to reveal itself. The man flashing a dazzling smile at the press was indeed the Prime Minister. He'd been voted in last year and was proving pretty popular. Especially with the female voters. Personally, I thought he was a bit of a git.

And yet I still remembered the old guy so clearly. He'd not been so popular. His grey hair and sullen smile didn't play well with the voters. It didn't play with anyone at ARES either. He's been the one who'd put the agency on lockdown: introducing all the security; bringing the NSOs in; insisting on complete containment. He was paranoid about everything.

Someone had Shifted and the world had changed: all these new events rippling out from that one moment. Only I had no idea who or why.

I had to concentrate to hold onto the previous reality, which was the very thing I was trained not to do. Fighting against the current of a new version of the present could lead to a reality attack. And that could be bad news. I'd interviewed a Shifter, a kid who was only about eight, who suffered so badly from a reality attack after a Shift that he'd been locked up in a mental home. I worried that that's where I'd end up one day too.

I didn't know why I had this weird ability to remember alternatives for longer and stronger than anyone else. Most people just held onto glimpses, echoes, that they quickly dismissed. With me, the old reality didn't fade that easily. Sometimes, it was like waking up and not being sure if what you'd dreamt was real. It could take me days to sort through versions, finding places for all my memories. While for everyone else it just happened instinctively. A touch of déjà vu, maybe. A shiver down the spine as if someone had walked over your grave. And that was it. They just accepted the new reality as quickly as the old one collapsed. But not me. I had a serious problem with letting go. I'd never told anyone this, even Aubrey, but I felt this weird sort of responsibility, as if someone had to hold on to the old realities. If only just to understand why they'd come about.

I could feel the two versions of "now" fighting for place in my head. I wanted to hold on to both of them. The problem was, when a reality is shared by lots of people, it's so much easier to accept. The personal stuff, things that just happened to me or people I cared about, that I could hold on to for as long as I wanted. Much longer than I wanted in a lot of cases. But when it was something big, something public, when there were so many people observing the event, so many ropes pinning it in place, it became irresistible. And there wasn't anything much more public than a Prime Minister.

The Prime Minister stopped laughing and stretched out his hand to shake mine. I started to panic. If I shook his hand, it would make him real and harder to remember what had happened. I had to leave myself a message. Something that would put a pin in the old reality so I could work out if this new one was the better. I could hardly write myself a note. I looked at the guards in their black suits and wondered how they would react if I suddenly reached inside my jacket.

His hand was uncomfortably close now. I bit down on my lip. Hard. And tasted the coppery tang of blood. When my lip throbbed later it would remind me. I told myself over and over. Blood equals Shift. Blood equals wrong.

I reached out and shook the Prime Minister's hand. He had a firm shake and surprisingly cold hands. As his fingers closed over mine I suddenly couldn't remember why I was feeling so unsettled. He oozed natural charisma and it was clear why he'd won the election so easily. No, I was worrying for nothing. Not that I could even remember what there had been to worry about.

"Good to meet you…?" Miller said.

"Scott, Scott Tyler," I said.

"And you are?" he said, letting go of my hand and turning to Aubrey.

"Aubrey Jones."

"Wonderful. And hello you, little scamp," he said, ruffling Jake's hair. He half turned to Sir Richard and didn't bother to lower his voice. "I'll have to get a picture with this one later. Ethnics play well with my demographics." He wiped his hand on his trousers. "So about this power, this... sifting?" he said, as Aubrey and I stood looking at him open-mouthed. That's probably why I was so anxious earlier. He was a slippery git. But weren't all politicians?

"Shifting," Aubrey corrected him.

"Shifting, right. From what I've been told, you can undo any decision?"

"Pretty much," Aubrey said, her jaw tight.

"I have to say, I'm a little annoyed that no one told me about this before." He waggled a finger at Sir Richard. "But no matter. I know about you now. You kids should come in quite handy."

"We try and just keep them out of sight and out of trouble, Prime Minister. Controlled and regulated," Sir Richard said, sounding uncertain. "It's what ARES was set up to do."

"Yes, I'm sure that's right. And you're doing a fine job of it, I'm sure." Miller slapped Sir Richard on the arm. "Old Oxford boy, like myself."

Sir Richard forced a smile.

Old? Miller couldn't be much older than forty.

"So, only children have this ability?" Miller said, looking back down at Jake.

"Yes!" Sir Richard said, a little too quickly. Clearly Miller had not been briefed on Project Ganymede.

"Shame. Shame. Can you imagine it?" he said, looking wistful. "Changing any decision. I mean, the women alone..."

I saw Aubrey's fists tighten. If he wasn't the Prime Minister, I was pretty sure Miller would have found himself on the receiving end of a Jones special. "We try and use it for more important stuff, sir," she said.

"Oh, yes, quite right too. Quite right. It's just…"

Before he had a chance to finish, a second limo pulled up next to the first.

The doors opened and four kids who didn't look older than ten or eleven piled out. They wore green suits with high collars and small peaked caps with a red symbol on the brim that I couldn't quite make out. They had the glazed expression of a Shifter weighing up their options. They were scanning the area, taking everything in. After a moment, in which the Prime Minister rocked back and forth on his feet, and Sir Richard clenched and unclenched his fists, the children stepped aside and a small, elderly man, dressed in a simple blue suit with a high collar, slowly eased himself out of the car. Two men dressed in simple black suits, both of whom had suspicious bulges under their left arms, then stepped out of the front. The President of China wasn't taking any chances.

Miller stepped forward and introduced Sir Richard. President Tsing nodded slightly then stretched out his hand. Sir Richard took it and the two men shook. Although I noticed it wasn't Sir Richard's usual knuckle-crushing affair.

President Tsing then turned and walked towards us. He stopped in front of Aubrey and me, and bowed slightly. Not sure what to do, I bowed in return. The rest of the kids followed my example.

"I am interested to see what your ARES Guards are

capable of," Tsing said, turning back to the PM. "I had thought that only China had children with this special power."

"Ha! No, of course not. Yes, these kids from ARES play a crucial role in protecting our fair nation. As I am sure do your *Banjo Gongy,*" the PM said. I winced hearing his terrible pronunciation.

"*Banjai Gonsi,*" the President said. "It means Little Guards. And these little guards have saved my life more times than I care to remember." He smiled down at the boy next to him, who clasped his right fist in his left hand and bowed. The President rested a hand on his shoulder and the boy righted himself.

"And I feel quite the same about these kids. Isn't that right?" Miller reached out a hand and patted my shoulder. "Anyway, shall we?" He pointed towards the doors to the Pyramid. "After you."

Tsing nodded and wandered towards the glass doors, his hands clasped behind his back, walking slowly and taking everything in. His Little Guards followed him, their heads twitching as they looked left and right, watching for any danger.

"You two," the PM hissed, pointing at Aubrey and me. "Walk in front of me and act like you're ready to take a bullet for me, OK? Good."

He shoved me in front of him and we followed the President into the belly of the Pyramid.

The building was even more impressive on the inside. Three walls had been given over to apartments and offices. But the third wall was uninterrupted golden glass through which the grey city outside looked as if it was bathed in sunlight.

"The Pyramid isn't open to the public yet," Miller said. "We are a little behind schedule; you know how these things are. So you are one of the first people to see it. What do you think?"

"Impressive," said Tsing.

"Yes, it is, isn't it?" Miller replied. "I was involved in the initial planning, back when I was Minister for Culture. You should have seen some of the designs they put forward. One of them would have been the tallest building in Europe, you know. We'd have been able to see it halfway across London. But I was told it would have been a beacon for suicidal nutters and terrorists in planes. So I decided on this one. Yes, this building sends out all the right signals: that you don't have to be big to be impressive."

Tsing turned slightly and looked at the Prime Minister. "And of course, on your small island, space is such an issue." He turned back and continued walking.

I could hear Miller muttering something under his breath.

"The lifts are to your left. The observation deck is quite something," he said finally.

The lifts held ten people at a time, so there was a bit of fussing as we worked out who would go in which lift. In the end, Tsing went with his Little Guards in one and we went in the other.

"That jumped up little..." Miller said as the lifts whooshed upwards to the sixty-fifth floor. "If he thinks he can stomp over everyone and we'll just stand by... Small island. I'll give him small island!"

Thankfully, the lift only took a matter of seconds and we stepped out onto the observation deck almost on the very top of the Pyramid. It was about fifty foot square and empty apart from masses of potted plants.

"Wow!" gasped CP, taking the word right out of my mouth.

Through the golden glass you could see across the whole of London. The Thames looked like a glittering snake, cutting its way through the city.

"You can see HQ!" Jake said, running up to the window and pointing out to St Paul's Cathedral and beyond.

"Stay away from the windows," Miller snapped with more force than I thought was really necessary. He coughed and straightened his tie as Jake crept back, step by step, away from the edge. "Um, we had trouble with one of the panes falling out," Miller mumbled.

We all froze, suddenly aware that we were standing in a glass prism hundreds of yards high.

"I'm sure it will be OK now, just... don't touch anything."

The lift doors *ping*ed and we all turned to see Tsing and his guard. He was looking at his watch.

"There is an unnecessary delay of ten seconds between these elevators arriving on their designated floors and the doors opening. I would get your engineers to see to it," he said, stepping out onto the deck.

Miller's lips pursed so tightly, I thought they might disappear altogether.

I watched Tsing's face for any expression that might convey his wonder at the building as he looked about. But there was nothing. He simply walked around the room, hands still held behind his back, taking it all in. His guards were a little less stoic. I saw their eyes widen in involuntary awe as they looked out of the windows.

Miller glared at the President while Tsing gazed out across the city. Sir Richard looked from one leader to the other and eventually broke the silence.

"Mr President, tell us more about your Little Guards. How many children do you have in service?"

President Tsing stood with his back to Sir Richard, looking out of the windows. "Hmm, let me think? I have forty *Xíngdòngzh*⬚ in my personal guard. And about twenty thousand currently being trained."

"Twenty thousand!" I could see Sir Richard's huge jaw tighten. "That's… impressive."

Tsing half turned and looked over his shoulder. "We are a very large country, Sir Richard. And we have sophisticated techniques for searching out potential… Shifters, as you call them." The word sounded awkward on his tongue. "And you? How many Shifters are there in Great Britain?"

"Oh, in the thousands. I don't have the exact numbers to hand, but at least a few thousand," Miller butted in. "Isn't that right, Sir Richard?"

"Um. Somewhere approximating that number, yes," Sir Richard said, looking decidedly pale.

"And what skills do they have?"

"Skills, well… How about they give you a demonstration?" The Prime Minister clasped his hands on mine and Aubrey's shoulders, squeezing hard.

"What? Here?" Aubrey said, looking around at the glass walls and floor.

"Why not?" Miller shook us slightly.

"But what do you want us to do?" I said, as CP, Jake and the other kids looked at each other worriedly.

"I don't know. What has millions of pounds of

taxpayers' money trained you to do?" he said, looking angry, the overly large smile suddenly gone.

Jake raised a hand. The Prime Minister nodded at him to speak. "Um, we learn history and science and..."

"We learn how to fight," CP said.

"Is that so?" Miller looked at Sir Richard.

"Oh, yes. They have years of fighting training," Sir Richard said.

"Good. Well, how about one of you fight one of them?" He pointed at the Little Guards. "Would that be appropriate, Mr President?"

"Yes, quite appropriate." Tsing said something in rapid fire Chinese and one of the boys bowed and stepped forward. He couldn't have been older than twelve.

"You," Miller said pointing at me. "Why don't you show us all what the best of ARES are capable of?"

"You want me to fight him?" I said.

"Yes!" He smiled and then pulled me to one side. "And unless you'd rather make an absolute ass out of me in front of the President of China," he hissed from between clenched teeth, "I suggest you win."

I had to admit the thought of losing just to annoy him was tempting.

The spectators moved back to give us some space and the Little Guard stepped into the centre of the room and waited, his hands pressed firmly by his sides.

I unbuttoned my jacket and handed it to Aubrey.

"No Fixing, now," she said.

"Huh? Why not?"

"It's cheating."

"Just because you can't do it doesn't make it cheating," I mumbled to myself and approached the boy.

He looked even younger close up; his small mouth making a thin line straight across his face and his large eyes quivering slightly.

"It's OK," I said, quietly. "I'm not going to hurt you." I reached out my hand to shake his, the gentlemanly way to do things. Only he wasn't playing by our rules. He grabbed my hand and pulled me forward into his suddenly outstretched foot. I barely missed being kicked in the stomach.

I yanked my hand free of his and spun out of the way as he came at me with a series of spinning roundhouse kicks, one after the other. I managed to block the last one and countered with an elbow punch. It was soaring straight for his face when he Shifted and was back-flipping out of reach.

"OK, I can play that game."

I steadied myself, finding my balance and raising my fists in guard as I'd been taught. Acrobatics over, the boy slid his leg out low and stretched out his arms like a bird. This kid had some pretty sick moves.

I waited for him to come at me again. And he did. Faster this time. Fists flying, Shifting left, right, up, down. His actions seemed to flow into each other and I was just a fraction behind him, barely able to keep up.

I got in a lucky punch and knocked him to the floor, but before I'd had a chance to follow up, he'd flipped back onto his feet again and was coming at me. He was smaller and weaker than me, but he was quicker too. And it seemed we were evenly matched when it came to Shifting. I could Fix him and just get this over and done with, but I didn't think Aubrey would be too impressed. So, I had to find another way to win.

I changed styles, slipping out of kickboxing to try some Capoeira moves I'd been practising lately. This was more like dancing: fluid movements that were about avoiding your opponent's blows rather than blocking them. It was frustrating the boy as well as tiring him out. As I spun and dodged his punches and kicks, he continued to come head on, moving high then low, throwing everything he had at me. His breath was getting heavier and his blows clumsier. He tried a double fist punch and I flicked out of the way with a one-handed cartwheel. As soon as my feet touched the floor, I sprang back and caught his neck between my two legs.

The key with fighting another Shifter was to back your opposition into a corner so they would accept defeat rather than injury. Sometimes, done right, you wouldn't ever actually need to lay a finger on each other.

The boy struggled to be free of my hold. He should, if he had any sense, Shift to avoid me breaking his neck, but it would mean losing the fight. As I tightened my legs I suddenly realised he wasn't going to Shift. He'd rather die than back down.

I released him and jumped away. Was this kid really going to force me to hurt him?

I didn't want to embarrass him in front of his President and his friends, but I'd rather he were embarrassed than injured or dead even. He raced at me again and instead of blocking his blows, I simply scooped him up in my arms in a great big bear hug. His arms pinned to his sides and his legs kicking uselessly, there was nothing he could do to get out of it. And, so what if Aubrey thought it was cheating, I Fixed him, stopping him from Shifting. I wanted this fight over with.

He finally went loose in my arms and I set him down. He staggered back, his chest heaving from the exertion of the fight and the frustration of being beaten. Then bowed.

I bowed too, glad it was all over. The whole thing had shaken me. An image flashed in front of my eyes, an echo from the simulator.

I've wrapped my hands around Katie's neck and I'm squeezing, tighter, tighter.

"Nice job," Aubrey said, jolting me out of the memory. "Shame about the Fix at the end," she whispered into my ear as she handed me my jacket.

"It was either that or really hurt him," I said.

"Well done, Tyler. Very well done," Sir Richard said, slapping me on the back. He looked very, very relieved.

"Is that it?" The Prime Minister said, looking at his watch. "Well, I had been expecting a slightly longer display, but yes, well done everyone. Most, um… impressive." He grasped my hand and leant forward a bit so only Aubrey and I could hear. "Well done on beating the little yellow bastard."

Aubrey and I gasped at the same time. I pulled my hand out of his and stepped away not knowing what to say. What do you say to something like that? He was beaming as if nothing was wrong while smoothing down his hair.

"No hard feelings, hey, Mr President? Your boy put up quite the fight himself."

I saw the boy return to his place by the President's side, bent over, head down. And I noticed rather than take his previous position in front of Tsing, he'd dropped in at the back. I felt a pang of guilt for shaming him in front of his leader.

"Yes, Ken-ze Tsing did a fine job," the President said.

"Ken-ze Tsing?" Sir Richard said. "Your son?"

The President nodded and I saw Ken-ze Tsing's cheeks darken. I hadn't just shamed him in front of his leader. I'd shamed him in front of his father. And for what? To make Miller happy? Screw that.

I closed my eyes, playing out the fight in my mind. There had been a moment when Ken-ze had me, just before I'd changed styles. I focused on that.

When I opened my eyes again, Ken-ze was standing by his father's side, beaming proudly. The winner of the fight.

I had a pang of regret, but when I looked at the outraged expression contorting Miller's face it was more than worth it.

"Well, would you look at the time," Miller said, not even bothering to look at his watch. "I'm sure we all have places to be. Shall we?"

Miller strode back to the lift and got in the first one that arrived with Sir Richard. He punched the close button before anyone else could get in. Just as the doors closed, I saw him turn to Sir Richard and start shouting.

I hoped my little Shifting trick wasn't going to cost ARES too badly.

President Tsing took the next lift with his Little Guards. As the doors were an inch apart, Ken-ze stopped them with his hand. He said a few words to his father, who nodded, then stepped out of the lift.

Ken-ze walked up to me and bowed. "Thank you," he said, the words slow and practised.

"That's OK," I said. "It was a close fight anyway. You're really good."

"I train. A lot!" He smiled. "It is my greatest wish to protect father. My duty. Today, you have made him proud. I am in your…" He bit down on his lip, trying to find the word. "In your debt."

"No debt, Ken-ze. Just take care of yourself. And of your father," I said.

He bowed again, and went back to the lift to join his father and the rest of the Little Guards.

"That was really sweet of you," Aubrey said, squeezing my hand.

"Well, you know me. I'm a softie."

"You're a numptie, more like," Jake said. "I can't believe you threw the fight."

"Hey, sometimes you have to lose to win."

The kids all looked at me.

"That makes no sense at all," CP said, shaking her head.

CHAPTER EIGHT

——

The cool air outside the Pyramid was an instant relief. A larger crowd of people had gathered and were being kept at a safe distance by police. Press photographers tried to lean over the barriers and were being pushed back. There was a flash of camera bulbs as they raised their cameras high in the air while calling the Prime Minister's name. He raised a hand and waved at them, keeping up his profile.

All eyes in the crowd were on the PM and the President. Apart from one man. He was tall, so tall he could see over the gathered people without straining. But that wasn't what caught my attention. It was because he was staring straight at us. No, not us. He was staring at Aubrey.

He had dark, closely cropped hair, heavy stubble and light grey eyes, that weren't blinking. There was something familiar about him. I looked from him to Aubrey. She hadn't noticed the stranger, she was too busy rolling her eyes at Miller's media-whoring antics.

When I looked back the man was gone. I was trying to seek him out in the crowd when I saw a blur of movement from the left. Both the Little Guards and the Prime Minister's security team flinched. It was just a small girl wearing a rabbit mask running towards us holding a bright yellow stuffed bunny.

"Stand down, everyone," Miller said, with a laugh. "It's just a little girl." He bent down as the girl approached. "And hello there. What's your name?"

The little girl said nothing. She just waved the teddy at him.

"Is this an Easter present?"

The girl nodded.

"Is this for me?" Miller said.

The girl hesitated. Looked from Miller to the bunny and then shook her head. She pointed at President Tsing who was standing behind Miller.

"Oh, right. It's for him, is it?" Miller said with a sniff. He straightened up a looked over at the President. "Seems you have a fan, President Tsing."

The old man walked forward and bent low to greet the little girl. She copied him, giggling as she straightened up. She then stretched out her hand and gave him the toy.

"Thank you," he said, accepting it solemnly with both hands. "I will take good care of him."

The girl giggled again and then skipped away, back towards the crowd where she was met by a young girl with long, light-brown hair. I couldn't see the other girl's face as she had already half-turned and was walking away.

Tsing tucked the bunny under his arm and headed back to the limo. Just as the door was opened for him, he started to cough. A small cough at first, as if something was irritating his throat. But it quickly became heaving and desperate. He held onto the car door, wheezing and gasping for air.

The Little Guards ran to him, looking frantic and confused. They called out to him in rapid Chinese and I could tell they were begging him to tell them what to do. He pushed one of the girls aside, as if she were the one denying him the air, knocking her to the ground.

The President clutched at his throat and the bunny he'd been holding fell to the ground. I could see it had specks of blood on its yellow fur. Blood was flowing from Tsing's eyes and his nose. His face had gone pale and the bags under his eyes were sagging lower than they had any natural right to do. His mouth was hanging low on one side, as if he was made out of wax and was melting. White bubbles formed around his mouth and he was thrashing his limbs as if being electrocuted.

"Um… Somebody?" Miller said, staring at the President, unable to move.

The Little Guards were screaming and panicking now. Each of them shouting at the other.

"What's happening to him?" CP asked, sounding as scared as I felt.

"I don't know. Someone help him!" I shouted, desperate to make whatever was happening stop.

Ken-ze ran over and started shouting at me, tears falling down his cheeks.

"I don't know what you're saying," I said.

He shook his head and scrunched up his face, as if he was trying hard to remember something. He clenched his fists and banged them against his legs, hard. "No move. No Shift!" he said, finally.

"You can't Shift?" I said.

Ken-ze nodded frantically at me and pointed at the other guards who were now trying to hold Tsing up. The President's eyes were rolling in his head and his lips had gone a terrible shade of purple.

"None of you can Shift?" I shouted.

Again Ken-ze nodded, even more furiously this time.

"Scott, are you Fixing?" Aubrey said.

"What? No. I mean, I don't know," I said.

Was I? Was I holding events in place? That only happened when I wanted to keep a reality in check. But why would I want the President to be writhing around in pain on the floor?

"Stop it!" Aubrey shouted at me.

"I'm not doing anything," I shouted back.

I kept looking between Ken-ze's terror-filled eyes to the President who was thrashing on the floor.

Miller was backing away as if worried he might get some of Tsing's blood on his too-shiny shoes.

I closed my eyes and tried to Shift, sorting through the day's events. Trying to think of something I could undo to stop all of this. But with all the screaming and panic I couldn't focus clearly.

"I'm sorry about this, Scott," I heard Aubrey say, just before I felt pain exploding in my jaw.

Lights sparkled behind my eyes and my knees crumpled under me. Everything tilted and I could see Aubrey shaking her hand like she'd hurt it and the Little Guard bowing low in front of her, thanking her for something.

My shoulder hit the pavement, followed by my head.

"At least you won't remember," Aubrey said, as I blacked out.

A moment later I was standing upright again, next to Aubrey, CP and Jake. The Prime Minister was pacing back and forth looking furious.

I looked around. Tsing and his Little Guards were nowhere to be seen. I stretched my jaw, expecting pain. It was fine.

"Right, I've had enough," Miller said, "We've waited an hour and he's not coming. That rude, slitty-eyed bastard. Well, see how he likes our treaty now." He stormed off to his limo without so much as a backward glance in our direction, muttering all the way.

"Who isn't coming?" I said softly, but no one answered.

Sir Richard turned to us. "None of you are to talk about what you saw or heard today, do you understand me?"

"You mean we're not to tell anyone that the Prime Minister is such a tool that the President of China stood him up?" Aubrey said.

Sir Richard wagged a warning finger at her. "Not a word." He took a deep breath and closed his eyes. Then walked off to where his car was waiting.

"What a dick," Aubrey said when we were alone again.

"Which one?" Jake asked.

Aubrey rocked her head back and forth, considering. "Both of them."

The kids all laughed. I shook my head, trying to settle everything back into place.

So the President hadn't turned up. Which meant we hadn't all watched his face melt off. Which must have meant his Little Guards had been able to Shift, after all. And all because Aubrey had knocked me out with one punch.

No wonder I felt dizzy.

"What was that 'You're not the Prime Minister' gag all about?"

"Huh?" I looked at her. "Oh, I don't know…" I felt a dull ache in my lip. "Did I get hit in the mouth?"

"Hit? No. Scott, are you OK?" Aubrey said.

I tongued the ragged hole in my lower lip and tasted blood. Blood. Something was wrong. Something I had to remember. The Prime Minister. The Shift.

"I can't believe I forgot!" I shouted. "That guy isn't the PM. Or at least he wasn't this morning. It was another guy called Vine who was the Prime Minister. But on our way here it all changed. And that!" I said, pointing at the Pyramid. "That was not here either."

"Scott, keep your voice down," Aubrey said, nodding to the cadets, who had wandered off to check out a fountain in the courtyard.

"But a minute ago the President of China was dying, right in front of us." I pointed to the ground where he had been writhing and foaming at the mouth. There wasn't a single mark. "And his Little Guards couldn't Shift because I was Fixing them and you hit me."

"I hit you? Calm down, Scott. I can't understand a word you're saying," Aubrey said.

"But don't you see? Someone Shifted and the bloody Prime Minister changed. That's… Well it's huge."

"Not necessarily, it could have been a really small Shift. Or Scott, you could just be confused. Remember your training – just let it go." She squeezed my arm, trying to make me calm down.

"I'm not confused," I snapped. "It happened. I know you can't remember, but that's not my fault. And I kind of wish you wouldn't keep trying to make me forget. Because I don't want to."

I felt a buzzing in my head as if I was listening to music too loud and couldn't concentrate. Aubrey trying to reassure me, the kids play fighting, and the light reflecting off the Pyramid seemed too strong.

"I have to… I have to go…"

"Scott, wait!" Aubrey called after me.

"No. I just have to be alone!" I shouted.

I stormed off and headed for Tower Bridge. At least that hadn't changed.

As I walked, banging into people I only half saw, I sorted through my memories, trying to distinguish the old from the new.

I kept seeing Tsing's face, lips curled back in pain, a silent scream escaping from his mouth. But I knew that he was safe. His Little Guards had done their duty and he'd avoided danger by simply not turning up. OK, so the Prime Minister had been insulted. Far better that than the previous reality. As for the change in Prime Minister, for some reason it was that Shift that troubled me even more.

I had shadowy images of Benjamin Vine, the man I remembered as Prime Minister: at press conferences, on news shows, standing outside Number 10. But slowly all of those moments were wiped away and replaced with images of James Miller, the shiny jerk I'd just met. The ripples of reality settled and I could see things a little more now. I started to compare the two realities. We were still at war in Afghanistan, Miller refusing to pull our troops out, whereas Vine had brought that fight to an end six months ago, preferring to concentrate on the issues at home, such as making sure everyone at ARES behaved. Miller had recently signed some big deal on climate change, a deal I seemed to remember Vine not being able to get heads of state to agree with. Other than that, I didn't really know. I made a mental note to start taking a more active interest in politics in the future.

It didn't really matter to me what Miller had or hadn't done. Or that life at ARES was back to normal, without Vine interfering. All that mattered was that the leader of the country had changed because someone had Shifted. I didn't care what Aubrey or anyone said, I wasn't going to let this go.

It took me over half an hour to get back to ARES, and Aubrey was already at her desk. She looked up as I approached.

"Scott, are you OK?" she said, sounding relieved. "I was worried about you."

I placed a cup of takeaway coffee from her favourite café on the table in front of her. My peace offering.

"I just needed to clear my head."

"And is it clear now?" she said, keeping her voice low.

"Not really."

She took a sip of the hot coffee. "Vanilla sprinkles?"

I nodded. "Of course. They're your favourite."

"I'm sorry I wasn't much help earlier," she said, pulling her chair closer to me. "It's just so weird, you know? You remembering all this stuff everyone else forgets. I just don't know how to deal with it."

"How do you think it makes me feel?" I said, rubbing at my pounding temples.

She looked left and right, checking we weren't being watched, then reached out and squeezed my hand.

"Let's find this old PM of yours." She nudged me out of the way so she could get to my keyboard and launched the ARES database. "What was his name?"

"Benjamin Vine," I said, giving her a grateful smile.

A rattle of keys and a file came up.

Dr Benjamin Vine. GP. Born 1968. Married to Marie Vine, nee Lay. One daughter: Charlotte Vine aged eighteen.

"His daughter. She's not dead," I said, pointing at the screen.

"That must be nice for her," Aubrey said.

"No, I mean, you told me she'd died in an accident. It's why he went into politics."

Aubrey opened her mouth to protest and then thought better of it. "Obviously not in this reality. What else can we find on her?"

Aubrey did a second search, her fingers dancing across the keyboard, this time for Charlotte Vine. There was even less information on Charlotte. Her birth date, schools she'd been to, and a picture of her from an article in the local press about a school trip accident. I scanned the article. They had been rock climbing and Charlotte's rope had snapped. Luckily she'd only been a few feet off the ground when she fell, so escaped with just a sprained knee. The picture showed her standing on a cliff edge, blonde hair blowing in the breeze, one knee bent as if it was causing her some pain. She was wearing climbing gear and a hard hat, and her arm was thrown around another girl who had long, frizzy hair that fell over her face.

"Seems like a pretty average girl," Aubrey said.

"Apart from the whole coming back from the dead thing," I said.

"So someone Shifted and the accident never happened?"

"But why now?" I said. "Why did the Shift happen today? Why not six years ago straight after the accident?"

Aubrey shrugged. "Sometimes it takes Shifters time to find their way around events. They probably don't even remember making it now."

"And what about the attack on the President? They have to be connected somehow."

"It could just be a coincidence. But think about it. In the old reality two people died. In this one, everyone's OK. Charlotte and the President are still alive and relations between China and the UK are preserved. That has to be a good thing, doesn't it? Whoever made the Shifts, even if they were connected, they did them for a good reason."

"I guess," I said.

"I hate to say this, but you really just have to–"

"I know." I shut down the file and forced a smile. "Let it go."

Only there was no way I was going to.

"Should I report it? I mean, the attack? If someone tried once, they might try again?" I said.

Aubrey sucked at her lip, thinking. "The Regulators will have probably registered the Shift anyway. But maybe leave out the mysterious Shifter stuff. Just say the attack happened and the Little Guards took care of it."

I was already typing away, trying to get down every last detail before I forgot it.

"It will mean revealing to Sir Richard that you can remember old realities. Are you prepared for that?" Aubrey said, fiddling with a pen on her desk.

I hadn't thought about that. I just wanted to unload this weight onto someone else. Someone who could do something about it. But maybe it was time I told. Maybe it could be of some use to the agency.

"Not really," I said. "But I can't keep something this big just between me and you. I feel like I have a duty."

Aubrey laughed, but her smile didn't quite reach her eyes. "Oh, ARES sure has its hooks in you, Scott."

I tried to laugh as well. But she was right. I was an agency man through and through now. "Towards the true way." I really believed in that.

"Well, luckily Sir Richard is still at Number 10 being debriefed by the PM. Maybe you can slip that report on his desk and escape before he has a heart attack." She mimed clutching at her chest and I laughed. For real this time.

I didn't have a choice, not really. I had to tell someone. Besides, I'd feel better with one less thing to worry about.

After I finished my write-up on the events at the Pyramid and left it on Sir Richard's desk, the rest of the day was spent sorting through other business. We got the psych evaluation back on Jack Glenn: definitely exhibiting the first signs of psychosis. They were going to remove the transplanted brain tissue and hopefully that would mean he was back to normal. It would also mean he wouldn't be able to Shift again. But that was no bad thing. I marked his file "completed" and got on with the backlog of other things I had to do that had nothing to do with Project Ganymede.

By the time I finally finished it was already 6pm. Most of the other kids had either gone home or back to the dorms, and my head was pounding.

"I hate paperwork almost as much as I hate field-work," Aubrey said, stretching out her arms behind her head. "And Sir Richard just can't get enough of it."

"Mmm," I said, only half listening. Aubrey didn't know how lucky she was. The amount of paperwork in the old reality was way worse.

"You're really stimulating company today, Scott, you know that?"

"I'm sorry. I'm just really tired," I said.

"Well, go home and get some rest. That's what I'm going to do." She stood up and pulled on her jacket. Looked around the room quickly and, seeing we were alone, planted a soft kiss on my lips. "Try and sleep," she said, gently thumbing my cheek.

I watched her walk away, her jacket slung over her shoulder, the laces of her boots trailing behind her. They certainly wouldn't have been allowed under the iron rule of the MOD. Or the mask of make-up she wore that kept the world from seeing the real her.

Things were back to normal now we had a new PM. I should be grateful. I should be. But something didn't feel right. I kept prodding at the old memory, like a hole in a tooth. Like something was rotten.

I hit "submit" on the report and shut my computer down. I knew it was late, but I really needed to clear my head. Which meant going for a run.

Outside the building, I tightened up the laces on my trainers, pulled on my backpack, and went. It didn't matter where. In fact, the thing I'd discovered about free running, the important thing, was not knowing where I was going. I'd just run till my heart started pounding in my chest and my lungs started to burn. I'd turn left or right, race down a side road, leap over walls and down staircases and find myself somewhere I'd never been before.

I felt the pavement beneath my feet, each pounding step sending shockwaves up my legs and into my body. I vaulted over a railing and rolled as I hit the street below, the momentum bringing me back up onto my feet. It sometimes felt as if free running had been made for Shifters. You took a risk – running full speed at a wall or launching yourself off a roof – and for most people it only paid off some of the time. Me? I could make sure that every move, no matter how dangerous, resulted in a safe landing.

A group of school kids sitting on a wall shouted something as I approached. I sprung off two walls, pulling off a sweet Tic Tak, leapt over their heads and was gone before they'd recovered.

It was seven miles to home. On a good day it took me just over an hour to get back. Except when I got really lost and had to unravel my path. That happened a lot when it was dark and I would follow some lights ahead and end up... somewhere. Tonight, a full moon was rising in the east. I made sure it was directly behind me and headed west. My only focus was not focusing. Not choosing. It was the only time when I wasn't trying to plot every single decision in my life. The only time when I felt free.

The further I got away from ARES the further I got from the pressure that I wasn't only responsible for my actions, but the actions of so many other people. It was crushing. And I was so tired. All the time. The nightmares were getting worse. I kept having one where a burned and scarred Abbott would come to me and say "What have you done to me, Scott? What have you done to yourself?" And he'd remind me of all the things I'd done while on the simulator one by one.

Along with all the stuff that had happened today, I wanted a moment that belonged to just me. Where I couldn't affect anyone and they couldn't affect me.

A cat wandered in front of me and hissed as I sprung over it.

I took a left, sliding over the bonnet of a car that blocked my way. It blasted its horn. I started to recognise roads, and knew home wasn't far away, which always made it harder to stay in the moment.

I turned right, into the alleyway that would lead to my road, and slammed into a man who I knew hadn't been standing there a second before.

CHAPTER NINE

I staggered back, my fists raised instinctively, and glared at the stranger.

He had badly cut dark hair and looked like he'd shaved with a knife. His grey eyes bored into mine.

"You," I said, recognising him now, both from outside the Pyramid earlier and from the club a few days ago. "You're a Shifter."

It wasn't a question. I was sure I'd sensed a Shift when he'd appeared at the top of the alley. An adult Shifter. Was it possible that the man we'd been hunting for had come for me?

"Anderson?"

The man flinched at the name and batted his hands in front of his face, as if trying to ward off invisible attackers.

"Are you Frank Anderson?" I said.

"No!" he roared. "Never. Never. Killer."

He was clearly unhinged. Late stages of psychosis most likely. I'd have to get him back to ARES for an eval. "It's OK," I said, sliding off my backpack. "I'm going to get you help."

I looked down to find my phone and suddenly my bag was wrenched out of my hand and thrown away.

"I don't need help. I'm here to help you. Help you help her," he said, his face an inch away from mine. His breath stank.

I stepped away, looking to my bag behind him. I could easily overpower him and get it back. But I wanted to take this one nice and slowly.

"It's OK, Anderson."

"Stop. Stop saying that name. I'm not Anderson!" He flinched again, holding his hand to his head. As he brushed the shaggy strands of hair away from his forehead I couldn't see any scar. But it had to be Anderson.

"Sure," I said softly, as if trying not to spook an animal. "What shall I call you then?"

"Jones. My name is Jones. Captain Thomas Aubrey Jones."

I let what he'd just said sink in. Then snorted. "Aubrey Jones? Yeah right." How he knew Aubrey's name I didn't know. Or where I lived, for that matter. But I was sure he was the man we'd been hunting for and I was going to bring him in. I laid a hand on his arm, in preparation to cuff him. I just had to get to my bag. He was faster than me. He twisted out of my grip, grabbed hold of my hoodie, and pushed me up against the alley wall.

"She's dead. She killed her," he said, stinking spittle covering my face.

"Who's dead?" I said, still shocked from how quickly he had moved. I had to focus harder, to find a Shift that would get me out of this situation.

"She died in my arms. Only a child. So tiny. So perfect." He let go of me and looked down at his empty hands.

"Who?" I said, readjusting my hoodie and slowly sliding away.

He looked up at me, tears filling his eyes. "Aubrey. Aubrey is dead."

My mouth was suddenly dry. "She... she can't be. I just left her."

"Because the witch brought her back. Killed her, then brought her back. Wicked witch. Wicked. She made me her flying monkey." He flapped his arms up and down, mimicking a flying thing. "She took my hope. My hope and my heart. Opened up the box and it flew up and away. Like Pandora. Like a monkey. Pandora, the witch."

The fact he was clearly insane made up for the terror that had gripped my heart when he said Aubrey's name. I took another step towards my bag.

"You have to stop her," he said. "Not me. Not me. I have to stay away. To protect her. She'd take my baby away if I so much as tried. But you..." I froze in reaching for my bag as he looked at me again. Grey eyes the colour of a stormy sea. He reached out a gnarled finger. "You can stop her."

"Stop who?" I said, hoping to placate him just long enough for me to call in back-up.

"The witch. The witch that killed my Aubrey. My daughter."

"Your Aubrey? Are you... are you saying you're Aubrey's father?"

"Captain Thomas Aubrey Jones, Mapper, Fifth Class, reporting for duty." He stamped to attention and pulled a salute that Sergeant Cain would have been impressed by.

"Look, I don't know what you're playing at. But Aubrey's father wasn't a Shifter. He was a waster who walked out on her when she was four. Now, I'm going to reach into my bag here and–"

He squatted down so his face was level with mine. "I had to leave her. It broke my heart. But the witch made me. She took my child. She took all the children. Now you have to stop her."

"OK, sure," I said appeasing him. "I'll stop her. Where can I find this witch of yours?" I was scrabbling around in my bag, trying to find either my phone or my cuffs.

"Over the rainbow. Red and yellow and blue and green. Green. You have to find green." He was staring ahead, gazing into whatever madness he was seeing.

"I have to find green. OK," I said, nodding. My fingers were just on my phone. I looked down to grab it.

"Don't forget green," I heard him say.

When I looked back up, I was alone in the alley.

I ran to the end of it and looked left and right. Nothing but empty streets.

He'd vanished.

"Damn it!" I said, kicking the wall.

I called ARES anyway.

"Good evening, the Academy for Revolutionary Engineering Sciences?" the voice on the other end answered.

"Scott Tyler, Fixer, Third Class. Put me through to the Regulators."

A few beeps later and a female voice answered the phone. "Speak."

I rolled my eyes when I recognised the voice. "Lane," I said. "It's me, Scott."

I heard her grunt from the other end. "What is it now, Tyler?"

"I need you to run a cross check on a location for an unlicensed Shift."

"As if I didn't have enough to do."

"What is it?" I heard Lottie's voice in the distance.

"It's Tyler. Got himself in trouble again," Lane said, not even bothering to cover the mouthpiece. "Go on then, Tyler."

I checked my phone and read out the GPS coordinates of my location. I heard the rattle of keys from the other end of the phone.

After a minute, Lane sighed. "Nope. Nothing registering in that location. Is that all?"

I hung up without giving an answer.

No Shifts registered. How was that even possible? I'd sensed the Shift myself. Whoever he was, I'd just let him slip through my fingers.

I picked up my bag, threw it over my shoulder and headed for home. At least I knew what he looked like, that was one thing. But what all of that crap about Aubrey had been I didn't know.

I kicked at the ground, so annoyed with myself. I couldn't even think of a Shift I could make that would allow me to get the upper hand on him as I'd spent the last hour consciously not making any choices. I'd screwed up big time.

I crossed the road and looked at my house and the houses next to it. It filled me with a mild sense of relief. Whatever else happened to me this place stayed unchanged. The same mid-range cars parked in the driveways. The same doors painted a series of safe yet stylish colours picked straight out of catalogues. The same middle-class families going about their business behind those doors. Funny, how I used to hate this place, how turning into the top of my road used to make me feel sad and pathetic and like my life wasn't going to go anywhere. Now, I embraced the boredom.

"I'm home," I said, as I let myself in.

There was no response. Mum and Dad were shouting at each other from the kitchen. I really needed a glass of water, but I just couldn't face them, not tonight.

I walked upstairs, my legs like jelly, to the top of the landing. As I walked past Katie's room I heard a soft sobbing from inside.

I hesitated for a minute outside, letting my breathing calm down. She probably didn't want me bothering her. She probably just wanted to get on with feeling miserable for herself. I know I would. But she was my little sister and I couldn't just let her be alone.

I knocked softly.

"What?" Katie shouted.

I opened the door slightly and pushed my head in. "Hey," I said.

"Hey," she said in return.

There was no point in asking whether she was OK. Or if Mum and Dad were driving her mad. Of course she wasn't. And of course they were.

"How was school?" I stepped inside and closed the door behind me.

"Sucky."

"What happened?" I sat on the side of her bed and picked up one of her teddy bears and stroked its ears.

"I got into St Francis."

"What? I didn't know you were applying."

"Yeah, Mum made me. Went on and on about my future. So I sat the exam last week and got in."

"That's amazing."

"Only they're not giving full scholarships. Which means Mum and Dad will have to pay. Which is why they're screaming at each other again."

"Mum and Dad are screaming at each other because of Mum and Dad. They'd be screaming if you didn't get in as well. I guess they just like to scream." I took hold of her teddy's arms and used it as a puppet version of Mum and Dad freaking out.

She laughed a little. "I don't even want to go to that stupid school. Only weirdoes go there."

"Hugo goes there," I said.

"And?"

She had a point. "You don't have to go if you don't want to, you know?"

"Are you kidding me? They'll make me. I'll get the talk about not wasting my life like Dad from Mum and the one about not squandering my potential from Dad. I wish I'd never sat the stupid exam." Katie scrunched up her eyes and clenched her fists hard. Like she was willing herself to undo the exam. Suddenly everything went quiet downstairs.

I felt a flutter in my stomach and looked at my little sister.

"Katie, did you just…"

It couldn't be. Had my sister just Shifted?

"Did I just what?" she said, her big blue eyes clouded with tears.

I heard a thumping and Mum started yelling at Dad again.

"Nothing. Don't worry." My ability to sense Shifts was way off. Lucky I was a Fixer rather than a Spotter. I ruffled Katie's hair and stood up. "I need a shower."

"You're telling me!"

I threw the teddy at her head. She caught it and squidged him under her chin. It reminded me of the yellow bunny from earlier. I wondered if the girl with the bunny mask still had it out there, somewhere.

"You can't change it, you know?" I said.

"Change what?"

"Mum and Dad."

Her forehead wrinkled and she scrunched up her little nose. "You're so weird, Scott."

"You don't know the half of it," I said as I closed her door behind me.

Back in my room, the buzzing in my head was louder than ever. How and why had Anderson tracked me down? What did he want, apart from spewing crazy stuff about witches and rainbows? And what did he want with Aubrey?

I kept hearing the name "Thomas Aubrey Jones" echoing in my head. What if... what if he hadn't been lying?

I pushed a pile of folded clothes Mum must have left on my desk onto the floor, pulled my laptop out of my rucksack and ran a search for Thomas Aubrey Jones.

A file came up, with a picture of a young man wearing an ARES uniform. The picture must have been taken decades ago judging by the uniform and haircut. I looked at his dark hair, slicked over his forehead, his grey eyes, and imagined the face older, scarred and covered in dirt. It was just possible it was the man I'd met.

I slumped back in my chair. Had Aubrey's dad really been a Shifter? It did run in families, I knew that much. Like Jake and Rosalie.

All of the information on Thomas Jones was redacted. Blacked out with a thick pen so all I could read was his name and rank: Mapper, Fifth Class. That was high ranking. I didn't know anyone in ARES higher than Fourth.

"No," I said out loud, shutting down the file. It couldn't have been. The name Thomas Jones hadn't been on the list of candidates for Project Ganymede. And I was almost certain I'd sensed the man in the alley Shift. Almost certain.

But maybe I'd been wrong. There'd been no register of the Shift. Maybe he'd just been able to move that fast naturally.

I dropped my head into my hands. Nothing was making any sense. On top of the mess in my head over the man in the alleyway, the memories of Vine as Prime Minister and the attack on the President were eating away like at me like a maggot.

To distract myself from stressing over Captain Thomas Jones, or whoever he really was, I pulled up another search: Benjamin Vine.

The files Aubrey and I had been looking at earlier appeared again. I enlarged a photo of Vine at a village fête, mentally layering the old image I had of him over the one on screen. The memory I had of him was of a stern man. Tired and worn out and always sad. But in this picture, as he held up what looked to be a Victoria sponge, he looked so happy.

I launched the file of Charlotte Vine and stared at the image of her on the edge of a cliff till I could see it when I closed my eyes.

Why wasn't this enough for me? A good thing had happened and yet here I was picking at it like a scab. A dead girl had been brought back and was now living a life of meaning and value. A President had not been killed on foreign soil. Whoever had made the Shifts had brought about a better reality. Did I want to take that away just because I wanted things to stay as they were? Maybe Aubrey was right about Fixers being weird because we don't like change.

She was right, I should just focus on the job at hand. Anderson. I should also tell Aubrey about how I'd met him. If that really was him.

I pulled out my phone, brought up her number, then stopped. What was I going to tell her? That a man claiming to be her father had turned up and told me she was dead?

If I called Aubrey at – I checked my watch – close on midnight, she'd freak. No, I'd have to wait. I'd tell her in the morning. I should just try to get some sleep and maybe everything would make sense tomorrow.

I closed down the computer, pulled off my clothes, and threw myself into bed.

"Green. Don't forget green," the man's voice echoed around my head.

As I lay there, the memory of another "green" came into my mind. Benjo Greene. The cannibal who'd been Abbott's henchman, doing his dirty work for him. The man who'd tied me and Aubrey up and threatened to eat our brains.

I'd had my revenge on him, just like I had Abbott.

Bile rose in my mouth as I remembered the report from Greyfield's – the photo of a charred body found strapped to a metal gurney. Mr Abbott, the head of the Regulators. The man I had killed. There was a second picture in the file Sir Richard had made me read, scouring my face for the slightest twitch that would give me away. The second picture was of the body of Sergeant Cain, a man who had been my teacher and friend and who had died trying to protect me.

I'd spent the first few weeks after the fire trying to find a way I could bring him back. Aubrey and I had talked it over and over, trying to find a Shift to undo. But anything we could think of would either end up with Aubrey being operated on or us never uncovering what had been going on.

"Cain wouldn't have wanted that," Aubrey had said. "He'd rather have died than that." And I agreed.

Only two bodies had been recovered. Greene's body had never been found. We'd assumed that it was because it had been burned up. All that fat would have made him go up like a candle. He was dead, I was certain of it. Certain.

I threw my arm over my face and willed myself asleep. Maybe by tomorrow I'd have forgotten all about Vine and the attack. And as for the man in the alley, well, I wouldn't let him get away a second time.

I took a deep breath and tried to let it all go.

Half an hour later I was standing outside Benjo Greene's building.

CHAPTER TEN

The building was covered with large stickers declaring it to be "dangerous" and "condemned". I peered in through one of the broken windows and saw nothing but darkness inside. Nothing stirred. Not even a bird.

What had I been expecting, really? Benjo up on his sofa, tucking into a fresh brain dipped in mayonnaise? The man was dead. Coming here to an empty warehouse wasn't going to make me any more sure of it. And yet, I'd had to come.

You're an idiot, Tyler. What are you?

I leaned my head against the window and was about to Shift my decision to come here, when I heard a squeaking from inside the abandoned warehouse, the high-pitched sound carrying on the still night air. It had to be a mouse, or a rat. That place had to be filled with them. But if I just took a quick look inside…

I checked the street was empty and ducked under a strip of cordon tape, yanked aside a plank of wood covering over the doorway, and squeezed myself inside.

It took a while for my eyes to adjust to the darkness.

The only light in here was the shine of the moon breaking through from the gaps in the roof overhead. The old machinery and piles of rubbish I'd seen the last time I'd been here had been cleared. The warehouse was empty.

That was it. I was done. I closed my eyes and felt for the decision that led me here. With a thought I would be back in my bed and hopefully asleep.

"I wondered when you'd come looking for me."

The shock of the voice made me jump so much, I almost fell over. I spun around to where the small, croaking whisper had come from. Out of the shadows stepped a man. At least, I thought it was a man.

He was a bag of flesh and bones. Even in the half-light I could see folds of skin hanging low on his cheeks. Only the black, button eyes looked familiar.

"Benjo?"

The last time I'd seen him he'd been munching his way through a table of surgical tools. It didn't look as if the meal had agreed with him.

He must have lost at least twenty stone. Although it had left him with rolls of skin, now hanging empty around his body.

He chuckled, the sound a wet, horrible rattle in his throat. "Who else did you expect?"

"You escaped?" I said finally.

"No thanks to you," he said. His voice was dry and speaking seemed to cause him pain. His dark eyes were madder than I'd ever seen them. "How did you do that to me? How did you make me do… those things? And poor Abbott. Perhaps I should have tried to save him. But the fire was so strong. He died screaming your name, Scott Tyler. Did you know that?"

Heat burned at my cheeks, but it wasn't as bad as the ice in my stomach. Guilt.

"Where have you been for the last six months?" I asked, avoiding his question.

"Here. Hiding. Waiting."

"Waiting for what?"

"For you, my fresh Shifter. Only…" he sniffed at the air. "You're not so fresh now, are you? Reckon that power of yours is running out. Tick tock. Tick tock." He rocked his head back and forth, the action sending the flap of skin under his chin swaying. He stopped and smiled, his mouth a dark hole, then took a jerking step forward.

I fumbled inside my pocket for my phone. "Don't move. Don't even breathe!" I shouted, suddenly realising I hadn't actually planned for what I would do if I found Benjo.

"Oh, don't worry. I won't put up a fight." He stood with his hands by his sides, looking up at the holes in the roof.

I punched the number to speed dial ARES and the call was answered after two rings.

"Scott Tyler, Third Class. I need immediate assistance. Grouber & Sons Upholstery, East Street," I said to the ARES receptionist on the other end of the phone.

"The Regulators will be with you in five minutes," her soothing voice came over the phone. "Anything else I can help you with?"

I hung up.

"Third class? Impressive. I always knew you'd go places," Benjo said, a small grin hitching up one side of his drooping mouth.

"Just shut up. Don't say a thing."

"Oh, but I've been so lonely. With no one here to talk to. Just me and my rats." He held out the furry body of a rat. Small bites had been taken out of its stomach.

I turned away in disgust.

"Don't look away, Scott Tyler. You did this to me. You," he shouted, throwing the rat at my feet. "I've been forced to live off rat's blood and marshmallows. Eating causes me pain. You've robbed me of my only pleasure."

"If that means you can't eat people's brains any more, I don't know if I feel too bad about it. You're a killer, Benjo. And you expect me to feel sorry for you?"

Benjo snorted. "I would never expect someone like *you* to feel anything other than disgust. You were always so limited in your understanding."

He was right. I did feel disgusted by everything he was and everything he'd done. But I felt sorry too. And terribly guilty as I looked at him, almost buried under the weight of all his useless skin.

"The Regulators are coming and we're going to take you in and you'll be punished for your crimes."

"Good."

I blinked, confused. "Good?"

"Yes. Good. It's so cold here. And damp. And I can't go anywhere without people pointing and screaming. No, a nice clean cell and soft, squidgy prison food… Yum, yum." He said it with a glazed look on his face, as if he was describing a beach holiday.

I couldn't quite believe that he was here. As much as I'd come here looking for him, I hadn't actually believed I'd find him. I was coming just to put my mind at rest. Like when you worry you've left the iron on and you know, really, that you haven't, but you just have to check. But it seems as if I had left it on after all. And maybe I'd found the answer to my questions right here.

"Was it you?" I said.

"Was what me?"

"The President of China. The Shift today. Was that you?"

"Now, what would I want with the President of China? His Little Guards on the other hand, now them I'd like to get to know."

He made a slurping noise as he took another step forward into a beam of moonlight. I almost retched. Half of his face was a puckered mess of scars. The red flesh oozed in the pale blue light.

"Oh, you like my new look, do you?" he said, gesturing to his face with a wave of his hand. "Seems flames don't agree with my complexion."

"So, was it you?" I said, swallowing the vomit that had risen in my throat.

"I don't know what you're talking about. I haven't been able to Shift since our last meeting."

"What? Why not?"

"Entropy, I guess. Caught up with me at last."

There was a crash from behind me as the Regulators broke through the door and piled in, the beams of their torches slicing up the darkness.

"It's OK," I said, "It's under control."

But they weren't listening. They were in mission mode.

"Down! Down!" One of them started screaming, pointing her Taser in Benjo's face. I recognised Lane under the visor.

Before even waiting for a reaction, she pulled the trigger. Two darts attached to wires shot out of the end of the gun, and embedded themselves in Benjo's unscarred cheek.

He sighed, reached up a hand, and pulled the darts away, leaving two red holes in his face.

I saw Lane hesitate. The Taser had had no effect on him at all.

"Just get down, Benjo," I said.

He shrugged, and slowly, as if it was causing him terrible pain, lowered himself to the floor.

Lane leaned over him. "Hands behind your back," she shouted.

"I'm not sure you're going to want to do that," I said. But she ignored me and cuffed Benjo.

"Now, on your feet," she shouted.

"Um," Benjo's muffled voice came from the floor. "We may have a problem."

"Feet! Now," Lane shouted.

"Do we have a problem?" a second Regulator said, coming to stand next to Lane. She pulled her visor off, letting her lank hair fall free. Great, Lane and Lottie to my rescue. I was never going to hear the end of this.

Benjo huffed and wiggled around like a landed fish, but utterly failed to get to his feet.

"We're going to have to help him up," I said, already wishing I hadn't bothered calling the Regulators in. "How many of you are there?"

"A unit of six, as standard."

"That might just be enough. Guys, get over here."

The four other Regulators who had been making sure the rest of the building was clear walked over. I bent over and took Benjo's elbow. Lane took his other arm and Lottie took a leg, twisting her face away from him in revulsion. The other Regulators reluctantly took whichever bit of Benjo's body they could reach. None of us wanted to touch him.

"OK, on three. One. Two. Three."

We pulled. Even with the weight loss, it was still a struggle to get him to his feet. But finally we managed it.

"OK, take him in," I said, wiping my hands on my trousers.

"What's going on, Scott?" Lottie asked. "Who is this guy?"

"Benjo Greene. He was connected with the Ganymede Project and is responsible for the death of at least five Shifters that we know about and who knows how many we don't."

Lane and Lottie turned to look at him as he shuffled off, smiling at the Regulators around him.

"Try not to get too close," I said. "He likes to lick people."

They both groaned in disgust.

"Don't worry, I'm not going anywhere near him," Lane said.

Benjo stopped at the doorway, and no matter how much the Regulators shoved him, he wouldn't be budged.

He turned back to look at me. "Will you be joining us, Scott?" he said, as if he was just heading into dinner rather than being arrested.

"Oh, don't you worry, Benjo. I'm not done with you yet."

"Good, I look forward to having a nice chat. It's been a while." He smiled. His remaining teeth shone in the moonlight. "And bring marshmallows. I have developed a taste for marshmallows."

I watched him go and wondered if he was telling the truth about not being able to Shift. If it wasn't him responsible for what had happened today, then who was? And had the man in the alley's warning not to forget green just been a coincidence? It had to be.

I took a deep breath and climbed out through the broken door.

CHAPTER ELEVEN

"I wasn't sure you'd come and see me," Benjo said.

"I said I would."

Benjo was even more repulsive in the bright lights of the interrogation room. He sat, blinking like a mole, his thighs sagging over the edge of the small seat. His skin, which had once been rosy and pink, was now grey, bordering on green. And the burn scars on the left side of his face were oozing. He was a shadow of his former self.

"And you are a man of your word, isn't that right, Scott Tyler? A man whose word cannot be broken."

"What's he on about?" Lottie asked, angrily.

I didn't want anything connecting me to that night at Greyfield's and how I'd been able to bend reality to my will.

The experience had been terrifying and yet thrilling at the same time. It had taken me two weeks before I'd dared try to bring it on again. I'd focused on trying to make Max get me a cup of coffee. Nothing had happened. I still wasn't sure how I felt about that. Relieved? Or sad that all that power had gone.

"How am I meant to know what he means?" I snapped at Lottie. "He's a nutjob."

Lottie shrugged. "I'm not going to argue with that. Anyway, he's all yours. You've got ten minutes and then we're taking him to processing." She closed the door and I heard the security locks clunk closed.

I was alone with Benjo once more.

I couldn't face sitting near him, so instead I leant up against the mirrored wall, clutching the Project Ganymede file to my chest, trying to stay as far away as possible. "So it's true then? You can't Shift?"

"You think I would be here if I could? You think I would be like... this?" He held up his arms, the wings of flesh wobbling.

"I guess not."

"Oh, but I can still Fix. Isn't that strange? Not that I could Fix you, Scott. Isn't that right? You're more powerful than any of us."

"Shut up."

"Oh, I see. You don't want anyone to know." His eyes lit up with delight. "Well, you can trust me." He held up a bony finger and pressed it to his sagging lips. "Shush," he hissed. The sound set him coughing, a wet, gurgling sound.

I turned around and stared into the mirror because I couldn't face looking at him. Only it was worse looking at myself.

I looked pale and tired and I really needed a shave, something that I was still trying to get used to. I remember when I was jealous of boys at school who bragged about their facial hair. Now it was just a pain. But it was my eyes I didn't want to look too closely at. I looked down at my feet instead.

"So, come on then, Benjo. You said you were waiting for me. What did you want to tell me?"

"Tell you? Oh, nothing. I have nothing to tell you. Do to you? Now that is a different matter. I've been dreaming about what I would do to you. That's what kept me alive, living in my hole with... with only my rats for company." He sniffed and when I looked back, big pearly tears were falling down the deep creases in his face.

I forced myself to remember how he'd almost killed Aubrey, remember the deep red scar she hides under her fringe, and I didn't feel quite so bad.

I pulled out the chair and sat down in front of him. "The brains in your place, Benjo. We retrieved them months ago and identified your victims. You killed five Shifters and those are only the ones we know about. You want to tell me about the others? Or don't you remember them?"

He sniffed a bubble of snot back into his nostril and stared at me. "Oh, I remember every one. Even ones I had to go back and put right. I can hold onto the memory." He leant forward as far as he was able given the chains pinning him to the chair and I could smell his rotten breath. "You can do that too, can't you?" he whispered.

"So, are you going to tell us then?" I said, desperate to keep the conversation on track.

"I killed you, you know? And your pretty friend. I can remember it all so clearly."

"That was a drug-induced dream, Benjo. It never happened. And it's never going to happen. Now are you going to tell us how many deaths you've really been responsible for?"

"Where would be the fun in that?"

I'd had enough of him. He was never going to tell us about the other people he'd killed. And I wasn't even convinced he wasn't lying about remembering them. I would pass him back to the Regulators and let them process him. I didn't care what happened to him. I only wanted to never, ever see him again.

To finish, I asked him the question I asked every man I'd interrogated over the last few months, not really expecting any useful response. "Frank Anderson. Do you know him or where we could find him?"

I was sure it had been him in the alley. The fact he'd been able to track me down so easily was unsettling. Best I find him before he found me again.

Benjo flopped back in his chair, making a loud slapping noise as flesh connected with flesh. He tilted his head and smiled, revealing stained and pointy teeth. One of his canines was missing. "What do you want with Frankie?"

"You know him then?" I said, a swell of hope rising. If Benjo could really lead us to Anderson we could put it all behind us. We could know for sure if there were any more Shifting adults out there. Anderson held the key to it all, I was certain of that. "Where can I find him?"

"Him? You want to find *him*?" Benjo smiled even wider, happy that he was the one back in control. "Why should I tell you that? You of all people? Why should I tell you anything?"

He had a point. I had absolutely nothing to offer Benjo. I wasn't even going to tell the Regulators to go easy on him. He deserved everything he got and more.

"Don't think you can slime your way out of punishment again, Benjo."

"Oh, I don't doubt that. It's what comes after my punishment that I'm interested in discussing."

"What is it you want?" I said.

"Well, I'd really like a nice nibble on your frontal cortex, but I guess that's not going to happen."

I gave him my most unimpressed face. "How do I even know you have any information, Benjo? You weren't a part of Project Ganymede."

"No, but Abbott told me all about it and all of the players involved."

I wished Aubrey were here. She'd know how to handle this mess. Maybe I should have woken her up after all. Maybe I should just come back tomorrow. I gathered up the paperwork, closed over the file, and stood up.

"I want to be buried with my father," Benjo said just as I turned my back. Simple as that. He said it with no swagger or whine. Just a simple statement of fact.

I turned to face him.

"I'm dying. It's obvious isn't it? My life's just slipping away from me. Seems my slow-ageing genes were no defence against you." He smiled, not evil or scary. If anything, he was looking at me with respect.

"So, that's all I ask. When the time comes, your doctors don't chop me up and examine my brain. You let me be. And you bury me with my father."

"And in return?" I said.

"I'll tell you about Anderson."

"I don't know if I can do that," I said. I was sure that the docs would love to get their hands on this guy to try to unravel what made him tick.

"Oh, I think you'll be amazed at what you can make people do when you put your mind to it, Scott. I know I was. In fact, I've been dying to tell everyone just how persuasive you can be."

So, that was what he was playing at. He would tell everyone about what had happened and what I'd been able to force him to do. Most likely no one would believe him. But I wasn't willing to take that chance.

"I'll see what I can do," I said.

"That's all I ask."

"You've had your ten minutes, Tyler," said Lane, opening the door. "We're taking him down to processing."

"Just give me another minute." I ignored her sigh. "Now, it's your turn, Benjo. We had a deal."

Benjo pouted his lips and looked up to the ceiling a picture of perfect coyness. "I can't tell you where to find Frank…"

"Then what the hell was that all about?"

"But," he continued, looking back at me. "I can tell you that you're looking in the wrong place."

"What do you mean? We've been looking everywhere for him."

"Exactly. You're looking everywhere for *him*."

"Come on. Time's up." Lane said. She unlocked the chains and pulled Benjo to his feet.

I didn't know what Benjo was on about and I was fuming I'd wasted time pandering to his requests. Only…

"Wait!" I held up my hand to stop Lane and looked at the smug grin on Benjo's face. "Him? We're looking for *him* in the wrong place. Are you saying Frank isn't a him?"

"I suggest you start looking for *Francesca* Anderson, nee Francesca Kingly, in Africa, the last place I heard she was. She has a thing for little lost children," he said. "But then, who doesn't?" He winked, the fold of his eyebrow melding in with his cheek. "But be careful, she has a way of getting under your skin. Not as stylish as my method, but still. Effective."

"Get him out of here," I shouted. "And if I ever see him again, I'll kill him."

"I look forward to it," Benjo said, before he was pulled away.

CHAPTER TWELVE

I stood alone in the small room trying to gather my thoughts. The idea of Anderson being a woman just hadn't occurred to us. But maybe Benjo was lying. He could just be messing with me.

I pulled up my tablet and did a search for Francesca Kingly. And there she was, smiling out at me from the screen. A young woman in ARES uniform. How could we have been so stupid? Anderson was obviously the name she took after getting married, which she must have done between leaving ARES and signing up for Project Ganymede. That, combined with the fact we'd been looking for a man, meant we'd never have found her if not for Benjo.

I sensed a change in the light and turned around. The back wall that was usually a full-length mirror was now smoked glass, still dark but clear enough to see through. Standing on the other side was Sir Richard. He'd been watching the whole thing.

He leant forward and pushed a button on the control panel in there. His voice filled the tiny room, reverberating through hidden speakers and sounding like he was coming from all angles at once.

"I'd like to see you in my office, Tyler."

He pushed another switch and the glass returned to its mirror state, reflecting back my face, which was a picture of shock.

I played back my conversation with Benjo. Had I given myself away? How much could Sir Richard have worked out? And what was he doing at work this late?

I paused before knocking on his door. Up until now I'd managed to stay off his radar. I kept my head down and my boots polished to a reasonable shine and he'd ignored me. Just as I wanted it. But it looked as if he wasn't going to ignore me for much longer. I thought about Shifting and avoiding this whole mess. But if I'd never gone looking for Benjo we'd still be looking for Frank Anderson, the man. Maybe I would remember that Anderson was a woman after Shifting. But I didn't know if I could take the risk.

Sir Richard must have heard me shuffling outside. "Come!"

The door creaked as I opened it. I swear it never creaked when it was Morgan's office. Either Morgan junior had kept the hinges oiled or Sir Richard had got someone to make it creak, just for the extra intimidation factor.

"Sir?" I said stepping inside. He was sat behind his desk on the phone to someone.

"Do you think I'd be calling at 2 o'clock in the morning if it wasn't important? Get her in here now!" he shouted into the receiver before placing it back in the cradle and turning to me. He looked tired, not surprising given the time.

"Pull up a seat, Tyler," he gestured at one of the leather-covered chairs in the corner. I dragged it closer to his desk and sat down. The seat was so low, I could barely see over the top of his desk.

"So, interesting events took place at the Pyramid today, it seems," he said, tapping the brown covered folder on his desk that contained my report.

I was regretting ever telling him. "Yes, sir."

"Any idea who the attacker was?"

"I don't know. One second President Tsing was holding a toy rabbit, the next he was…" I closed my eyes, trying to block out the images.

"And you remember it all. Even after the Little Guards made their Shift. You remember?" he said, leaning forward in his chair.

"Yes, sir. Seems so," I said.

"And has this always been the case, this ability of yours?"

"Pretty much, sir," I said.

He let out a snort of air and sat back in his seat. "You're not the only one, Tyler. I worked with a chap who could remember the old realities. Name of Cooper."

"Really?" I said, hopefully. Maybe my ability didn't make me into a total freak after all?

"Yes, odd fellow. But one of the best Fixers ARES ever had," Sir Richard said.

"What happened to him?"

"Oh, he ended up in an asylum. Quite mad. There's a reason we train you to forget past realities, Tyler."

"Yes, sir. So I understand."

"But in this case it has proved useful." He tapped at the folder. "I'll inform the Prime Minister. It might help

ARES gain a little more favour. If the attack had been successful the outcome would have been catastrophic for international relations. If we're lucky, we might just be able to take credit for stopping it." He slid the report out of the way and started scribbling on a pad of paper.

So that was his game? He'd say that it was ARES members who'd saved the President. I didn't really care as long as it meant I could get out of here.

"Will that be all, sir?" I said, after the sound of scratching ink pen became too much to bear.

"Not quite," he said without looking up. "Mr Greene is a very interesting character is he not? And it seems you two have met before."

"I, er, I had a run in with him in the past, sir."

"And this was at Greyfield's? Oh come on, Tyler," he said, re-capping his pen. "I know you were there. I've known all along. I have reports of you running around asking people where you could find Ms Jones the day that the place went up in flames. And I know she was there. And I know that you are a very determined young man, ergo... I was just waiting, no hoping, that you might tell me yourself." He steepled his fingers under his huge chin and for a moment looked just like his son.

"Yes, sir. I went to try and find Aubrey. I didn't tell you because I was worried about getting into trouble."

"Oh, you're not going to be in any trouble. At least not if you just tell me everything that happened."

"I don't know what you mean, sir."

He pinched the bridge of his nose as if trying to hold back a headache. "Stop playing the fool, boy. We both know that something very unusual occurred that night. We found Abbott's charred body tied to a machine and it was clear that he could have let himself out if he wanted. But he didn't. At first we thought the SLF might have been responsible for his death. But I questioned Isaac Black myself."

"You spoke to Zac in the cells?"

"Cells? What are you on about? I spoke to him a few weeks after the event when he was issued with a Shifting license."

For a moment, the two versions of Zac's fate flickered in my mind. In one, he'd been arrested for unlicensed Shifting and locked up in the cells downstairs. In the other, the reality we were in now, he'd gone legit, got a license and used it to become hugely successful playing professional football. Yet more ripples peeling off from the Shift at the Pyramid.

"Oh, yes. Of course," I said, trying to gloss over my confusion.

"He was very helpful. He said he'd had a change of heart about ARES and was willing to help us in any way he could. Especially given that was the only way he was going to get an official license for Shifting. Anyway, he said he had nothing to do with Abbott's death and I believed him. When we questioned the soldiers who were on duty that night, they said that they'd found themselves acting against their will, leaving their posts and in some cases, falling asleep on the floor. And they all said they'd seen a boy matching your description walk by them and they'd not been able to stop you. Not a single one. Can you explain that to me?"

"No, sir, I can't."

"You mean you won't." He glared at me through narrowed eyes. "Do you have any idea how much pressure

I am under to maximise the performance in this place?
To prove that we are actually of some use? If Miller had
his way every one of you children would be locked up
and experimented on. Poked and prodded like lab rats.
He wants to do more than control your powers, he
wants to weaponise them, do you understand? It's lucky
he listens to me. I'm all that stands between you and the
operating table and all because I have promised to give
him what he's after. Answers.

"We have never truly understood the Shifting power,"
he continued, stroking his moustache. "There are theo-
ries and speculations. Some feel that it is simply what it
is, while others, Mr Abbott included, believe that there
is yet more to be discovered. Untapped reserves of power
that would only be revealed in the right circumstances.
What do you think, Tyler? Do you believe we've discovered everything there is to know, or is there yet more to
find out?"

I mumbled something about not being sure.

"I used to think that the power was fleeting, limited.
But after the research uncovered with Project
Ganymede I'm not so sure. And maybe you hold the key
to that. You and what happened that night."

"I don't know what you mean, sir. I went there, got
Aubrey out and then left."

I was a terrible liar. My cheeks were burning and I
had to hold on to the edge of my seat to stop my hands
from flapping around my mouth.

"But of course there is the footage from the security
cameras."

My quick intake of breath was a total giveaway. I
didn't know about the cameras. Or at least, I assumed

if there had been any that the fire would have destroyed any footage.

He continued to stare at me, stroking his long chin in slow repeated movements. "But maybe we won't need that."

There was a knock at the door.

"Come!"

I turned around, relieved that someone was coming and I might have a chance to get out of here and call Aubrey and we could work out a plan. Only it was Aubrey at the door.

She looked tired, she'd clearly left her flat in a rush and hadn't had time to put on her make-up or do her hair. She also looked scared. Her body was stiff and shaking slightly. Her eyes darted around the dark room and finally found me. When they did, she let out a loud sigh and her shoulders dropped.

"Scott, you're OK," she said.

I stood up as she ran forward and threw her arms around me. I returned the hug, resting my chin against the top of her head. I was so tired, so empty after everything that had gone on today, I just wanted to stay like this and let everything else fade away.

Sir Richard coughed his disapproval and so, reluctantly, I let her go and sat back down.

"Thank you for joining us at such short notice, Jones," Sir Richard said, not sounding grateful at all.

"The person who called told me that Scott was in trouble," Aubrey said.

I looked back to Sir Richard, wondering why he'd summoned Aubrey and just how much trouble I was in.

"Oh, not really, Jones. Take a seat. We're just going

over the events on the night of the thirtieth of September last year."

"Again? I've told you everything already," Aubrey said, deciding to stay standing. She rested her hand on the back of my chair.

"Ah, but you neglected to tell me that Mr Tyler was with you that night. Don't bother trying to deny it," he said, before Aubrey had a chance to speak. "Tyler himself has admitted to it."

She scowled down at me and I knew I was going to get a serious talking to later about how I had to learn to keep my mouth shut.

"And now I would like your help in piecing together some of the events that took place that night," Sir Richard said.

"I don't know what you mean, sir," Aubrey said, her mouth a small pucker of irritation.

He raised himself up out of his chair till he was towering over both of us. "No more games now, do you understand me? You will tell me what went on or I will make you." Spittle flew as he roared at us.

Aubrey backed away. "Sir, I don't know what you—"

"Enough!" he bellowed. "I had hoped it wouldn't come to this." He pulled open one of the drawers in his large oak desk. Aubrey and I exchanged a look that said a lot about wanting to get the hell out of here. When we looked back to Sir Richard he was holding a gun.

It was an old fashioned pistol, the kind you saw soldiers wear for ceremonial occasions. But that didn't mean it wasn't still deadly. Sir Richard had clearly taken good care of it. Its dark barrel shone with a purple sheen from being polished time and time again.

He flipped open the cylinder and slotted a brass bullet into one of the chambers. I stood up and backed away from the desk. Aubrey was on the other side of the chair and I reached out my hand, trying to reach hers. Our fingertips barely touched.

"Sir, I'm sure there's been some misunderstanding."

With a flick he closed the cylinder over and pointed the gun, first at me then slowly he moved it so it was pointing at Aubrey.

"Actually, Tyler, understanding is exactly what this is about."

"Please, sir. Put the gun down," I said, holding out my free hand to try and calm him.

"Make me, Tyler." He kept the gun pointing directly at Aubrey but he was looking at me. "You can, can't you? What was it Greene said? That you'd be amazed at what you could make people do if you put your mind to it. Well, go on then, Tyler. Amaze me."

There was a small click as he cocked the firing trigger back. I moved, hoping to put myself between him and Aubrey but he flinched. "Don't move, Tyler, or it's over." His voice was steady although his hand was shaking.

I looked at Aubrey. Her eyes were wide, but she didn't look afraid. She had her chin lifted and her shoulders back.

Shift, I thought. Don't be stubborn. Just Shift. Only she wasn't moving. I looked back at Sir Richard.

"I don't know what you're asking me to do, sir."

"I'm asking you to stop me."

I took a step towards him, reaching my hand out for the gun. "Not like that. With your mind, boy!"

"I... I don't know what you mean. I can't make you do things. No one can."

"You're a bad liar, Tyler."

I looked from Sir Richard and back to Aubrey. She turned to me and smiled. "Go on, Scott. It's OK. Do it."

"Yes, come on. I haven't got all night."

So, he wanted me to force him to stop. Like I'd forced those men in Greyfield's. Like I'd forced Abbott to kill himself.

I dipped my head and stared at Sir Richard, trying to summon up that strength inside me. Tried to direct my will at him. "Put the gun down," I said.

Sir Richard raised an eyebrow. "Nope, you'll have to try harder than that."

I tried again, searching inside myself for any vestige of that power. "Put the gun down," I said, louder although even less certain.

Again nothing happened.

"Come on Scott, you can do it," Aubrey said, and her brow was furrowed above her nose like when she's really confused about something.

I shook my head. I couldn't. I couldn't do it. A tear of frustration rolled down my cheek.

Suddenly Aubrey changed. Her confident stance was gone and her eyes widened in fear. She looked from me to Sir Richard, her head shaking. "No, no."

I didn't know if that was directed at me or at him. Why didn't she just Shift?

"Well, Tyler. Seems as if you need a little more motivating."

His finger twitched and I reached out, trying to stop him, putting everything I had into a single thought. My blood was thudding in my ears and I felt my heart tighten as if it might never beat again.

I roared it as well as thinking it. "Stop!"

Click.

The hammer connected. But the gun didn't fire.

None of us moved for a minute. Sir Richard still had the gun pointed at Aubrey's head, my hand was still reaching out to him, while Aubrey shook, tears rolling down her face.

Eventually, Sir Richard lowered the gun and laid it on the table. He placed a single brass bullet next to it. He'd never even loaded the gun.

"You may go," he said, as if nothing more had happened than a usual status report.

Aubrey didn't wait to be told twice. She spun around and charged out of the room. I couldn't make my legs work. My hands were shaking and I was having trouble breathing.

"Oh and Tyler. I want you to make the attack on the President your top priority. The file on Project Ganymede is shut, do you understand?"

He didn't even bother to look up at me. He just sat back in his chair and started scribbling notes with his gold pen. I wanted to grab it off him and stab him in the throat with it.

When I finally made it out into the corridor Aubrey was nowhere to be seen. But her jacket, her Bluecoat, was lying on the floor in an abandoned heap.

CHAPTER THIRTEEN

I let myself into Aubrey's flat with the key I knew she hid over the mantel of the door. Getting in downstairs had been easier still. I just pushed all the entrance buttons and waited till an annoyed, half-asleep voice swore at me and buzzed the door open.

I flicked on the lights in her hallway and walked down into the kitchen. I'd persuaded her to pay the electricity bills just so I could come around with my projector to show her some classic monster films. We'd turned her living room wall into a cinema screen and we'd watched movies all night long.

The clock in the kitchen hadn't told the right time in weeks, but it was still feebly trying to tick away. Maybe Aubrey had gone for a walk? Or gone to Bailey's to try and relax? She wouldn't be too long, I was sure of it. I checked my watch. Nearly 3am. She'd be back any minute. The look on her face right before she ran out had been really scary though. Filled with fear and disappointment and it all seemed directed at me. I tried to tell myself I was being paranoid. That of course it was

Sir Richard she was furious with for pulling that stupid stunt with the gun. She probably just needed a rant and a hug and she'd be OK.

I placed her Bluecoat over the back of the single chair in the tiny kitchen and sat down to wait. As the minutes ticked past, I pulled the jacket sleeves around me.

What had Sir Richard been up to, I wondered. Now that I'd failed his stupid test would he forget about what Benjo and the guards at Greyfield's had said and just leave me alone? Or would tonight be the first of many attempts to try to make me reveal my power? Whatever he wanted, it hadn't worked.

But why hadn't it worked?

I'd always thought that it would be there when I needed it again. Just waiting to be called upon, like some comic book super hero. "If you need me, you know where to find me." But tonight, I'd really, really needed it. And nothing. I wasn't sure which was worse. The nightmares I was having about what I'd made those men do, or the realisation that I'd never have that control again.

I heard a rattling at the door and jumped out of the chair.

"Where have you been?" I asked, and instantly regretted sounding like a nagging spouse.

"What are you doing here?" Aubrey said, as she let herself in.

"I was worried about you."

"Yeah, well you needn't be." She kicked off her boots, threw her keys on the floor and went into the lounge. I ran back into the kitchen, grabbed her jacket off the chair and followed her into the front room.

"You forgot your jacket."

"I didn't forget it, Scott. I quit. I don't want anything to do with that place or that man again. Can you believe him? What an arrogant arse. I didn't think anyone could be worse than his son. But apparently I was wrong." She wasn't meeting my eyes.

"Aubrey, it's OK. Calm down."

"Don't tell me to calm down! I will not calm down."

"So stay pissed off. Just tell me this: why didn't you Shift?"

She spun around and glared at me. "Why didn't I..."

I sensed I'd said something really stupid, but I didn't know what. "Yeah, why didn't you just Shift when Sir Richard pulled the gun?"

She ran her fingers through her shaggy hair and her fringe remained standing upright, revealing the thin red scar that ran from temple to temple. "You just have no idea, do you?" she said, shaking her head.

"So tell me." I held her wrist and pulled her close to me.

"You're an idiot, Scott Tyler, do you know that?"

"Yes, you tell me all the time."

"I didn't Shift because I couldn't. Because when they called and said you were in trouble I thought you were... I don't know. Hurt? Dead? So, I didn't stop to think. OK?"

She sounded as annoyed with herself as me. Annoyed that she'd been stupid enough to race into a situation without planning her options and all because she thought I might be hurt. I fought back a grin.

"It was like when I heard about Mum all over again," she said, turning away from me. My smile froze on my lips. "I remember when Abbott called me back to HQ because he had to tell me something about my mother, and I just knew. I knew she was dead. So when I got that call tonight..." She chewed at the edge of her thumbnail. "God, I need a cigarette."

"It's OK. I'm OK."

"Yeah? Well you're not the one who had a gun pointed to your head. You're not the one who thought you were going to die. You're not the one who was..." She looked at me, eyes brimming with tears.

"Who was what?"

She bit her bottom lip. "Nothing. Forget it." She wiped her eyes with the cuff of her sleeve.

I tried to wrap my arms around her but she shrugged me off. "Aubrey, look at me. I'm sorry," I said.

"It's not your fault he's an evil git."

"I don't mean I'm sorry about him. I mean I'm sorry about me. I'm sorry I couldn't stop it."

She fiddled with a book on her shelves, trying to fit it in the row of other books packed tight between the two ends. It wouldn't go.

"Aubrey," I said, resting my hand on her shoulder and turning her to face me. "I tried."

Aubrey sighed and wrapped her arms around my neck. "I know you did."

I rested my forehead against hers. "I don't know what happened. I don't know why I couldn't do it again."

"Maybe whatever it was, was just a one-off thing. Maybe it only works if you've just come back from the dead. Who knows? I just hope we never have to find out," she said.

"I'm so sorry he did that to you, because of me."

"I'm the one who should be sorry. I shouldn't have expected anything of you."

"I was so scared," I said, lifting her chin to look at me.

"Me too," she said.

We kissed, our mouths slotting together, comfortable and familiar. She tasted of mint and alcohol.

"You were at Bailey's?" I said after we'd pulled apart.

"Rosalie says hello. And Jake wants to know how we're getting on with Project Ganymede." She still sounded annoyed, but her guard was back up, the emotion she'd revealed hidden away again.

I remembered my meeting with Benjo. "Actually," I said. "I have a lead on that."

"What?"

"Anderson is a she."

"What?"

"Frank is short for Francesca. And Anderson is her married name so no wonder we couldn't find her on the ARES database."

Aubrey shook her head. "I can't believe I didn't think of that!"

"None of us did. But it's OK, now we know we can track her down."

"How did you find this out?" Aubrey said, still sounding annoyed with herself and a little annoyed at me for getting the first breakthrough.

"Um…" I started. I wasn't sure if I should tell Aubrey about Benjo. Not after the day she'd had. But she'd find out soon enough. "You're probably going to want to sit down," I said, leading her towards the sofa.

"Scott?" she said, warily. "What have you done?"

"I've not done anything. Only…"

"Only what?"

"Only I found Benjo. He's alive."

She gasped, her hand flying to her mouth.

"But it's OK," I said. "He's in an ARES' cell now. I arrested him."

"But he's dead. You said he died in Greyfield's. That you made him eat his tools."

"He escaped."

Her breathing was ragged, her pale face flushed with anger. "After what he did, to us, to those kids, to Heritage! He deserves to be punished," she said standing up, fists curled into tight balls.

"He has been, Aubrey. He's a broken man."

"I'll break him again," she said.

She paced back and forth in front of her bookshelves. Suddenly, she stopped and looked at me. "How did you know?"

I stood up and joined her. "It's a little complicated."

"Well, I should say so. Someone we thought was dead is now alive. Did he come after you or something?"

It had just been a coincidence that the man from the alley, the man claiming to be Aubrey's father, had said the word green. He couldn't have meant Benjo Greene. It had just set off a chain of thoughts in my mind. I wasn't going to tell Aubrey about the man. She'd had a crappy enough night.

Then a book on her shelf caught my eye. I reached out and pulled it out.

A hardback, golden-bound edition of *The Wonderful Wizard of Oz*.

"What's this?" I said, opening it.

"What do you mean? It's a book. Don't change the subject."

On the first page, underneath the title, there was a scribbled note.

"A heart is not judged by how much you love; but by how much you are loved by others."
To my heart, my hope, my Aubrey. Love always, Dad xxx

"Your father gave you this book?"

She grabbed it off me. "So what? It was the only thing he ever gave me."

The wicked witch. The flying monkeys. It was all making a kind of weird sense.

"What's this all got to do with Benjo?" she said.

"Your father, Aubrey. He led me to Benjo."

There was a loud bang as the book fell to the floor. "You saw my dad?"

"I think so. Thomas Aubrey Jones?"

She gasped at the name.

"Captain Thomas Aubrey Jones, Mapper, Fifth Class?"

Aubrey's brow furrowed and she shook her head. "No, he was just a guy. Some loser guy who walked out on my mum. He wasn't a Shifter."

I looked at the book on the floor. "I'm not sure, Aubrey. I think he was. I did a search on him on ARES' database…"

She ran back into the hallway and pulled her tablet out of her bag. Her hands were trembling still, but I didn't think it was from anger now.

"I never thought…" she said as she turned the table on. "I mean, I Googled him, I just never." Her words caught in her mouth as the picture of Captain Thomas Jones appeared on the screen.

She stared at him. And now I saw the resemblance was unmistakable. He can't have been much older than her when the picture had been taken.

"No," she said finally, and threw the tablet on to the sofa. It landed face up, Captain Jones still staring out at us. "No!" she said, louder this time. "Because, if he'd been a Shifter – a Mapper – he would have known."

"Known what?"

"The consequences," she said, her voice broken by emotion.

And I knew she meant her mother's death. Her own burning guilt. The one thing she never talked about.

"He said he had to leave to protect you."

"Protect me?" she said, a hopefulness creeping into her voice. "From what?"

"I don't really know what he was saying, to be honest. He was a little…" How was I going to say this? "A little mad."

She walked over and picked the book back up, brushing her hand over the embossing on the front. "I always wondered where he was," she said, so quietly I could hardly hear her. "What he was doing. If he ever thought about me. Why he'd just left me alone. When I was little, I used to dream he'd come and find me and take me away. Like some knight in armour, you know? But when I got older, I decided Mum was right about him. He'd never wanted me or her. I hated him so much, I thought if I ever did see him, I'd…" She bit down on her bottom lip so hard I was worried she'd draw blood. "So why now?" she said. "Why you?"

I shook my head. "I don't know. He was babbling all

this weird stuff about a wicked witch having taken all the children and Pandora…"

"Pandora?" she said.

"Yes, but he wasn't making much sense. He went on about a box of hope and how I had to find green. And, well, green made me think about Benjo and how we'd never found his–"

"I remember hearing something about Pandora," Aubrey said, ignoring me and picking up her tablet. "A charity for Shifter kids. Lane told me about coming across it when she was in Africa. I remember because I asked her if it had anything to do with saving pandas and she laughed so hard I thought she was going to choke."

I tried to hold back my own grin.

"What?" Aubrey said, annoyed. "I didn't know you don't get pandas in Africa. Look, I'm a bloody good Shifter, right? I never bothered much with zoology. Stop smirking."

I tried.

"Pandora Worldwide," she read out from a website she'd just pulled up. "Providing hope for lost children. There's stuff here about how long it's been running, how many children it's helped," she muttered, scanning the page. "Here!" she said triumphantly. "It was set up by a woman called Francesca Goodwin. Francesca! You were right. And would you look at that?"

She handed me the tablet that was showing a picture of a woman. She was gazing into the camera, a soft, almost sad smile on her face. It was the same face I'd seen before from the ARES' files, only older. She had a long, thin nose, large full lips and scar on her forehead that managed to make her look even more beautiful somehow. Highlighting her otherwise perfect face.

"Goodwin?" I said. "Not Anderson?"

"Maybe she married again. I don't know. But look at her scar," Aubrey said tapping the picture.

There was no denying it. This was the woman we were after.

"It could just be a coincidence."

"Another one? Like Greene was a coincidence? I don't believe it. He was right," she said. "He wanted us to follow the trail to Pandora. To her."

The excitement in her voice made my stomach twist. Because I knew it wasn't the idea of finally finding Anderson that interested her. It was finding her father. I shouldn't have told her. I should have lied. I should have kept my stupid mouth shut. The idea of her seeing that broken, crazed man, rather than the knight in shining armour she'd dreamt about as a kid, was crushing.

"She doesn't look much like a witch," I said.

"He said she'd taken all the children?" Aubrey asked. I nodded.

"Well, that's what she does."

"To help them," I said, pointing at the website. "To give them their hope back."

"We can't be sure unless we go and see for ourselves," Aubrey said and I couldn't read her expression. Was it anger or hope?

I shook my head. "No way. Sir Richard told me that the Ganymede file was shut. That I was to focus on the attack on the President."

"Oh, come on Scott!" she shouted, throwing her arms in the air. "You were the one who wanted to find Anderson. Unfinished business, remember? What was it you said you wanted? Closure? Well, maybe if we take Anderson in, you'll get it. Maybe you'll finally sleep again."

She was wrong. The closure I needed had nothing to do with finding Anderson and bringing her to justice. It was about me and what I'd done with my power. In fact, I wanted to forget all about Ganymede and Greyfield's and Abbott and everything that had happened that night. For the first time in months, I felt like my power could be put to some good use in finding whoever tried to kill the President.

"He won't be there, Aubrey," I said, and she flinched as if I'd slapped her. "I'm sorry. But if you're hoping to find your dad, he won't be there."

"Why not?" she said, fighting back the tears that threatened to come again.

"Because he said he had to stay away from you. If that man even was your dad and not some nutter." I took her hand in mine, marvelling at how tiny it was.

"But we could try," she said looking up at me, her eyes glittering like still pools.

Any resolve I had melted.

"OK," I said, letting out a long sigh. "I'll tell Sir Richard that Anderson is tied up in the attack somehow." Aubrey smiled. "But," I added quickly, "when we're done you have to help me find out who was really responsible."

"Shifter's honour," she said, holding up three fingers.

"There's only one problem," I said.

"Which is?"

"You quit," I pointed at her jacket, which I'd thrown over the arm of her sofa.

She picked it up, brushed dust off the arms, then slipped it on. "Well, maybe I can hold on for a little longer."

CHAPTER FOURTEEN

The building looked ancient. More like a castle than a stately home.

I'd driven this time. Although I wished I'd let Aubrey take the wheel. The whole way down she'd huffed and rolled her eyes at how slowly I was going.

"This is going to take forever," she said, when we had just got onto the motorway.

Turned out, she was right. We'd got stuck in the worst traffic I'd ever seen and the journey that should have only taken two hours ended up taking five.

My legs were aching by the time we pulled into the long driveway. I parked in front of the house and killed the engine. The sudden silence was eerie. I was used to the constant noise of London, the background buzz of life. But here, I couldn't hear anything but the ticking of the engine cooling and the wind blowing in the trees.

"We're here," I said, unnecessarily, as I opened the door.

Aubrey jumped out of the van. The gravel crunched loudly under her feet. She looked up at the house and whistled. "Fancy," she said.

"Spooky," I said. "So how are we going to play it this time?"

"Well, I guess we start by knocking."

We stepped up onto the porch and I reached out to the brass lion's head. I jumped as I heard a scream in the distance that sounded like a child being murdered.

"What the hell…?"

"It's just a peacock," Aubrey said, laughing at me.

She pointed at a scrawny-looking peacock. Its beady eyes were trained on me. I raised the knocker and let it fall. All I needed now was for the door to creak open and reveal a hunchback.

Instead it was opened by a small girl, with enormous hazel eyes and a hairless dolly tucked under her arm. She was sucking her thumb.

"Kushi! What have I told you about opening the door?" A tall, dark-haired woman wearing a pair of green combats, no shoes and a large scarf strode into the hallway.

She patted Kushi on the head and pushed her gently away. The little girl waved the hand of her plastic doll at us. Aubrey waved back. The girl burst out laughing and then ran away through one of the many doors in the hallway.

"Sorry about that, we don't get many visitors. Especially not from ARES," she said, eyeing our Bluecoats.

"Are you Francesca Goodwin? Previously Francesca Anderson?"

"Yes," the woman replied. "How can I help the old agency today?"

"I'm Aubrey Jones and this is Scott Tyler," Aubrey said. "We'd like to have a word with you."

"Aubrey Jones?" Frankie said, tilting her head and looking intently at Aubrey. "What a... lovely name. Come in. I'll make you some tea if you like?"

Aubrey gave me a look that I struggled to read. But as far as I was concerned, tea was a good sign. Number four had made us tea.

"That would be lovely, Mrs Goodwin," Aubrey said, barely hiding her distrust of the woman.

"Oh, call me Frankie," she said, waving away Aubrey's formality. "Everyone does."

We followed Frankie into the hallway, through a long room lined with shields and swords. A group of kids ran past, chasing each other, their high-pitched laughs echoing around the room.

Frankie didn't even tell them to slow down, she just laughed along. She was not like any of the members of Project Ganymede we'd come across so far, that was for sure.

She led us down a narrow flight of stairs into a huge kitchen. Two boys of about twelve or thirteen were sat on either side of the wooden table playing cards. They had black hair and wore shabby, loose fitting T-shirts and scuffed trainers. They were engrossed in their game and didn't look up as we came in. I watched as the cards that were already on the table suddenly flipped, replaced with another set. The kids were definitely Shifters. The boy on the left threw his hands up and started complaining loudly in a lyrical language I couldn't understand. Arabic maybe?

"Boys, behave now. We have guests."

The two boys turned to face us and I had to hold onto the doorframe to stop myself from falling over. It looked as if a large part of both their foreheads had been crushed. I heard Aubrey let out a tiny gasp next to me and was glad I wasn't the only one shocked.

Frankie picked up a fallen card from the floor and placed it back on the table. "This is Hamid and Hazid," she said pointing from the boy on the right to the boy on the left. "They were born joined at the head."

"Siamese twins?" Aubrey said, finding her voice.

"Actually, we prefer the term conjoined twins. Siam, after all, no longer exists. I found them in a souk freak show in Marrakech three years ago. Half-starved, they were forced to beg tourists for food. Shocking, just shocking. Luckily, I was able to bring them here and after a great deal of medical consultation, they had the separating operation a year ago and seem to be doing fine."

"Pleased to meet you," Aubrey said, shaking their hands. "I'm Aubrey and my silent friend over there is Scott."

I managed to let go of the doorframe and waved.

"You're both Shifters?" Hamid asked, his English perfect despite a strong accent.

"Yes, we work for ARES."

"Can you do this?" Hazid asked. He turned and focused on his brother who was wearing a blue top.

Hamid sighed. "Stop showing…"

But before he had a chance to finish he was suddenly wearing a red top. Hamid shook his head and scowled at his brother who was now laughing. Hamid in turn squinted his eyes and suddenly Hazid was wearing a baseball cap.

"Boys, stop it. You'll only end up fighting again."

"What's going on?" Aubrey asked.

"When they Shift, they change each other's decisions," Frankie said, filling up a large kettle under a tap. "A side effect of the separation."

"But... that's incredible," Aubrey said.

"Yes, the power to change what other people do. Quite incredible."

Aubrey threw me a quick look before Frankie turned around. "Unfortunately, all Hazid and Hamid use it for is to annoy each other. Isn't that right, boys?"

The two boys were now smacking each other around the head.

"I give up!"

Frankie walked over to them and pulled them apart. "You two. Rooms now. And I want you on your separate sides as we discussed."

Hamid and Hazid sloped away, nudging each other as they did. I didn't speak a word of Arabic, but I spoke sibling well enough to understand what they were saying.

"So, how do you take your tea?"

"White and one sugar for me please," Aubrey said, watching Frankie through tight eyes. It was clear she didn't trust her one bit.

"Oh, just white for me. I'm sweet enough already," I said automatically.

Frankie smiled kindly and finished making the tea. Aubrey just shook her head.

"So, you haven't just come here to visit the charity, that much is clear," Frankie said handing us our mugs.

"It's about Project Ganymede," Aubrey said.

Aubrey and I both watched Frankie, looking for anything. A flinch, a twitch, a grimace that might give her

away. There were two usual responses when we confronted the members of the project: tears and screaming.

"Oh, I've not heard that name in a long time,"
Frankie said casually, readjusting her scarf. "What
about it?"

Aubrey blinked, looking surprised. "So you were a
part of it?"

"Yes. I was one of the first candidates." There wasn't
a hint of embarrassment. Clearly Frankie hadn't known
what the project really involved. At least if she was in
the first phase of the project we didn't need to worry
about the cortex bomb. Dr Lawrence had only put that
little back-up device into his later subjects.

"And so you're a Shifter?" I said.

"Well, yes. I can Shift. But I tend not to. I find that it
leads to unhappiness – never settled with your decisions.
Never happy with your lot. I reserve the power for life
and death situations only. And I don't face too many of
them around here." She smiled and it was infectious.

"What exactly do you do around here?" I said.

"Oh, that's simple. I find abandoned and endangered
Shifters and bring them here. I have a leaflet around
somewhere." She started digging around in a pile of
papers on the dresser behind her and pulled out a slim,
folded flyer. "For fundraising purposes. No mention of
the Shifting power in there, obviously. I just talk about
the street children and the child soldiers desperate for a
home. I set up Pandora after my second husband died,
leaving me all alone in this place." She indicated the old
building. "I think without the project to keep me going
after he'd passed, I'd have just given up and died myself.
Hope, you see. That's why I called the charity Pandora.

The last thing left in Pandora's box of evils? Hope. It's what this place has given me. And what I hope it gives the children."

"How many kids do you have here?" Aubrey asked.

"Twenty-eight at the moment. But sometimes, it's as many as fifty. I've had nearly two hundred children pass through here, all needing some kind of special help. It's terrifying what some people will do to children. But we do what we can to help them recover and go on to lead productive, valuable lives. No one is forced to do anything against their wills here. That's one of our most important rules. Everything has to be their choice. How else can they really come to grips with their powers otherwise?"

"Are you able to help everyone?" I asked. "I mean, all the children here."

"We try. But sometimes, the children just have to learn to live with what has happened to them. Even with their powers, they're just children after all." Frankie looked me with kind, sympathetic eyes. And I felt like I wanted to tell her everything. Not just about Ganymede, but about me and what I'd done.

"Do any of the children from here go on to join ARES?" Aubrey asked.

"Well, not many of the children I look after are really suited to the agency life. They've not had any real structure and so the limitations placed on them during training can be unsettling. Besides, given what most of them have been through they're not all entirely, how should I say, stable. Their powers often manifest in rather unusual ways."

"Like Hamid and Hazid?" I said.

"Exactly. And I've had other children through here who've had other unusual skills. I help them come to terms with their power until entropy takes it away, and then I help them integrate back into real life."

"Here in the UK?"

"Sometimes. Sometimes I try and take them home."

"When there's a home for us to return to." A skinny girl with dry, frizzy hair in a long plait and dark, deep-set eyes walked slowly into the room. She was so pale I could make out the veins in her thin arms and it looked as if she hadn't eaten properly in months.

"Ah, this is Ella," Frankie said, reaching up and taking the girl's bony hand. "She's been with me the longest. How old were you when I found you?"

"Six."

"Yes, six. Drug lords in Guatemala had massacred all of her family. And she was crying over the body of her mother. And even at that age I could sense she had the power to Shift."

"You're a Spotter?" Aubrey said.

"Oh, a little, I suppose. Although at ARES my official title was Mapper, Fifth Class."

Fifth Class. Just like Aubrey's dad, I thought. Had they known each other? And what had happened to make him hate Frankie so much? I couldn't imagine this woman ever doing anything bad.

"Although after Project Ganymede those boundaries seemed to blur somewhat," Frankie said with a wave of her hand.

"Speaking of the project, there are some questions we have. Although I think we should probably talk in private." Aubrey looked at Ella.

"Anything you can say to me you can say to Ella." Frankie let go of Ella's hand.

There was something about the girl I couldn't put my finger on. It was as if I'd seen her somewhere before. "Well, the men," I said. "I mean the other people who were a part of the project have been experiencing some side effects. Mental issues."

"The psychosis? Yes, I saw some of that when I was on active duty with men. Some of them didn't take to the programme as well as the others. But what has that got to do with me?"

"We wanted to check that you'd not been experiencing anything like that and..." I looked to Aubrey, uncertain how to continue.

"We need carry out an evaluation. ARES feels it's not safe to have adult Shifters."

Frankie laughed. "Sir Richard is happy to trust children with this power and not adults? Come now, that seems rather silly."

I saw Aubrey's jaw tighten. "It's more to do with how the power was obtained."

"I don't understand."

"How much do you know about the project? About the operation you had?" I said quickly, sensing Aubrey's increasing tension.

"Not a huge amount. I was told that they were able to stimulate the part of the brain that controlled Shifting. I assumed it worked like a pacemaker."

I took a deep breath. "There's no easy way of saying this, and believe me, I've tried lots of different ways, but I'm just going to come out and say it. You've had part of a child's brain placed in yours. They cut out the bit of the brain that controls Shifting and gave it to you."

"What happened to the child?" Frankie said, her voice suddenly dry.

"Brain dead," Aubrey said.

Frankie's eyes darted from my face to Aubrey's. "I don't believe it. Dr Lawrence. He wouldn't."

"He did. The files are all here." Aubrey pulled out a brown file from her bag and passed it over. "Besides, we saw the evidence with our own eyes."

"Did you ever meet Mr Abbott?" I asked.

"The head of the Regulators?" Frankie said distracted by the paperwork she was flicking through. Her face became paler with each page.

"Yes, he recently decided to start the programme back up again. He'd carried out the procedure on three of his men and had planned to carry it out on many more."

Frankie pushed the folder away as if it disgusted her and placed her hand over her mouth.

"I'm sorry. I had no idea. But I don't know what I can do about it now." She sat up straight and fiddled with her mug, spinning it around on the table. "However I gained this power, I have used it for good. Isn't that what matters? In the long run?"

"Maybe so, but we need to carry out a psychiatric evaluation, to make sure that you're not suffering from the same symptoms as the others," Aubrey said.

"Yes, I understand. But is there any way this evaluation can be done in the morning? I have a very important event to be at tonight and I have to get ready. A huge amount hangs on me being there. For the future of the charity and, well, you understand?" She smiled at me and I wondered if it was the tea causing my stomach to heat up all of a sudden.

It was a struggle to take my eyes off her. The other Ganymede men we'd interviewed had all talked about Frank Anderson like some kind of hero. A saviour. Back when we'd thought Anderson had been a man, I'd imagined some muscle-bound superhero. Frankie was slim and delicate and yet there was still something of the comic-book heroine about her. I had to try really hard not to imagine her in skin-tight Lycra.

"I don't think…" I started to say when Aubrey cut me off.

"Sure. Tomorrow would be fine."

I looked at Aubrey, wondering what was happening. I didn't want to have to drive all the way back only to return in the morning.

"Marvellous," Frankie said, standing up. "Why don't you stay here for the night, there's plenty of room. It will give you a chance to meet all the children."

Aubrey stood up too. "Sounds like a plan."

I stayed sitting and looked from Aubrey to Frankie, there was definitely something going on here and I was missing it all.

"Well, make yourself at home. Ella," she turned to the pale girl. "Show Scott and Aubrey around, will you."

It wasn't really a question. I saw a look flit across Ella's face. Uncertainty? Annoyance? Whatever it was, it was just the tiniest flicker and then her still expression was back.

Frankie readjusted the scarf around her neck and smiled at us. I could see how that smile could win over politicians and warlords alike. She turned and walked back up the stairs, her bare feet padding on the slate floor.

"We just have to get something from the van. Scott?"

Aubrey grabbed the back of my jacket and tugged at it. The bench scraped on the floor as I pushed it back to stand up.

"Yes, something from the van…" I said, as Aubrey half dragged me out of the door. "What's going on?" I hissed as we were clear of the kitchen. "I'd thought you'd want to be well clear of this place. I know I am."

"And miss a chance to have a snoop around? No chance." Aubrey tested door handles as we walked back the way we'd come. Each door opened up, revealing another ornate room. Apart from one. "And what do we think is behind here?" Aubrey said, grinning as the door refused to open.

"Oh, I don't know? A cellar where they keep all the kids who stick their noses in," I said, looking around to make sure we weren't being watched.

Aubrey reached into her jacket and pulled out a slim leather pouch. Inside it was a set of thin tools, the kind of things a dentist would use to inflict the most pain possible. She selected two and set to work on the door. I was too busy watching her at work, so I didn't hear the soft footsteps behind us.

"You're not allowed in there."

We both jerked around, Aubrey hiding the lock-picking set behind her back. "Oh, we were just trying to find the bathroom."

"Both of you?" Ella said, tilting her head like a bird.

"I was helping," I said, stupidly.

"Well, the bathroom is second on the left up there."

Ella pointed a long thing finger up the corridor. "That room that you're trying to get into is a broom closet. Maria our housekeeper keeps all her cleaning stuff in there. That's why it's locked up."

If Ella thought we were up to anything strange, her face didn't show it. It didn't show anything.

"Right, second on the left," Aubrey said and headed off in that direction.

Ella and I stood, waiting. I hummed uncomfortably, while she just stared at me. There really was something niggling me about her.

"Have you ever been to ARES?"

"No," Ella said. "I received all my training here."

"Oh, it's just, I thought…" I thought I recognised her, but it must have been someone else. Besides, with my ability to remember past Shifts when no one else could, I was constantly finding myself thinking people were familiar when in reality, in the new reality, we'd never actually met. "Nothing," I said. "Never mind."

It was quite a relief when Aubrey returned from the bathroom, picks safely tucked away once more.

There was something creepy about this girl. About this place. The sooner we could get this evaluation done with and I could go back to focusing on the President, the better.

CHAPTER FIFTEEN

The house was enormous. Every time I thought we'd got to the end of it, another room appeared, as if had been tagged on to the one before like an afterthought. Long, thin corridors lined with flaking wood panelling led from one huge room to the next and children seemed to be hiding in every nook and cranny.

I waved at a boy who peered out from behind a green-leather sofa. He let out a squeak and scuttled away.

"Is Frankie the only adult here?" Aubrey said, watching the boy disappear through a doorway.

"There's Maria, the cook and housekeeper," Ella replied.

"No men?"

"Not since Mr Goodwin died, no."

"Oh." Aubrey sounded disappointed. And I understood why. She'd been hoping that her dad would be here. This wasn't about tracking down the last member of Ganymede for her anymore. She was on a new mission.

Me, I just wanted to get the job done so I could start hunting for the President's killer. Aubrey's dad had been wrong. Frankie was the least wicked person I'd ever met.

There was another thing that still kept niggling at me. I was sure I'd seen Ella somewhere before.

"Have you lived here ever since you came to this country?" I asked her.

"Since Frankie found me, yes," Ella said.

"And do you like it here, out in the middle of nowhere?" Aubrey said. "With nothing to do?" Aubrey wasn't the biggest fan of the countryside.

The girl stopped and gazed up at the arched ceilings as if it was the first time she'd really looked at them. She tucked a curl of hair behind her ear that had escaped her Alice band.

"I don't know anything else," she eventually said, then set off again, pointing out paintings and statues on the way. We passed one wall lined with maybe a hundred frames containing butterflies of every colour. They looked as if they might fly away, if not for the brass tacks stuck through their bodies, pinning them in place. They gave me the creeps too.

It was a relief to get out to the gardens.

A bunch of kids of all ages were kicking a football around the large lawn. They were good, too, better than I'd ever been at football. Although it was clear a few of them were cheating by Shifting. One of them kicked the ball from the middle of the pitch. It went soaring over the heads of the other children and straight into the back of the goal.

"That's Prestige," Ella said, pointing at the goal scorer. "Our newest guest."

Prestige had dark skin that glowed golden in the low

sunlight and a delicate face, which seemed at odds with his broad and muscular frame.

"He was conscripted to a children's army in the Democratic Republic of Congo," Ella explained. "He'd been about to kill the warlord who killed his family and kidnapped him when Frankie arrived and stopped him."

"And killing the warlord would have been a bad thing how?" Aubrey asked.

"He'd already seen enough death. Besides, if he'd gone through with it, he would have been a killer too. No better than the warlord."

I looked closely at him and realised what was odd. He wasn't smiling. Even after that incredible goal, there was no celebrating, no rubbing it in the other children's faces. He just picked the ball up, ran back to the centre, and kicked off again.

"And that's Daniel, Klaus, Felicity…" Ella reeled off a list of names, pointing out the rest of the kids in turn. "They've all been here for years. And there, watching the game, is Kia."

I followed Ella's finger to see a slim, young girl, her enormous smile visible even from this distance. The girl had golden skin and long dark hair, which fell in front of her face as she jumped up and down, cheering the game on. The ball was kicked offside and Kia ran after it.

A couple of the kids waved at Kia to come join in. Her face lit up as she kicked the ball back and started to run towards the game. Then she stopped and looked down at her hands as if something was wrong with them.

The Shift was one of the most jarring I've ever seen. One second, there was a beautiful slim Asian girl standing there. The next, it was a young Asian boy, with short hair, long jeans and a Chelsea Football Club shirt. But the same attractive face. I knew that they were the same person.

I turned to look at Ella with my mouth open wide. Aubrey was just watching the football match that was going on.

"Did you sense that?" I asked Aubrey.

"That boy's Shift. A little. What about it?"

"But she…"

Aubrey looked up at me, her brow wrinkled in confusion. "She? What do you mean?"

I looked back to the boy who was dribbling the ball across the grass. A second boy came in for a tackle, but the boy who had been Kia hoofed the ball just in time. It went just wide of the posts. He laughed loudly and ran after it.

"But a second ago…"

"You remember?" Ella asked, her expression now a mirror of mine. "You remember Kia?"

"Of course I do. She was just standing there cheering," I said, pointing at the spot on the sidelines.

"What are you two on about? Who's Kia? I thought you said his name was Pia?" Aubrey said.

"It is. He's Pia and Kia. Depending on his mood," Ella said, brushing her frizzy hair out of her eyes.

"You mean he's a she?" Aubrey said, looking back at the boy.

"No. It's a bit complicated," Ella said. "She's transgender sometimes. Not others."

"And what, he just changed his decision to become a she? Just like that? Just so he can play football?" I said.

"Oh, he does it all the time. One second it's Kia. The next it's Pia," Ella said with a wave of her hand, as if changing sex was no big deal.

"Are you guys saying that that boy is a girl?" Aubrey said, pointing at Pia. He'd just tackled Prestige and was dribbling the ball down the pitch.

"Only sometimes," Ella said.

"But how?" I said. "The second law of Shifting. You can't undo a Shift."

"Frankie said it's because it's such a huge choice with so much uncertainty involved, there are lots of chances to change it. Plus, the choice was sort of made for him, where he grew up, his parents thought it would be the best way for him to make money. It was Frankie who explained that it was up to Pia now to decide. One day, he'll have to settle on one or the other. But I think he likes the freedom of it now."

"I'd like to meet her," Aubrey said.

"You will," Ella said. "Kia will be back any minute."

"Yes, but I won't remember that she was a he, will I?" Aubrey said.

"I suppose not," Ella said.

"But you can?" I asked Ella. "You can remember the old reality?"

She paused before answering, as if she wasn't sure she was supposed to say anything. "Yes," she said softly.

"Oh," Aubrey said, looking from me to Ella and back again. "Guess you're not the only one then after all, Scott."

I stared at the girl in shock. I'd never met someone else like me. Before I had a chance to say anything more, Pia came running over.

"Do you want to join us?" he said, holding out the ball to me.

"Oh, no. I'm fine thanks. The last time I played football I nearly broke my nose."

He smiled and turned to Aubrey. "How about you?"

She looked at Ella and me, then back to Pia. "Sure, why not?" she said, taking the ball. She threw it up into the air, headed it perfectly back onto the pitch and ran after it. Pia smiled in delight and followed on.

"Frankie told me I wasn't to tell anyone," Ella said a few minutes later. She and I were sitting on a bench watching what had now turned into a football match the likes of which I'd never seen.

Hamid and Hazid had joined in. Originally, the twins had been put on opposing teams, but they kept cheating by Shifting each other's decisions, making them miss the ball. They had to be separated three times before they were put on the same team. The little girl we'd seen earlier, the one who answered the door, had also joined in. Although she didn't do much kicking. She just ran after the ball like a small dog, baying with laughter, her doll trailing on the ground behind her.

Aubrey had gone in goal. She was amazing – mostly because she Shifted so effortlessly that she hardly missed a ball – and I loved watching her laugh. I think she'd only joined the game to give Ella and me some time alone.

"Why weren't you supposed to tell anyone?" I asked.

"I don't know. I think Frankie thought it would..." She hunted around for the correct word. "Unsettle people. That other Shifters wouldn't like it if I could remember the decisions they'd undone. The bad choices they'd made."

That made sense. Aubrey was the only person who knew about my ability – unless you counted Benjo and Sir Richard, and I was trying not to think about them – and I knew it weirded her out. Maybe she'd become so used to erasing her mistakes that the idea of someone who wouldn't forget them was scary.

Perhaps this was why I thought I recognised Ella. That the nagging feeling I knew her was really just me sensing we shared this same ability. Although if that was the case, wouldn't I have felt some sort of connection between us? A kinship? Whereas the exact opposite was true. Even though she was sitting just a few feet away from me I felt completely cut off from her. She was distant and untouchable.

"It's not easy, is it?" she said, looking down at her hands, which were folded neatly in her lap. "Remembering."

A flash of memories hit me. The crash with my sister. The knife in the chest. The President's bubbling face. All realities I couldn't let go of. "No. Not always."

I heard a high-pitched scream and looked back to the pitch. Aubrey was carrying Kushi, swooping her around like she was flying, while the rest of the kids laughed and whooped. Even Prestige, the stern soldier, was close to smiling, the simple act restoring his youth to him. "Looks like Kushi scored," I said.

Only Ella wasn't sitting next to me anymore.

"Come on, now!" she shouted to the group. "Time for dinner."

They ignored her and continued with the game. The sun was slowly disappearing behind the turrets and chimneys of the house, casting long, snake-like shadows across the grass. The kids raced in and out of them, moving from dark to shade as they chased the football.

"I won't tell you again," she said, not shouting now, but in a voice that seemed to carry across the grass and made all the kids stop and turn. Pia pulled the football out of Hamid and Hazid's hands, who were fighting over it again, tucked it under his arm and walked back towards the house.

Aubrey put Kushi back on the ground. The little girl took Aubrey's hand and looked up at her, an enormous grin on her face.

"I see you have a new friend," I said to Aubrey as she walked over. Only it was Kushi who answered.

"I'm going to show her my dolls."

Aubrey was dragged away before she had a chance to protest.

I fell back a bit watching them all head towards the house. Children from all over the world who had found themselves a home here. It was pretty amazing, what Frankie had done for them. She'd given them the chance to change their lives.

I looked up at the sky. The first few stars peeked out from behind a scattering of clouds.

"Beautiful, isn't she?"

I jumped when I heard the voice behind me and turned to see Frankie gazing up at the sky as well.

"I'm sorry?"

"Venus, the Goddess of Love," she said pointing at a pinpoint of light nearest the moon. "There's something special about knowing she's the first light to greet us each night."

I couldn't take my eyes off Frankie. Her tanned skin seemed to glow in the moonlight. "I guess."

"Did you know you can perform the Double-Slit Experiment using the gravitational lensing of fourteen billion-year old starlight around intervening galaxies?"

"Huh?"

"Don't tell me they're not teaching the Double-Slit Experiment at ARES these days?"

"No... I mean, yes, they are. But with lasers. Not starlight."

I'd been taught all about the quantum physics experiment that shows how light acts as both wave and particle. But where it got really weird, and why they taught it in ARES basic training, is because the behaviour of light alters purely through the act of it being observed. Just like how our decisions could change when we focused on them.

Frankie looked up again at the night sky. "It's the same experiment. Only instead of slots, you determine which direction light bends around planets. Amazing, isn't it? To think that you can decide whether a photon was emitted as a particle or a wave fourteen billion years ago. And its application to Shifting is staggering. Just how far back can our influence go?"

"But we can only change our own decisions. Which means we can only influence things within our own lifetime. Right?"

"Perhaps," Frankie said, looking at me now with the same curious gaze she'd turned on the planet. "But what if we could learn how to amplify our power, beyond our own petty concerns and choices, and influence great events? Why, the potential could be limitless."

"Do you think that's even possible?"

"I've seen enough to know there are special Shifters, for whom the normal rules don't apply. Those with a certain strength of character that enables them to lead where others follow."

She knew. I didn't know how. But it was clear from her expression – eyebrow raised, a half-smile hitching up the corner of her mouth – that she knew about what I'd done at Greyfield's. But what did it matter anyway? After facing Sir Richard's gun it was clear the power had gone and wasn't coming back.

"Yeah, well, maybe those special Shifters are just freaks."

"If by freak you mean extraordinary, then I would agree with you."

"But what if their power only works in extraordinary circumstances, like when mothers can lift cars off children caught in a crash or when…" I was about to say "when people are about to die". But I'd already given too much away. "Or whenever. What good is it to anyone?"

"You read too many comics, Scott. The potential for greatness lies within us all." She took a step closer to me. "In some, more than others."

She tapped my chest with a strong finger. It felt like a shock of electricity passing into me. "See those trees over there," she removed her finger and pointed to two dark shapes on the lawn.

I could only just about make them out in the moonlight.

"The ones that looks like spirals?" I said.

The kids had used them earlier as goal posts and I'd wondered about their weird shape. All the other trees and bushes in the grounds were left to go wild. But these had been pruned into perfect geometric swirls.

"Yes. I had them planted last year and I hate them. The gardener insisted. He said they would give structure to the garden and I didn't think it was important enough to argue."

"What about them?" I said.

"I want you to Shift them for me."

"What? But... but I can't Shift your choice," I said, stumbling over my words.

"Try. I had a choice between those arrogant symbols of man's mastery over nature or two simple silver birches. And now I think on it, I'd rather go with the birch."

"So, why don't you just Shift?"

"Because I want you to do it for me." She laid her hand on my chest again and I was very aware of the beating of my heart under it. "Imagine the birches. Think about their slender trunk and frail, paper-like bark. Imagine them right there." She raised her hand to my chin and turned me to face the spirals in the dark. "Focus, Scott. Will them to change."

"But I ca–"

She cut me off with a finger to my lips. "I know you can do it," she whispered into my ear, her soft breath tickling the hair on the back of my neck. "I believe in you."

Those words sank into my brain like a coal through butter. If she believed in me, then maybe, maybe I could do it after all.

I turned and faced the trees. Black spirals punched out of the dark.

I blinked and when I opened my eyes again the spirals

were gone. Instead, there stood two tall trees, their silver bark catching the moonlight.

Frankie made a soft humming noise, as if she'd taken a bite out of something delicious. She leant in and kissed my cheek. "Well done. Now you'd better get inside or all the food will be gone."

I nodded dumbly and stumbled forward.

"Oh and Scott," Frankie said as I started to walk away. "Best you don't tell anyone about this. Best you just forget all about it."

"Sure," I said, and the buzzing confusion in my head slipped away and was replaced with a warm glow.

CHAPTER SIXTEEN

The dining room echoed with shouts and screams as all the kids tucked in to whatever Maria loaded up on their plates. From what I could tell, some of them were eating their puddings before their mains, but no one was stopping them.

Ella led Aubrey and me to a table with Prestige, Pia, Kushi, and Hamid and Hazid. It was a little like being back at ARES, with all the freshers. Only even more chaotic. Frankie had been right when she said the children here could do whatever they liked.

I watched the kids, while picking on a bread roll, and wondered just what they'd all been through. The boy from the Congo looked the most damaged. But all of the children had hollow looks in their eyes if you looked deep enough. Even little Kushi who was now chatting away with Aubrey while feeding her doll crisps would sometimes pause and stare into the distance before snapping back and continuing to babble.

"Enjoying dinner?" Frankie said, walking down the stairs. She wasn't in bare feet anymore. In fact she was in high heels and a long black dress that clung to her hips. I had to work hard to swallow my bread.

The children nodded their approval, their cheeks bulging with food.

Ella, who'd been just picking at a salad stood up. "Are you going already? I'll have to go get changed."

"Sorry, Ella," Frankie said, rubbing the girl's thin arm. "But I told Pia I'd take him with me tonight."

Pia jumped up out of his seat. "Do I need to change?" He tugged at his grass-stained football shirt.

Frankie considered the boy. "Yes, I think so. Something smart. Something striking."

Pia smiled and raced off out of the room. Ella was still standing up, her small chin bobbing up and down.

"Come now, Ella. I need you to stay here and take care of everyone. You're the eldest after all." Frankie leant over and placed a kiss on Ella's forehead.

Ella looked like she didn't understand at all. She spun around and stormed out of the hall.

Frankie looked as if she was about to follow Ella, then shook her head slightly. "I want you all to behave for our guests," she said to the children. "Make them feel at home, OK?"

"Yes, Frankie," the kids sang in unison.

"Good. I'll be back before midnight and I want you all in bed by then."

I craned my neck to watch Frankie walk back out of the room. I could just see her heels reflected in one of the large mirrors in the next room. Shortly, they were joined by a two brown shoes poking out from under a pair of grey trouser legs. Pia had changed in super quick time. As I watched, the brown shoes vanished and were replaced by a pair of purple heels. It looked as if Frankie was going to be taking Kia instead.

I looked back at the kids who had stopped talking. I wondered if they'd sensed Pia's Shift. Then Hamid flicked a pea at Hazid's head and everything was suddenly back to normal.

Through one of the large stain glass windows, I saw the shadow of Ella. It looked as if she had her face in her hands.

"You go keep the poster girl for anorexia busy," Aubrey said, nodding towards the windows. "I want to see what's really in that room."

Aubrey stood up before I had a chance to protest.

It was cold outside. The bitter February wind cut through my jacket and hoodie. Ella was standing against the wall, her thin arms wrapped around herself. I could see her shoulders shaking.

"You OK?" I said.

Ella spun around so fast it made me jump. "Oh," she said when she saw me. "It's you." She wiped her eyes with the back of her hand.

"Er, yeah. Not some killer ninja. Ha, ha." I forced a laugh but Ella's expression remained unchanged. "So were you supposed to go with Frankie tonight?"

"Yes. She normally takes me. Or she used to."

"So, what changed?" I said, stepping next to her and staring out into the moonlit lawn to try and see what she was looking at. As far as I could see, there was nothing there. Just two silver birches quivering in the breeze.

"I got old."

"You're kidding me. You're what, fourteen?"

"I'm sixteen," she snapped.

"Oh, right." She certainly didn't look it. I had been trying to be nice when I said she looked fourteen. I'd had her placed at thirteen tops. "But why does that matter?"

"I suppose I'm not as much use to her now."

"Oh, cause the little kids do better with the donors?"

"I guess." Ella wrapped her arms tighter around herself and in the pale light I could see the hairs on her arms were standing up.

Reluctantly, because I knew I should rather than because I wanted to, I slipped off my jacket and handed it to her. "Here. You look cold."

She looked at the jacket for the longest time as if it were a puzzle she was trying to work out. Then looked up at me and smiled. The first smile I'd seen from her. She had really tiny teeth and too much gum. But it was a nice smile anyway.

"Thank you," she said.

"No problem," I said, regretting the decision instantly. It was really cold out here. I even thought about Shifting and taking it back. But she looked so happy as she slipped her arms into the sleeves that I couldn't bring myself to do it. "I'd better get back inside," I said, feeling worried that if I stayed out any longer she might actually open up and then where would I be?

"Oh, OK," she said, looking genuinely upset. She went to take the jacket off.

"Nah! You can give it back to me later. Just don't get any ideas that you're a Bluecoat though." I laughed. And then felt like a fool.

"A Bluecoat?"

"An officer at ARES." She still looked blank. "Never mind," I said. "Just give it back when you're ready."

I returned to the dining hall, but Aubrey wasn't back yet. I hoped she wouldn't be much longer. I didn't want to spend any more time with that creepy girl and her dark, penetrating eyes.

I sat back down, rubbing my cold fingers between my knees. Ella returned a few minutes later, still wearing my jacket, and gave me a small smile. I tried to return it. As long as she stayed in the hall where I could keep an eye on her that would be fine.

Finally, after what seemed like an age, I felt a tap on my shoulder.

"What took you so long?" I said, probably too loudly.

Aubrey slung one leg then the other over onto the bench, kicking me in the shins. Whether it was on purpose or not, I didn't know. "I found Frankie's office," she whispered, leaning into me.

"And?"

"And nothing. Just piles of paper on the charity."

"What were you expecting, Nancy Drew?" I asked. "Her broomstick?"

"Ha, ha," Aubrey said, not amused. "I don't know. Something that might lead me…" Her voice trailed off.

I reached under the table and took her hands in mine. "I'm sorry."

"It's OK," she said, but her hitched smile relayed her obvious disappointment. Then her eyes fell on Ella, still wearing my jacket. She lowered her head and raised an eyebrow.

I shrugged. "You said keep her busy."

The hall was mostly empty now as the children went off to play or do homework or whatever it was they got up to here.

The kids from our table hadn't moved and were busy clearing all the plates by passing them all to Kushi, who stacked them up on the end.

"What's going on?" I asked.

"Cards," Hamid said. "You wanna play?"

"Sure," I said. "Why not?"

"You got money?" Hazid said.

"You know what Frankie said about betting for money," Kushi said, wagging a finger at him.

"OK, then. No money. We play for honour!" Hamid said.

"Honour and cheesy puffs," his brother said, and the other kids laughed.

I accepted the cards I was dealt with a little trepidation. Because I knew when Shifters played cards all rules were off.

The game was a weird version of poker, with rules of the kids' own making. Aces were low and high, depending on your hand and you could pull one card from your neighbour, just to overcome the Shifting advantage. We were using cheesy crisp puffs as betting chips.

I looked at the hand I was dealt. Threw away three cards and pulled three more. I'd just thrown away the card I needed to make a half-decent hand. So I Shifted and only threw away two cards. Looking around the table it looked as if the rest of the players were all going through similar choices: Shifting and Shifting again, till they were happy with their cards.

"So, why didn't you go with Frankie tonight, Ella?" Hazid asked, pulling a card from Ella's hand and scowling at it.

"Like she said. She wanted Kia to go instead," Ella said.

"Do you normally go with her?" Aubrey asked, taking a card from my hand. She'd just taken a king, messing up the flush I was going for. Only she Shifted and this time took a jack. She smiled.

"She always takes at least one of us," Hazid said, picking up a card and holding it to his chest.

"She took me to London this week," Kushi said, throwing down a card. "It was fun!" She held her cards up to me so I could choose one. I went for the card on the end and got a nine of hearts.

The dealing and deciding was over. Now it was time to show our hands.

In turn, each of the kids lay down their cards. I was to go last. Unsurprisingly, there were some pretty amazing hands. So far Kushi was winning.

"Well, you got me," I said, throwing down my cards without turning them up. I had a royal flush. More than enough to beat Kushi's hand. But I couldn't do it. "I'm out."

Kushi squealed in happiness and dragged all the cheesy crisps towards her. She picked up a handful and squashed them into her mouth.

"No fair," Hamid said. "Now we can't win them back."

"You were never going to win them back," Ella said. "Not till you learn to stop fighting among yourselves. You're brothers. Doesn't that mean anything to you?"

Hamid and Hazid looked at each other for a moment, then back to Ella. "No," they said in unison. And returned to the game.

Ella looked up to the ceiling and shook her head. "Why me?" she said.

"Stop looking at my cards!" Hazid shouted at his brother.

"If you didn't wave them about so much, it wouldn't be so easy."

Hazid stared at his brother's cards and suddenly instead of having five, he had three. Hamid then threw them at his brother and the two started to fight again, before being pulled apart by Ella. Kushi took advantage of the distraction to steal another handful of crisps from the middle of the table.

It looked as if the game was over.

I checked my watch. It was 9pm.

"God, I'd better call home. Tell them I won't be back," I said. "Um, Ella, can I have my phone? It's in the inside of my jacket."

"Oh," she said, reaching inside the coat. "Is this it?"

I'd kind of hoped she'd give back the jacket too. But the phone would have to do for now.

I took it off her then stood up and walked into the other room for a bit of privacy. Only there were a few girls in here, doing each other's hair. They giggled as I walked in.

I kept going, through the room with the huge mirror and back out into the entrance hall. I pulled open the large front door and went outside. It was totally dark now, the only light coming from the glowing screen of my phone.

I pulled up the menu and hit the button for "home". It took a while for anyone to answer.

"Hello," Katie said.

"Hey, sis. It's me."

"Scott," she said, sounding genuinely pleased to hear from me. "Where are you?"

"I'm in the middle of bloody nowhere," I said, looking out at the blackness ahead. "Some great big stately home in Sussex."

"No fair, you get to have all the fun, while I'm stuck at home with Them."

As if on cue, I heard Mum scream something at Dad.

"I'll be home tomorrow, and we'll do something, just you and me, OK? Anything you want," I said.

"Anything?" she said, sounding mischievous, and I was already regretting it.

"Within reason."

"There's this new ride–"

I cut her off with a groan. I hated roller coasters, but Katie loved them.

"You said anything I wanted."

"OK," I said. "But I'm not going on it with you."

"I wouldn't want you to. You'd only end up throwing up on me."

I went to protest, but there was no point. She was right. "Listen, Katie, I won't be coming home tonight. It's a work thing."

"Oh, yeah, a work thing. Say 'hi' to your work thing for me."

I heard another crash from the other end of the phone.

"Katie, go into my room, and on my desk are my new headphones. The noise cancelling ones."

"The really expensive ones?"

"Yeah. Well, you can have them. For tonight."

"Can I have your iPod too?"

"I guess."

"Good, cause I've already loaded it up with all my songs. You have sucky taste in music."

"Night, Katie."

"Night, Scott."

I looked down at the screen of my phone as I hung up. I really should do something to try and help her. Something to try and help my parents. Maybe there was a Shift I could make. But every time I thought of one, I just saw Katie's broken body under the truck. Better leave things as they were.

"I was coming to check on you," Aubrey said, as I walked back in the front door. "Everything OK?"

"Yeah, probably didn't even need to bother though."

"Must be nice. Having someone to worry about you," she said, crossing the hallway.

"I worry about you," I said, taking hold of either side of her jacket and pulling her towards me. "Besides, Katie is the only one who worries."

"That's enough."

I stifled a yawn.

"Still tired?" Aubrey asked.

"Always. Where do you think we're going to sleep?"

"You can sleep in my room. We can have a slumber party!" Kushi said, suddenly appearing from behind Aubrey's legs.

"Um, I think we need to get some sleep, but thanks. Another time," Aubrey said, patting her head.

"There's a spare room across the hall from me. I'll show you. Come on."

Kushi grabbed Aubrey's hand and dragged her up the

stairs. I followed her. She ran as fast as her little legs would carry her and we had to walk quickly to keep up. She led us all the way up the spiralling staircase to the very top of the house.

"This is Hamid and Hazid's bedroom," Kushi said, throwing open a door to a largish room. I peered in and saw that the room had been split in two using a large sheet of wood. One single bed was pushed up against the right hand of the divider, while another bed was pushed up against the left hand side. I imagined the boys sleeping, their heads separated now by an inch of plywood.

"Kia sleeps in there." She pointed at a third, small room, which was covered in posters of what I guessed were Asian pop stars, and cartoon kittens.

"Cute," Aubrey said and turned to leave.

As I went to follow, the room changed as wherever she was, Kia changed back to Pia. The pop stars were replaced with pictures of flashy cars and even flashier footballers. One of the players grinned down at me, all muscles rippling and slicked back blonde hair. None other than my old nemesis, Zac Black. He'd used his official Shifting license to become lead striker for Chelsea Football Club. The git. Quite the change from his alternative life in the cells at ARES, waiting till entropy set him free. Now it felt as if he was watching me everywhere I went; staring up at me from newspapers and down from aftershave ads. I hated him more than ever.

I quickly closed the door before Aubrey could see the poster. It was weird, but she'd been happier when Zac had stayed on the wrong side of ARES. Now he was using his power to become rich and famous, she couldn't even bear to say his name.

Kushi then showed us her room. It was an explosion of pink. Pink walls, pink duvet covers and pink curtains. She didn't have many belongings from what I could see. But those that she did have were mostly pink.

"And you can stay in there." She pointed at last to a door at the far end of the hall. "If you need a dolly to sleep with you can have one of mine."

"We'll be fine," Aubrey said. "And you should go to sleep too. It's past your bedtime."

"Will you read me a story?" Kushi asked, her wide eyes getting even wider still. Who could say no to a face like that?

"OK. Just one," Aubrey said.

We walked into the room and Kushi bounced into the bed, kicked off her little red shoes and pulled the duvet over her, not bothering to change out of her dress.

"Do you have any books?" Aubrey said, looking around.

"Um… no," Kushi said.

"Then how can we read you a story?" I asked.

"Make one up!" Kushi said.

"I'm not very good at that," Aubrey said, looking at me for help.

"Oh," Kushi said, her little face looking crestfallen. Then she perked up. "That's OK. I am. I'll tell you a story."

"That's a great idea," Aubrey said, sitting on the floor in front of Kushi's bed. I followed her example.

"There once was a princess who lived in a faraway land," Kushi began. "Only she didn't know she was a princess. Her parents both died when she was really little, and she was left wandering the dark forests on her own. At night, she would sleep in tunnels under the ground to stay away from the monsters that came out at night. But sometimes, the monsters would find their way into her tunnels and she would have to fight them off. And that made her very scared. She was very tired and very hungry. Then one day, a queen from another land found her curled up under a tree and she picked her up and carried her home. And told her that she could be her princess as she didn't have any of her own. And the little girl lived happily ever after. The end."

"That's a lovely story. Thank you, Kushi," Aubrey said.

Kushi smiled, happy with herself. She rubbed at her eyes and lay down on the bed.

"Where are you from, Kushi?" I asked.

"Frankie says she found me in a place called *Ulaanbaa-tar.*" She stretched each syllable out, making each a last for ages. "Sounds funny doesn't it? Like a name from a story. I can't remember it," Kushi said, her voice now slurring with sleep. "I remember the tunnels where I used to sleep. They were warm but they smelt funny." She yawned and pulled her dolly up under her chin and closed her eyes.

Aubrey stood up and pulled the duvet to cover her. We tiptoed out, quietly, turning the light off as we left.

"She slept in tunnels?" I said.

"And had to fight off monsters."

I looked back at the sleeping girl and wondered if she had nightmares too.

"So, do you want to do any more exploring?" I said, as Aubrey closed Kushi's door.

"No," she said, leaning back against the doorframe, knee bent, boot resting against the wood. "I'm done.

You were right. Frankie doesn't have anything to hide. I don't know why I thought I'd find answers here." She pushed off and walked away. "No, the sooner we're out of here the better."

I couldn't agree more.

Then I turned to look at the door to our bedroom.

CHAPTER SEVENTEEN

The room was tiny, maybe six foot by ten, with only a small, single bed pushed up against the far wall. It had a bright patchwork quilt thrown over it. So small and snug. Hardly enough space for one person, let alone two.

I coughed. "I can sleep on the floor."

Aubrey tilted her head and fixed me with a smile that made my knees go instantly weak.

I watched her slide off her jacket and her boots, kicking them both off without bothering to undo the laces. I copied her, throwing my hoodie over a chair in the corner and struggling to undo my trainers. I had to bend over and undo a knot that was refusing to release, and by the time I'd stood up again, Aubrey was standing bare legged, only her ARES T-shirt on.

I stared at her legs, my eyes running from her ankles, up her knees and to her thighs.

"It's freezing!" she said, jumping onto the bed and diving under the covers.

"Is it?" I just about managed to croak. I didn't know

about freezing. My face was burning so red I thought it would be enough to heat the room.

Aubrey popped her head out from under the covers and blew her tousled hair out of her eyes. "Are you going to stand there all night?" She patted the bed next to her.

It took an extra effort to struggle out of my trousers and I hesitated for a moment over whether I should keep my T-shirt on or off. I decided to keep it on. Then I sat down on the bed. Aubrey shuffled over towards the wall, giving me space and I climbed in next to her.

We lay there, staring up at the ceiling, and I was intensely aware of the presence of her leg next to mine. Its softness and smoothness. It seemed to radiate heat.

The cracks in the ceiling looked like faces grinning down on us. One of them looked disturbingly like Hugo.

Aubrey rolled over onto her side and pulled my arm up and over her shoulder, so she could tuck herself under it.

It's going to happen, I thought. It's actually going to happen.

Don't be stupid, Scott, I thought straight after. It's never going to happen.

I felt Aubrey's leg glide over my calf and she shuffled up the bed slightly so that our faces were just inches apart. She rested her hand on my chest.

I twisted my head around, careful not to make any movements that might dislodge her leg from where it was currently resting so perfectly, and looked into her eyes. She smiled.

It was going to happen.

I brushed her hair out of her eyes and stroked my thumb down the side of her cheek. She nestled her face into the palm of my hand before copying my action: stroking my face with a single finger. It stopped on my lips. I opened my mouth the tiniest fraction to kiss her fingertip.

I lowered my head and we kissed, gently at first and then steadily more deeply. I could feel her heart pounding against my chest. Or was it my heart pounding against hers? It didn't matter.

She stopped kissing me and tugged at the neck of my T-shirt. I wrenched it off and threw it on the floor, before diving in to kiss her again. With one hand entangled in her cropped hair, I slid my other hand down her back, feeling the slight bump of her bra strap underneath her T-shirt, until I felt the damp heat of her skin at the base of her spine. I drew her closer and she made a small moaning noise deep into my mouth. She bent her leg, so it was now wrapped around my thigh and rolled over on top of me.

It couldn't happen.

"Wait. Stop." I pulled away from her kiss.

"What's wrong?"

"Nothing. God, absolutely nothing."

"So shut up." She bent down, kissing me deeply. My whole body was shaking. I wrapped my hands around her waist, and felt the pulse in her stomach. I gently lifted her up and back onto the mattress beside me.

"What?"

"I'm sorry, I can't," I said. Hating myself. Wanting to punch the stupid bit of my brain that was making me say what I knew I was about to say.

"Did I do something wrong?" Aubrey sat up, pressing

her back into the wall behind her and pulling the quilt up to her chin.

"No. Of course not."

"You don't want to?" She blinked and looked a little bit scared and yet angry at the same time.

I took her face in my hands. "No, of course I want to. Argh! You have absolutely no idea just how much I want to."

"Then what?" she said, quiet as a whisper.

"I need to know you want to."

She pulled away from my hands and shook her head. "What bit of me half naked in your bed are you not getting? I want to, OK?"

"But what if you regret it? Not tonight but tomorrow. Or next week. You'll Shift." She let out an exasperated sigh, but I pressed on. "You will. You know it and I know it. You might change your decision to be with me tonight."

"So what if I do?" I could tell I'd made her angry.

"I'll remember, Aubrey. Only I will remember. Can you imagine what that will do to my head? Knowing that you regretted being with me. Knowing you changed your decision. It would be like... I forced you or something." I covered my face with my hands.

"Scott," she leaned forward on her knees and pulled my hands down. "Scott, listen to me. It's going to be OK. I'm not going to change my mind."

"Can you promise me that? Can you promise me that you don't make every single decision in your life knowing that if it doesn't work out you'll just Shift?"

"Scott, why are you being like this?"

"Because I want to know you're one hundred percent certain?"

"Who can be one hundred percent certain of any-thing?" She threw up her arms in frustration.

"I can," I said, looking deep into her green-flecked eyes. I wanted to fall into them. "Every day, I get up and I have to reassemble my life. Sometimes, it's just tiny things, like some guy I knew was a Regulator the day before is gone, having Shifted along the way. And I miss them. Actually miss them. Even though I know I've never actually met them. Other times, I close my eyes and when I open them again I don't recognise where I am. In the blink of an eye the whole world can have changed. And only for me. It's like building your house on sand. I never feel safe. But there's one thing I am absolutely cer-tain about. One thing solid that I can build the rest of my life around. You." I tucked a lock of hair behind her ear. "If we're going to do this, I need to be sure you're sure. Absolutely sure. And that I won't wake up tomor-row and it will all be gone. Because, I just... I just couldn't cope with that."

She bit her lip and sat back on her heels. I could hear a tree branch tapping on the window outside. It sounded like fingers drumming impatiently. Although I was happy to wait all night. She looked down and tugged at the hem of her black T-shirt. I had my answer.

"I'm sorry," she said.

I wrapped my arms around her and pulled her into a hug, before leaning my chin on the top of her head, feel-ing her warm breath on my bare skin.

"You have nothing to be sorry for." It was almost a relief. Almost.

I could wait. I would wait. Because I knew I was lucky just being with her. Luck. That reminded me.

"I have a present for you," I said, letting her go. I leaned over onto the floor and dragged my tangled trousers towards me. I dug around in the pocket and pulled out the thing I'd been carrying around for weeks, just waiting for the right moment.

"It's a bit lame," I said, sitting back on the bed, looking down at my closed fist.

"I don't care," she said, trying to pry my fingers open. I let her.

A single copper penny lay in my palm. I'd drilled a hole into the coin and strung it on a black ribbon. "It saved my life," I said, placing it into her hand. "I thought that maybe it might be good luck. Stupid, I know…"

She silenced me with a kiss. "I love it, Scott. I love… it."

She turned around so I could tie the ribbon around her neck. The coin hung just below the hollow at the base of her throat.

"I'm glad we came here," she said looking back at me.

"Even though you didn't find your dad?"

She nodded, her hair tickling my nose. "Do you think I'll ever find him?"

We lay back down and I slipped my hand under her neck, letting my fingers brush against her collarbone. "I don't know," I said. "But I know he's looking out for you."

It was a simple lie. It skirted over the reality that he was completely and utterly insane. But it made her happy. And for that moment, that's all I cared about.

She rested her head on my chest, twirling her fingers in the little I had going for chest hair.

"One day, I will be sure," she said, arching her neck to look up at me.

"Yeah? But maybe by then I'll have changed my mind."

She gasped in outrage and I laughed. "You git," she said, pulling the pillow out from under my head and hitting me with it. I pulled the pillow away and wrestled her back onto the bed, pinning her beneath me. I kissed her, slowly, savouring every second of it.

CHAPTER EIGHTEEN

"Morning," Aubrey said. She was propped up on one elbow, the light breaking through the yellow curtains throwing her into shadow. "Sleep well?"

"Yeah, not bad," I said, yawning and realising that I had slept well. Really well. Probably for the first night in months. Contentment radiated from somewhere deep inside me. I felt as if I was lying in a warm bath, only I was actually on a small and rather lumpy bed.

"You?" I asked.

"OK. Only, you snore."

"I do not."

"You do. Like a little piglet. It's kinda cute."

I pulled the quilt over my head in shame. "Shut up!" I mumbled from under the covers.

"Come on, Pylon. Get a move on." I felt the bed bounce as she stood up. "The sooner we get this evaluation with the oh-so-angelic Anderson over, the sooner we can get back and…"

I pulled the quilt down a little and peeked over the top of it. "And?"

"Quit ARES and get on with the rest of our lives." Aubrey clambered back onto the bed and kissed me on the tip of my nose. "Isn't that the plan?"

I scooped the quilt over her head and pulled her back into bed. We lay under the covers, breathing in each other's stale morning breath and I didn't care. It was a perfect moment.

I didn't know what my life was going to be like without ARES. I guessed I'd have to go back to school and Mum and Dad could shout at me that they'd been right all along. Or maybe I'd just get a different job. Not that I was qualified to do anything accept catch unregistered Shifters. I'd been so obsessed about my past, I'd not given much thought to my future. But one thing I was sure of, it would be with Aubrey.

"Once you've helped me work out who attacked the President," I said. Aubrey rolled her eyes. "But you promised."

"OK. After that." She smiled and kissed me. And it felt like the first time we'd kissed all over again. "Come on," she said, pulling herself away. "We can't stay in bed all day."

"Oh!" I groaned. "Why not?"

"Because we have a job to do." She tugged the covers off me, leaving me with no protection from the chilly room. "Get your trousers on."

She pulled her own clothes on, tied up her big boots, and clomped out of the room. I scrambled into my own clothes and followed her.

The whole house was silent as Aubrey and I walked hand in hand to the kitchen.

"Stop grinning!"

"I can't," I said.

"Well try. You look like a mad man."

I pulled her arm behind my back, drawing her into me. "Mad about you."

"You are so cheesy, Scott," she said, but kissed me anyway.

We made our way through the house and to the kitchen where Frankie was already sitting, flicking through the morning papers.

"Good morning," she said cheerily, as we joined her. "How was your evening? I hope the children all behaved themselves."

"It was… fun," I said, smiling at Aubrey.

"How was your ball?" Aubrey said, nudging me to behave.

"Oh, productive but tedious. Lots of heads of state falling over themselves to be *seen* to do the right thing. Although actually making sure they live up to their promises is quite another thing. But I guess it's all worth it in the end. Coffee? It's from a project I fund in Ethiopia." She raised a pot of steaming black liquid from the stove and waved it at us. I could smell the smoky richness from across the room.

"Yes, please," I said.

"Oh, a package came for you early this morning." She gestured with the coffee pot to a large white polystyrene box on the table. It was covered in ARES stickers. "I didn't want to wake you." She handed me a mug of coffee, smiling. "I thought you could do with the rest."

Aubrey peeled off the stickers and lifted the lid on the box. Inside was a black computer screen and a tangle of wires. It looked a little like the simulators and the sight of the sensors sent a shiver down my spine. "It's the eval kit," Aubrey said.

"Oh, that's good." Frankie handed a mug to Aubrey.

"Yes, so we can do the evaluation and be on our way," Aubrey said placing the mug next to the box without even sipping at it.

"Why the rush?" Frankie said. "I would have thought it was good to be out of that building for a while. And away from Sir Richard. Does he still have that stupid moustache?"

Aubrey smiled despite herself. "He still waxes it every day."

"The man's an idiot. I remember he put me on detention for a week for sneaking out of dorms. When he was the one who'd shown us how to sneak out. Hypocrite. But then, as soon as a man gets a whiff of responsibility it's what it seems to do to them all."

Aubrey joined Frankie in sighing over the follies of men. I just stared into my mug.

"Why don't you do it, Scott?" Frankie said suddenly, her ice eyes boring into me.

"Huh?" I said looking up.

"The evaluation? Why don't you do it?" She smiled, and I felt my cheeks go warm.

"Sure!" I said, wanting to impress her.

"But you've never done one before," Aubrey said, uncertain.

"It can't be that hard. I mean, you do it."

Aubrey blinked and it took me a moment to realise why she looked so shocked. I replayed what I'd said and shook my head. "No, that came out wrong. I mean I've seen you do it." I covered my face with my hand.

Frankie laughed. "Oh, don't worry, I'm sure Aubrey knew you were only joking. I'm sure she knows you're perfectly capable. Take a seat." She pulled up a wooden chair and sat at the table. I glanced over at Aubrey to see if I was still in trouble. She skidded the box and her tablet across the table in my direction and narrowed her eyes at me. It was touch and go.

I took my seat as instructed, while Aubrey remained standing, and launched the application.

"Um, if you could place the electrodes on your temples," I said, trying to remember how the process worked. Normally one of the doctors at ARES carried out the procedure, although Aubrey had done the evaluation on number three.

Frankie did as instructed, lifting her honey hair out of the way. "And hold that silver thing." I plugged the wires into the tablet and launched the evaluation programme.

"So, Scott," Frankie said, curling her hand around the metallic cylinder. "You have my full attention. What do *you* want to ask me?"

What did I want to ask her? Not the stupid list of questions ARES had prepared for us, to reveal if a person had psychopathic tendencies, that was for sure. I really wanted to ask her something more important. More personal.

"How do you do it? This place. The children." I ignored Aubrey's little cough.

"It's easy when you know you're doing the right thing." The monitor bleeped into life. A steady, even line that meant she was telling the truth.

"But it must require a lot of strength. And to do it all

on your own, without a husband or a boyfriend. A beautiful woman like you, it can't be hard to find someone?" I sensed Aubrey moving out of the corner of my eye, only I didn't take my eyes off Frankie's face.

"Oh, you are sweet. But after my husband died, I decided to put my all into Pandora and the children. Theirs is the only love I need."

"Scott," Aubrey said. "Are you going to do the evaluation or not?"

"Huh? Oh, OK." I looked down at the list of questions I was supposed to ask. The first one seemed rather stupid, but I asked it anyway. "Do you ever feel that your accomplishments go unnoticed?"

"I wouldn't say I have that many accomplishments." Again, the readout of her brain activity and pulse remained steady.

I made a cross next to the question with my finger and asked the next one. "Do you ever feel that you are better than other people? Oh, that's just silly. You are better than other people. We won't bother with that." I marked that with an X. And the question after it, which asked if the subject ever found themselves feeling isolated from their peers.

"Scott, I think I should take over," Aubrey said, walking over and trying to pull the tablet out of my hand.

"I think Scott is doing just perfectly, Aubrey," Frankie said. And Aubrey backed up, one step at a time. I grinned at her and went back to the questions.

"I think we can skip most of these. Superiority, no. Disgust in your fellow humans, no. Oh, this is a good one. Do you ever experience fits of rage?"

"Well, I can get angry. When I see the injustice in the

world. But I wouldn't describe it as a fit of rage." The steady beeping of the machine sounded like birdsong.

I marked the final cross on the screen. There was something else I'd wanted to ask Frankie. Something that hadn't been on the list of questions. But I couldn't remember. It probably didn't matter.

"Well, I think that's everything, don't you?" Frankie said.

"Yep," I agreed. I quickly typed up a summary, about what an incredible person and upstanding citizen she was, hit the file button and watched as it was mailed back to HQ.

"Hang on, you've not asked all of the questions you're supposed to," Aubrey said, yanking the tablet away from me before I had a chance to stop her this time.

"I think Scott did brilliantly," Frankie said, peeling the sensors away from her skin, her eyes shining.

I beamed.

"Besides, you don't really think I'm a psychopath do you, Aubrey?"

Aubrey let the tablet drop back onto the table. "I guess not."

"Good. I'm afraid I have an important call to make, but stay as long as you like. Go for a walk in the woods. Relax a little." All of this was said directly to me and it sounded like the best idea ever.

"We should be getting back," Aubrey said.

"Come on Aubrey, chill out. You're so uptight."

"I'm… I'm what?" Aubrey stepped in close and whispered. "What's got into you, Scott?"

"You know what would loosen you up?" I waggled my eyebrow at her. Then slapped my hand to my forehead to stop it. What was I doing?

Aubrey straightened up, her face suddenly still and cold. "When you've stopped acting like an idiot, I'll be in the van." She spun around and stormed up the stairs.

I tried to stand to follow her, my stomach churning with guilt, but I found I couldn't move.

"Don't worry about her," Frankie said. "You know what teenage girls are like. All hormones. More coffee?"

My hands were already shaking from the strength of the last one, but I nodded my head for more.

"Ella is the same now she's going through entropy. It's such a strain, knowing that the thing that makes you special is fading."

"Ella is young to be going through entropy."

"She seems quite taken with you," Frankie said, ignoring my question.

"Who does?"

"Ella. It's nice for her to have people of her own age around. You should stay a little longer. Take her for a walk. She'd like that. You'd like that too, wouldn't you?"

"I, um…" I said. Something didn't feel right. I looked down at my hands shaking from too much caffeine. "Aubrey's right. We should head back."

"Forget about Aubrey," Frankie snapped and I looked at her once more. "Forget about her for an hour or so. She's not your boss. And after all, you're the more powerful Shifter; that much is clear. I can see you've been through a lot, Scott. More than Aubrey can understand, am I right?"

I nodded slightly.

"It's OK. I understand. That's what this place is all about, Scott. It's a safe haven for kids like you. Kids who've seen too much. There's a home for you here, if you want it. You just say the word." She patted my hand.

"That sounds good."

"Good," Frankie said, giving my hand a final squeeze. "Think about it. But first, take Ella out. She can show you our grotto out in the woods."

I would stay. I did want to go for a walk in the woods with Ella. What a brilliant idea.

"Yes. I'd like that."

"Wonderful. Ella will be so happy." Frankie stood up and crossed over to my side of the table. She laid her hand on my shoulder and gave it a squeeze. "You're a sweet boy, Scott. Do something for me, will you?"

I nodded. I would do anything for her.

"Don't change," her voice oozed like honey. "Stay exactly as you are."

I felt warm and safe and like I properly belonged somewhere for the first time in my life. And that somewhere was here with Frankie. Where she wasn't telling me what to do or who to be. She just wanted me to stay exactly as I was.

CHAPTER NINETEEN

As soon as Frankie had left the room that glowing feeling started to fade. I was trying to remember what I had been doing, like when you walk into a room and can't remember why you came in. There was definitely something I had to do.

"I forgot to give you this back."

I turned to see Ella at the foot of the stairs holding my jacket.

That's what I was forgetting. My jacket. I stood up and took it off her. "Thanks," I said. But still something didn't feel right. There was still something I was supposed to do.

"Frankie said you might like to see the grotto, out in the woods?"

That was it. I had to go and see the grotto. "Yes, I'd love that. Thank you."

Her face lit up and I felt that glow again.

I followed her out of the kitchen door and across the lawn. The dew still clung to the grass so the hems of my trousers were damp by the time I'd entered the woods on the edge of the grounds. There was a small, beaten path cutting between the trees. Birds sang in the branches and the sun broke through the canopy. It was a perfect early spring morning. But it didn't feel perfect to me. The trees seemed to be pressing down on me, watching me.

I stumbled over a tree stump and Ella caught my arm.

"It's just through here," she said, pointing at a break in the trees up ahead.

She pulled a bramble branch out of my way so I could get past.

The grotto was a small domed building, made out of stacks of white stone, about ten feet high and the same across. When she'd said grotto, I'd imagined the kind of things you saw in shopping malls, where you could tell Santa what you wanted for Christmas. But there was something Stone Age about this place. Something pagan.

Ella walked up the small steps leading to the arched entrance and waited for me. I followed her.

Inside, every inch of the walls had been covered in broken pottery and shards of glass. Reds, blues, yellows and bright greens. It was an assault of colour. A rainbow.

Why did that seem so familiar? "Who made this place?" I asked.

"It was here when Frankie moved in. We think it's as old as the house itself. Maybe even older. Some of the pottery used is Roman, see?"

She pointed at a triangle of broken red pottery which, I could see as I looked closer, showed a picture of a man and woman painted in black paint. It took me a while to realise what the figures were doing. When I finally did, I blushed and turned away.

Ella took a seat on a small metal bench under the single window. A wild rose bush crept its way in through the opening, and wrapped around the leg of the bench.

"I come here all the time," she said, looking up at the domed roof. "When I want to get away from all the little children. It's hard, being the only grown-up around here, other than Frankie."

"Grown-up, but you're still a kid, Ella."

"I am not. I'm a woman now." Her chin jutted in offended pride.

"Hmm, OK. If you say so. Me, I'm in no hurry to grow up. Sometimes, I wish I could go back and be a kid again. Six or seven. And just play all day. No worrying about exams or bullies. No ARES."

I saw a single square of mirror that had been used to tile the ceiling; in among all the colour it looked like a black hole. I moved and caught my reflection in it. I looked so very small.

"I don't remember much about my childhood," Ella said. "My earliest memories are of this place and Frankie. I think I remember my father's face sometimes. But then I don't know if it wasn't the face of the man who killed him."

I wasn't really listening to her. I was too busy looking at the fragments of images on the walls. "I guess you owe a lot to Frankie, then. I mean, she saved you and all?" I looked back to face her.

"I suppose," Ella gazed up through the window at where a bird was singing on a nearby branch. "She has made me what I am."

"Yeah, she's something. I've never met a woman like

her before. So…" I struggled to find the right word. "So forceful." That didn't seem right.

"It's been nice meeting you," Ella said, plucking a bud from the climbing rose.

"Oh, sure. It's been nice meeting you, too. I guess." There was still something about this girl I couldn't work out. Something so cold. So distant.

She stood up and walked towards me, holding the flower to her nose. "I've never met someone else like me. Someone who can remember. It's good to have someone who understands." She took another step forward and I could smell her perfume. Strong and floral. It stung my throat.

I sidestepped and walked over to the other side of the grotto. It suddenly felt really small. "Yeah, it's hard when other people don't get it."

"Like Aubrey? Does she get it?" She approached me again.

Aubrey? "Aubrey!" Her name was like glass of water in the face. "What am I doing here?" I said, looking around at the glittering walls, which felt like they were closing in on me.

Ella gasped, running forward and grabbing me by my shoulders. She pressed her chest into mine, pushing me backwards. I took a stumbling step and ended up falling onto the bench behind me. Ella sat on my lap.

"I have to go," I said, trying to push her away. For someone so small, she seemed unnaturally heavy.

"I thought you liked me," she said, her face uncomfortably close, her perfume choking me now.

"I do… It's just…" Her hand was curling in my hair and I slapped it away.

"I won't tell anyone. It's OK."

But it really wasn't OK. I couldn't move my legs and I was pinned to the seat.

"What's going...?" I didn't have a chance to finish before Ella's lips silenced me. I felt her tongue pushing into my mouth and her teeth scraping against mine. I could taste her perfume, sour and bitter and foul.

"Stop!" I shouted into her mouth, but I still couldn't push her away. I was gagging. Her tongue felt too large. Too heavy.

"Scott!"

Ella finally released me and we both looked to the small doorway of the grotto.

Aubrey was standing there, her eyes wide in shock, her perfect cupid lips open and wobbling.

"So, I don't give you what you want and this is what you do?"

I've done terrible things. I've seen terrible things. But the look on Aubrey's face before she turned away was the worst ever.

I shoved Ella off me and she landed heavily on the floor. I looked down at her, filled with rage and hatred and I wanted to hit her. I wanted to smash her stupid grindy teeth in for what she'd done.

"I'm sorry," she said, holding one of her frail hands up to her mouth. "She made me do it. She couldn't control Aubrey, so she made me..." She couldn't speak for sobs.

"What have you done?" I said. "What have I done?"

I ran out of the grotto, tripping on the steps and tumbling into a bramble bush. It grabbed at my shirt and I struggled to get free of it. Then I stopped, angry at myself for being so slow. It was OK. I could change all of this. I

was a Shifter. I slapped myself in the forehead, annoyed
at my own stupidity. I just had to Shift and then none of
this would have happened. I played back the last hour,
looking for that pivot point that I could tip. Saying "yes"
to the second cup of coffee. Agreeing to go for a walk
with Ella. I pushed at each in turn, expecting that flip of
reality.

But it didn't come.

I untangled myself from the brambles and stood up,
staring into the dark wood to where Aubrey had run. I
stayed there for at least a minute trying harder and
harder to find something to undo. But nothing changed.

I didn't have time to work out what was going on. I
had to catch up with Aubrey and explain, and then
when I was thinking clearly again, I could sort the mess
out. I raced down the path through the woods, leaping
over stumps and ducking low branches before finally
coming back to the playing field. I skidded around the
front of the house just in time to see the van speeding
away, Aubrey in the driving seat.

"Aubrey!" I screamed after her. But it was too late.
She was gone and it felt as if she'd wrenched my heart
out and taken it with her. I stood in a daze, not knowing
what had happened or what I could do about it. I had
to get back to Aubrey and explain everything.

I heard a crunch behind me. Frankie stood with her
arm around Ella's shoulder. Ella was looking at the
ground, her hair falling in front of her face so that only
the tip of her chin could be seen.

And now I knew where I'd seen her before. Why she
looked so familiar. She was the girl from the picture
with the original Prime Minister's daughter. The one

who'd been with Charlotte Vine the day she'd had her accident. The day that, in one reality, she'd died.

I was frozen to the spot, realisation sinking in.

"You should go home, Scott," Frankie said. "Now." She turned, leading Ella inside and shutting the door behind her with a heavy thud.

And I started running for home.

CHAPTER TWENTY

I ran.

Stones crunched under my feet as I left the house behind and hit the dirt track outside. My feet sunk into the mud, clinging to me and trying to slow me down. But I pushed on. Even when one of my shoes got stuck in the mud and almost came off. When I hit the main road, I got into my stride, picking up speed. The white lines cutting up the tarmac blurred past and cars honked and drivers shouted at me to get out of the way. But I barely heard them. I could only hear one thing: Frankie's voice telling me to go home. Without knowing how, I knew I was headed in the right direction, each pounding step bringing me closer to home. I ran up walls, vaulted off fences, threw myself over cars, all without really seeing them. They were just obstacles that stood between me and home. Once I was there, everything would be OK. Mum and Dad and Katie would all be waiting for me. I could see their smiling faces now, welcoming me home. There would be food waiting on the table and a hug from Katie and everything would be OK. I should never have been here in the first place. Once I got there, I'd never leave home again. The more I thought about it, the more frantic I became to get there. I ran faster than I'd ever run in my life. So fast I felt the rain sting my face like tiny blades.

After the first hour, time ceased to mean anything. Instead of being divided up into fractions of time, my life was defined by space. Inches. Feet. Miles. Each fragment bringing me closer to my only goal.

The siren call of home became deafening, drowning out all other thoughts. Aubrey and the mess I had made there, Ella and what she had to do with the Prime Minister's daughter, the President. None of it mattered. Only home.

Looking back, I realise I must have been running for six, maybe seven hours. The sky was getting darker and the streetlights had started to come on one after the other. I remember wondering if I was somehow turning the lights on just by passing them.

I tried to distract myself from the pain that was burning through my chest and legs by playing memories from home. When Mum and Dad came home with Katie, when she was just a little baby, and the first thing she'd done was throw up on me. When we used to play together in the tree house. How we'd curl up in bed at night with Mum and Dad and they'd read to us. Before all the shouting began.

And then there were the other memories. The ones people kept telling me to forget. To let go. Katie's limp, broken body under the truck. My mother's torn face as she screamed "murderer". And the deeper, darker things. The pain I'd caused them. The nightmares that wouldn't go away because they hadn't been dreams. They had been me.

By the time I reached my road, my feet had become balls of pain at the end of my legs, and my legs themselves were numb. I'd broken the wall ten miles back and was running on pure... pure what? Willpower? I didn't know what was driving me. All I knew was that I had to get home. I stumbled on a hole in the pavement and fell, crashing to the ground, both my knees making loud crunching noises. But still I had to press on. I dragged myself the last hundred yards, clawing at the tarmac till my nails snapped. When I touched the rough bristles of our welcome mat I collapsed, everything spent.

I lay there, jagged breaths slicing at my lungs. But while I was physically broken, my mind felt free. Like a great weight had been lifted from it.

"Frankie," I gasped. Frankie had done this to me. She'd done everything to me.

I managed to pull myself into a sitting position and leant against my front door, trying to stop my head from spinning. She'd put these ideas in my head. Made me stay when I'd wanted to leave. Made me run when I'd wanted to stay.

"Oh, Aubrey." I covered my face with my hands. Everything was a mess.

I heard a rattling behind me and before I could stop myself I fell backwards hitting my head on the wooden floorboards of our hallway. I removed my hands enough to see Katie standing over me.

"What have you done now?"

"Help!" I croaked.

Her annoyed expression changed and she seemed properly concerned. I must have looked a real mess to have inspired that in her. She bent over me and helped me sit up, propping me up against the wall.

"Scott, what's happened? What's wrong?" Katie said.

"Everything," I said. I wanted to cry, but there wasn't enough liquid left in my body to even produce tears.

"We have to get you upstairs before Mum sees you." She glanced over her shoulder at the closed door of the kitchen, before scooping one of my arms over her small shoulder and helping me to my feet. Every step was agony.

"I have to see Aubrey," I said, everything spinning.

"Shut up, Scott. You're not going anywhere. What have you been doing?"

"Running."

"Running? How far?" she said.

"About thirty miles, I think."

"What, are you mental?"

"I didn't have a choice," I said.

Each step of our stairs was like someone stabbing me in the thighs.

"You're freaking me out, Scott," Katie said when we finally reached the top.

"I know."

I just needed to sit down and think. To let the pain subside enough so that I could focus on a Shift that could make all of this go away. I needed to plot it, or else I could just make it all worse.

Katie helped me into my room and I collapsed on the bed. It felt like my ankles and knees had been ground into dust.

"It's OK, Katie," I said seeing her chew on her thumb-nail, which she only did when she was really worried. "Give me a second and I'll be fine."

A second is all I needed to wipe everything away. I closed my eyes and started going over the day in my mind. It had started as one of the best days of my life – waking up next to Aubrey – and ended as one of the worst. I kept seeing Aubrey's face over and over; her open mouth and the hurt in her eyes. I shook my head. I had to focus on my decisions and find the lever points.

I decided to do the evaluation. That made Aubrey angry. If I hadn't done that she wouldn't have gone off and I wouldn't have been left with Frankie or Ella for that matter. Bile rose in my throat as I thought about Ella. The evaluation. That was the decision to unmake.

I focused on that point. The echo of Frankie's voice, "Why don't you do the evaluation, Scott?" It became clear in my mind and I pushed, willing myself to make the opposite decision. Nothing happened. OK, maybe that wasn't a real decision. I'd been flattered and excited and so I hadn't thought through my options. A rookie mistake. But I could beat myself up about that later. For now, I just had to find another way around.

How about when I agreed to stay longer? I knew I'd been hesitant about it and when it came to Shifting, hesitation is your friend. Again I pushed. And again nothing. I flicked back through moments like sorting through a deck of cards; I was getting increasingly frantic as nothing was working. I went back further, the day before, the night before. I was even willing to sacrifice that night with Aubrey to have a chance to be with her again. Anything that would bring her back.

Nothing.

I sat up so fast it made my head spin. "I can't Shift!"

"What?"

I'd forgotten about Katie, who'd been sat on my bed-room floor all this time watching me mumbling to myself. But I was so panicked I didn't care. "I can't change anything. None of my decisions!"

I tried other decisions, stupid little stuff like what I'd had for breakfast three days ago, or which shoes I'd worn last week. Everything felt heavy and permanent. As though it was carved in stone.

"I'm stuck."

"Calm down," Katie scooted forward on her knees and rested her hand on my shoulder. "You're not making any sense. I'm going to get Mum."

"No!" I grabbed her T-shirt. "No… I just need…" I didn't know what I needed to do.

Was this it? Had entropy got me after all? I thought it was supposed to creep up on you slowly over years, like puberty. But this felt like a portcullis smashing down on me, cutting me off from everything that mattered in my life. Something had caused this.

Words echoed in my head.

"I like you, Scott. Do something for me. Don't ever change."

"She did it. She's stopped me Shifting!"

"Who did what now?" Katie said, leaning away from me. I didn't blame her. I was sounding like a madman. Like Aubrey's father. I should have listened to him, should have paid more attention to his warnings. Frankie was dangerous, perhaps the most dangerous person I'd ever met.

"She must be like me, Katie," I said. "She can make people do things. Like make me run, and Ella, and the PM's daughter. Oh, God."

The realisation hit harder than the pain. I slumped back onto the bed. I was pinned, like one of Frankie's butterflies in a frame.

"Just one choice. Let me change just one choice. I can make this alright." I was muttering now, not even making sense to myself.

"What are you saying?"

"I'm saying I can change my choices!" I snapped at Katie. "Change any decision I've ever made."

"People can't do that." Katie's voice was soft and scared. But there was something else there.

"I can, Katie. Or at least, I could. And now I don't know what's happening to me. I don't expect you to believe me. I hardly believe myself half of the time, but it's true."

I leaned up and reached out for Katie's hand. I just needed something solid to hold on to. Something real.

Katie took it, cautiously, as if she was scared of me. "I do believe you, Scott."

I looked down at our entwined hands, noticing how alike they were in ways. The same large knuckles from kickboxing training, the same little finger that bent at a weird angle.

"Sometimes," Katie said, squeezing my hand. "Sometimes I feel like everything I've done in my whole life is like an etch-a-sketch, you know? That I could just shake it and it would all disappear and then I could start over. But I'm too scared to even try, because where will I be? Who will I be?"

I stared at Katie's scared face and wanted the world to just stop spinning so I could get off. She was talking about her choices the way Shifters did. But it couldn't be. I'd always known the power to Shift ran in families. But not Katie. Not stubborn, brave, brilliant Katie. I couldn't believe she'd have a single thing she wanted to undo. No, I wouldn't believe it. Couldn't believe it. I didn't want this life for her. Chasing after madmen in the rain, being stabbed, blown up. I wanted Katie to stay exactly as she was. My Katie. My little sister.

"Listen to me," I said, wrapping my hand around the back of her neck and drawing her head against my shoulder. "You just don't think about it, OK? You know that dumb-ass fridge magnet mum has? The 'No regrets' one?"

Katie nodded, her forehead rubbing against my collar.

"Well, it's right. Don't be like me. Don't spend your life thinking about all the things you wished you'd done. You promise me. Don't look back. Just look forward. Always forward and everything will be OK, OK?"

"OK," Katie whispered.

There was so much I wanted to tell her. So much I had to tell her, but I just didn't have the strength. It would have to wait. First, I needed to speak to Aubrey and then I needed to face Frankie and work out what the hell she'd done to me.

But before that, I needed to sleep.

"Everything will be OK," I said, as I fell back on my pillow.

I didn't know how. But I had to believe it was true. Or else I knew I'd never get back up out of that bed.

CHAPTER TWENTY-ONE

My head felt less foggy in the morning. I was beyond tired and my body hated me: every movement was an act of revenge on its behalf. But the heavy pressure on my mind had lifted slightly.

I saw a glass of water sitting on the table beside my bed. Katie must have brought it in on her way to school this morning as it was still cold. I sipped at the water, the wetness stinging my raw throat and then glugged it all down. Next to the glass was a cereal bar and a small note.

I told Mum you were hung over and she's to leave you alone. K.

Where would I be without you, Katie? I thought. Had I been imagining things last night, or could Katie be a Shifter too? I didn't want to believe it. I didn't want my little sister to have to go through the things I had. But maybe I didn't have to worry. Maybe she was normal and I was just going mad. Aubrey would know. That's if Aubrey would ever speak to me again.

I'd left close to fifty messages on her phone throughout the night. The first was a desperate plea for her to speak to me. The last was just me sobbing into the handset. Now when I tried to leave a message there was just an annoying bleat and a digital voice saying "Mailbox full".

I had to get out of this bed and go find her to explain.

I dragged myself into the bathroom, each step a lesson in pain. I pulled off the T-shirt and jeans I'd slept in, the dried sweat making them stick to my skin, and turned on the shower. I clambered into the bathtub and sat down under the jet, not having the strength to stay standing. It helped, pounding my aching muscles, and afterward I felt, if not quite human, then at least a step up from vegetable. The walk back to my room was less agonising. I dressed in fresh jeans and T-shirt and gingerly squeezed my bruised feet into my socks and then trainers. The nails on both of my big toes had gone a scary shade of black. I'd deal with them later. For now, the only thing that mattered was Aubrey. I pulled on my Bluecoat, swallowed a couple of painkillers, and made my way downstairs.

"So, you're finally up then?" Mum said from the doorway. She had her arms folded across her chest and was staring at me. I was about to get a Talk.

"Yes, sorry, Mum. But I don't have time."

She harrumphed. "Look at the state of you. I thought that place would be good for you, Scott. But all you seem to do is crawl home in the middle of the night. Drunk, no doubt."

"Yeah, OK. Can the lecture wait till tomorrow? It's just that..."

"And that girlfriend of yours! Oh, don't pretend you don't know what I'm talking about. I've seen you with her. And her dyed hair and her smoking. She's a bad influence on you, Scott. You used to be such a good boy."

"Mum!" I snapped. "Don't. Trust me. Just don't." My hands were shaking in rage and I clenched them into fists.

"I'm only saying, you're very young to be just dating one girl. I'm sure there are plenty of nice girls–"

"Mum."

"Look at your father and me, we met when we were just sixteen and look how that turned out."

"But I'm not Dad. And Aubrey isn't you. We're nothing like you and will never be as bitter and cold and dead inside as you are!" I stepped in close to her and bent my head so I was staring straight into her eyes. "And if you have regrets about your life, that's your problem. Don't go trying to tell me what to do. I've had enough of that."

I stepped away and was out the door before she could even answer. Mum was another thing that I could deal with later.

I headed to Aubrey's flat first and let myself in. She wasn't home. I guessed, if she was trying to avoid me she'd have known this was the first place I'd have come. Maybe she was staying with a friend? And I had a pretty good guess about who that might be.

"Is Aubrey…?"

The slap came so fast I didn't even have time to block it.

"How dare you!" Rosalie snapped. "You pig. You absolute pig. And you know what's the worst bit? I thought you were different. But you're just like every other bloke, aren't you? Don't get what you want and so you move on. I can't believe you did that to Aubrey."

I pressed my hand to my pounding cheek. "Rosalie, it's not like that. It's all a huge mess and I have to speak to Aubrey."

"Well, she doesn't want to speak to you."

"Is she here?" I looked behind the bar at Bailey's to the door I knew led upstairs to Rosalie's accommodation.

"She's not here. And even if she was I wouldn't tell you, you... you pig."

"Please, Rose. You have to help me." I grabbed one of her hands in mine and squeezed it. "I don't know what's going on, but I would never hurt Aubrey, you know that."

"Yeah, well, you have." She pulled her hand free.

"But it wasn't me. Not really."

"Oh, what? Are you going to give me the 'you couldn't help yourself' story now? That this other girl just threw herself at you? You're a Shifter, Scott, none of that crap works."

"But that's the thing. I can't Shift!"

Rosalie's expression softened for a moment. "Entropy? Well, it serves you right."

"No, I don't think it is. Look, you just have to get a message to Aubrey for me; you have to tell her that Frankie did this."

"Frankie? Is that the girl?"

"No. Frankie is... look. Just tell Aubrey, OK? Tell her that Frankie is like me."

"Like you how?"

I shook my head, not knowing how much to reveal. I decided that things couldn't get any worse than they already were. "Remember Greyfield's? Remember how everyone just did what I said?"

"I… I don't know. It was all such a blur."

"I can make people do things, Rose. Or at least, I could. That night, I was able to make anyone do anything I wanted."

Rosalie laughed. "You?"

"Yes, me, really. But look. This woman we saw this weekend, she can do it too. And all of this mess is her fault."

"She made you kiss that girl."

"Not really. I don't know. But I know she's stopped me from putting it right," I said.

"I don't know, Scott. It all sounds like bull from where I'm standing. You're telling me you're a Forcer?"

"What's a Forcer?"

Rosalie picked up an already clean glass and started rubbing it with a tea towel. "I've only heard about them from Granny Bailey. She used to tell us stories about Shifters in the past with all these crazy powers. But I thought they were just stories."

"Maybe they are. I don't know, Rosalie. But just tell Aubrey, will you? Just tell her."

She hesitated, took a deep breath and then nodded. "OK, I'll tell her."

"And tell her I'm sorry and… and that I love her. And that I'll find a way to fix this."

Before Rosalie could answer the world flipped.

I wasn't standing in Bailey's talking to Rosalie. I was standing in ARES staring at a video screen surrounded by the rest of the agency. CP and Jake and the rest of the cadets were gathered. Something big was happening.

I fought off the nausea I sometimes got after experiencing someone else's Shift and tried to sort through the new reality. Maybe, whatever had changed would have fixed the mess I was in.

But no. All the events of yesterday were still in place. The only thing that had changed was that when I'd been on my way to see Rosalie, I'd been suddenly called into ARES because of an emergency.

I focused on the present and why I was here. The video screens were all tuned to the same channel showing a live news report. I tried to take in what the news anchor was saying.

"We have just received the tragic news that the President of China's son died in the early hours of this morning. Tsing Ken-ze had been in intensive care for the past forty-eight hours with suspected poisoning after attending a diplomatic ball. He was just thirteen years old and the President of China's only son. President Tsing will return to China tomorrow. But the questions today are: who did this and why? And what will it mean for the already strained diplomatic relationships between China and the UK, and the Prime Minister's environmental deal, that an attack like this was allowed to take place on our soil?"

I found I couldn't breathe through my nose. I sniffed and a ball of snot rolled back into my throat. My lips tasted of salt. I'd been crying.

"Scott, what's wrong?" I turned to see CP gazing up at me.

I couldn't believe she was asking me that. She'd met Ken-ze, she knew what a sweet kid he was. And then I realised she hadn't: none of us had. I was crying over the death of a boy I'd never known.

I wiped my eyes with the sleeve of my jacket. "He was just really young," I said.

"Yeah, he was only my age," said Jake, a slight catch in his throat.

CP patted Jake's arm. "My Nan always said God takes his favourites first."

"Yeah, well in that case God is a selfish bastard," I said.

CP stretched her hand up and clipped me around the back – as close as she could get to my head. "Consider yourself lucky my Nan isn't here or she'd have you over her knee for a comment like that."

"Give me a break, CP. I am having the worst day ever."

"Not as bad as the day he's having," Jake pointed back to the news report.

It was showing pictures of President Tsing coming out of the hospital, his head bowed, his steps laboured. It cut to a picture of Ken-ze in his Little Guards uniform standing next to his father, although no mention was made of his powers.

Why hadn't Ken-ze Shifted? He must have been able to prevent whatever had killed him. Or one of the other Little Guards. Why hadn't I done my job and found out who had been behind it? Whoever had tried to kill the President had gone after his son, I was sure. Or maybe the poison had been intended for his father and Ken-ze had died for the President just like he had been trained to do. Either way, it was my fault. I should never have listened to Aubrey and gone to Pandora. I could have stopped it. And now there was nothing I could do to put it right, thanks to Frankie.

Frankie. Hadn't she been at a ball two nights ago? A diplomatic ball? The one she'd taken Kia to. This couldn't be a coincidence. Just like Ella being with the PM's daughter couldn't be a coincidence either. Yet another death of a powerful person's child. Yet another connection to Frankie. I needed to get back to my desk.

"Tyler!"

I turned to see Sir Richard, his nostrils flaring above his moustache. "Where do you think you're going? We haven't had the briefing yet."

"Sir, I need to get some information."

"You need to stay right here."

I stopped and made my way back to the assembled kids of ARES, trying to keep my anger in check. Jake gave me an encouraging smile. He'd been on Sir Richard's bad side enough to know it wasn't worth it.

Sir Richard waved at the screens and someone silenced the volume. "OK, what we know is this. A Shift was made two nights ago in the same grid reference as this ball where Ken-ze was poisoned. It could have been one of the President's Little Guards trying to save their friend, or Ken-ze himself trying to avoid his own poisoning. Or, and this is what the analysts believe is most likely, the Shift might have come from the attacker, a rogue Shifter perhaps. We're looking into all the possibilities now."

"Any chance he can be returned, sir?" CP asked, her small voice carrying across the room.

"That depends on whether a Shifter was directly involved in his death and whether we can talk them round to changing what happened. First, here is a list of all of the guests at the ball."

"Can't we just rule out all the adults?" Jake said, taking hold of the piece of paper as it was passed to him.

"I'm not ruling out anything at this point. I want you to split the names between you and investigate them all. If any of their names pop, I want a Spotter on their case straight away. Speaking of which, where's Jones?"

Sir Richard looked to me. I kept my face as straight as possible. "I don't know, sir."

"Well, find her and get her in here. She's the best Spotter we've got. The rest of you, you know what you have to do, get to it. Oh, and Tyler. My office. Now."

I was handed a sheet of paper as I traipsed after Sir Richard. I scanned the list of guests at the ball. And sure enough, Francesca Goodwin was there.

"Sir," I said, following Sir Richard into his office. "Sir, I know who did this!"

"Oh yes, and who is that?"

"Francesca Goodwin AKA Frankie Anderson – the last member of Ganymede. She was at the ball two nights ago."

"Actually, it was Mrs Goodwin that I wanted to speak to you about."

"She's a Forcer, sir."

"And what, pray, is a Forcer?" Sir Richard said, stroking his moustache.

"Someone who can make other people do what they want."

"Really? And yet wasn't it you who tried so hard to convince me such a power didn't exist?" he said, with a smug twitch of his mouth.

"I was wrong. I was wrong about everything," I said.

"Well, I'm not doubting that. And I would also like to add that you are most certainly wrong about Mrs Goodwin. I met Frankie yesterday and she struck me as a most... impressive woman. I know she was involved in Dr Lawrence's schemes, but as your own evaluation shows," he pointed at a file on his desk, in which I could see the report I'd emailed in, "Frankie was innocent of all knowledge of the truth behind the project and she has gone on to live a life defined by charity and philanthropy. You say yourself she's a remarkable woman showing an excess of 'warmth and compassion'. Are these not your words?"

"They are, sir, but–"

"But nothing. There is no way she would be involved in Ken-ze death's or anyone else's death for that matter. Look at her!" He held up a picture of Frankie cut out from a newspaper, shaking hands with the Prime Minister. "Does she look like a killer to you?" He threw the clipping at me and I plucked it out of the air. I straightened it out and looked at her face more clearly. That incredible smile that everyone fell for. Even me.

"But it's her. She killed Ken-ze and I think she may have been responsible for the attack on the President. Or... or she made her children do it."

"Ridiculous. Frankie has dedicated her life to protecting children. She's hardly going to send us into a state of war now, is she?" He slammed over the file and threw it in the bin next to him. "If I hear that you've so much as looked at Frankie Goodwin you're fired. You're not to go anywhere near that woman or any of her children, do you understand me?" He was clutching the edge of the table so hard his knuckles had gone white. A bead of sweat rolled down his forehead and got lost in his moustache.

"I understand you perfectly." I pulled off my Bluecoat and threw it at him. "I quit."

"You can't quit. I forbid it," he bellowed as I stormed out of his office.

"Tough."

"Well, don't you come crawling back to us, do you understand me? And don't expect to get a licence for Shifting. You're on your own now, Scott Tyler."

"Fine by me."

I stomped to my desk, ignoring the curious looks from over the cubicles as I pounded past. I retrieved my laptop from my desk, yanking it away from the cables so hard I knocked my cup of pens over, and shoving it into my bag. The pens went rolling across the table and fell to the floor one by one.

I had some of the pieces. I just needed to fit them all together and find a way to stop Frankie. Maybe once I'd stopped her, and freed myself of her hold on me, I'd be able to undo all this crap. It was all I had to work with.

CHAPTER TWENTY-TWO

I didn't want to go home as I was certain that would mean another lecture from Mum. I needed to be alone. And if Aubrey wasn't going to use her place, I might as well.

I let myself in and headed straight for her living room where I knew the projector was. I'd not taken it home yet. Sometimes, when my head was a mess, it helped to look at things in a new way.

I took the poster of the fifty foot woman down off the wall and leant it against the sofa, fired up my laptop and plugged it into the projector. After a few minutes of whirring the thing came to life and an image started to form on the wall. I twisted the dial so I could see it more clearly. The picture of Charlotte Vine standing next to Ella.

There was no doubting it. It was her: the same frizzy hair in front of her face; the same frail, skeletal arms.

I returned to my computer and dragged the image to one side, then ran a new search, this time on suspicious deaths of politicians and their children. A few names of minor MPs popped up and I saved the files into a folder.

I broadened the search to include business people and people of power, not really knowing what I was looking for. More names appeared. Drug overdoses, car accidents. I added them to the file. I then started looking for accidents involving famous people and their children. I had ten more names. Nothing struck me as unusual, as in Shifter unusual. And why would it? If a Shifter had been involved there would be no trace at all. The old reality would be wiped away with a single thought.

ARES could trace the presence of Shifts with the quantum sensors, down to a location and time. But they still hadn't found a way of working out what that Shift had been or who had done it. All we had was a time stamp and a map reference on the log. There was no way Lottie or Lane would help me out, not after my dramatic exit today. If only I had access to the sensors myself.

"Hang on," I said out loud.

I punched the address for the sensor log into the search bar. It was supposed to only be accessed by the Regulators, but bypassing the security was going to be easy. Jake had taught me a few tricks about Shifting your way around passwords.

I let my mind clear and started typing, letting all the variants just flow out of me. It didn't take long before I was in. I made a note to tell Carl, our IT Director, to change his password. CARLSEXGOD was a bit too obvious. Once I had access, I cross-referenced the dates and times of the accidents and deaths with the sensor log. I got three matches.

A rock musician's son had broken his leg. An MP's niece had died when she choked on a chicken bone. And the MD of a multi-national corporation had been in a car crash with his son and daughter: only he and his daughter had survived. I then cross-checked the date Charlotte Vine had her accident. There was no registered Shift, but that wasn't surprising. The decision to kill her had only been unmade a few days ago. I added it to the folder anyway.

I discarded all the others and focused on those four accidents, arranging the files on my screen in a patchwork pattern. The faces of smiling children placed next to images of car crashes and emergency vehicles. I launched the internet again and found a news report from that day on Ken-ze's death and added that into the mix.

I used the mouse to move the images around on the screen, and watched as they floated across the wall in front of me. At the top was the picture of Charlotte Vine. Where it had all started. She was smiling, her arm wrapped around Ella's shoulder. I wanted to reach out and push Ella's hair out of her face just to prove to myself that I wasn't going mad. But I was certain it was her. So she had killed Charlotte Vine and then Shifted her decision only a few days ago. Maybe that had been her last decision before entropy finally took over, which might explain the delay. Perhaps, when facing the thought of living with that girl's death for the rest of her life, Ella had done the right thing? Is that why Frankie had stopped taking her to her balls? Had she been disappointed in her?

Next to Charlotte I dragged the picture of Ken-ze in his Little Guard's uniform. I stood up and walked closer to the images. I had sensed there was a connection and now I was determined to prove it. I reached into my back pocket and pulled out the strip of newspaper Sir Richard had thrown at me. In the picture Frankie had one hand resting on Kushi's head, while the other reached out to shake the hand of the man giving her the award. Her eyes bored into mine even through the grainy black and white print. I held it up to the wall, placing it in the centre of my spider's web of events. My arm broke the beam of the projector and the images of the children danced across my skin like glowing tattoos.

I needed something to hold the newspaper clipping in place while I thought. I looked around and saw a ball of Aubrey's nicotine gum pressed into an otherwise empty ashtray. I grabbed it, pressed it against the back of the picture and pushed it against the wall. Then I took a step back, watching the motes of dust floating through the projector beam.

Frankie. She was the centre of all of this. Somehow. But why? And how?

Why kill people if you were only going to undo it? I looked at Frankie's smiling face in the photograph, and of the other people around her, their hands pressed together mid-clap, like they were praying for her. Maybe I was wrong. Maybe everyone else was right and Frankie wasn't the bad guy here. Was she really just going around saving people and I was way off the mark?

I ran my palm across the hair at the back of my neck. Whatever Frankie was doing, it felt wrong.

I remembered the look on Ella's face when she was lying on the ground after she'd kissed me.

"I'm sorry," Ella had said. "She made me do it."

How many other things had Frankie made her kids do?

I looked back at the picture and focused on Kushi. A girl who had grown up fighting off monsters in tunnels and who was now living with a woman she thought was a queen. But maybe little Kushi was still in the clutches of a monster after all.

I looked closer at the picture, at something she was holding in her hand. It was hard to make out. At first I'd thought it was the doll she was never without. But now I could see it was a stuffed toy. A rabbit, maybe? Just like the one that had been handed to President Tsing by the little girl in the rabbit mask.

I shivered, as if someone had run an ice cube along my spine. Maybe Frankie wasn't doing any of this herself? Maybe she was controlling her children and making them do it, in the same way she'd controlled me.

I looked at the other three events I'd found, searching for any sign that one of Frankie's children had been there. Nothing that I could see. But that didn't mean they hadn't been involved. When the CEO had crashed, it had been to avoid a boy on a bike. That boy could have been one of Frankie's kids.

She'd been running the orphanage for ten years; over two hundred kids had passed through her doors. How many Shifts had she manipulated that I would never know about? How many lives had she altered?

I squatted back down on the floor next to my laptop and started flicking through the images again, staring up at the wall as they appeared and disappeared. Near misses. Recoveries in hospital. And these were the stories that had reached the newspapers. How about all the ones that had simply been wiped clean? Erased from history?

I heard laughter from the stairwell outside and I ran to the door and opened it, hoping that Aubrey had decided to come home after all. I leaned over the railings and looked down at the floors below. It was only the man from downstairs bringing yet another woman home.

"What you staring at?" he shouted up at me.

I straightened up and went back inside, closing the door heavily behind me.

I had to forget about Aubrey. It was breaking my heart, but this was bigger than us. I needed to follow my own way now. And that meant finding out what Frankie was really up to. I had to look her in the eye and say I knew what she was doing.

I thought about going back to Pandora. But that place was like a fortress and I'd be stopped before I even got down the drive. I needed to head her off somewhere neutral. And to find that, I needed some help.

CHAPTER TWENTY-THREE

This time I managed to block Rosalie's slap.

"Look, I'm a pig and Aubrey's not here and even if she was you wouldn't tell me. We've been through it all before."

"What are you on about? This is the first time I've seen you since Aubrey told me what you did. But you're right about one thing. You are a pig."

I sighed. There was no way I was going to convince her otherwise. "I need to speak to Jake."

"Oh, come here on official ARES business, have you? I have a right mind to pull him out of the agency."

"But I'm not with ARES any more."

"What?" Rosalie looked genuinely shocked.

"I quit. Now, can I speak to Jake? It's really serious. Bigger than me and Aubrey even."

Rosalie tilted her head and considered me. "OK. He's been punching me in the leg ever since you came in anyway."

Rosalie stepped aside and let Jake crawl out from under the bar.

"Seriously, Sis, you're mental," he said, rubbing his knees clean of dust.

"Hey, Jake," I said, his cheerful optimism infecting me a little.

He returned the smile with his usual grin. "Hey, Scott. Some show you put on today."

"You saw that then?" I said.

"Well, heard it mostly. I think half of London heard it," he laughed, but it was an uneasy, unsettled laugh. "You didn't mean it, did you? About quitting?"

"I'm afraid so. If Sir Richard is just going to stand in my way, I don't have any other choice."

Jake chewed on the inside of his cheek. "ARES won't be the same without you."

"Thanks, Jake," I said, ruffling his hair.

Rosalie slapped my hand away and flattened Jake's hair back down. "Well," she said. "Are you going to get to what you came here for?"

"I think I know who killed that boy."

"The President of China's son?" Jake said, his wide eyes going even wider.

"Yeah. Him and other kids too," I said, shaking my head. "So, I need you to hack into their diary. I've tried, but it's got really good security."

Jake looked a little disappointed. "Well, that's too easy. Come on up."

"This one thing and then you're out of here. Do you understand me, Scott?" Rosalie said, opening the bar hatch. "I don't want you dragging Jakey into whatever mess you've got yourself into."

I placed my hand against my heart. "I promise. I get these details and I'm gone."

Jake tugged on my sleeve and I followed him through the door behind the bar.

I hadn't been back here in all the time Rosalie and Jake had lived at Bailey's. There was a narrow set of stairs leading up to a large living room. Compared to the chaotic decor downstairs, this place was what my mother liked to call shabby chic. There was a tatty yet comfy looking sofa, scattered with pastel cushions. Rugs of all styles covered the old floorboards, making a patchwork of colours. A bunch of purple flowers in an old teapot sat on a large wooden table, which had been painted pale blue. There was only one word for this place, and that was written in large white, wooden print blocks on one of the shelves. Home.

"My room's through here," Jake said, leading me out of the living room and into a small bedroom. Jake had clearly decorated this place himself. A big metal STOP sign was pinned behind his bed, which itself looked like it was made out of scrap metal. And a light by the side of his table was made out of an old set of traffic lights. He flicked it on and it shone all three colours at once, giving the room a warm glow. It was almost as messy as my room at home.

"Whose diary do you need hacking?" he said, pulling up a car seat chair next to his metal desk. There were three computer screens on his desk, and each one flickered into life with the push of a button.

"A woman called Francesca Goodwin."

Jake flexed his fingers over his keyboard and started to type. Like watching any Shifter at work, it was a weird series of jarring movements, as each choice was wiped out and replaced with a new option. Jake, who'd never been the best fighter or the best Mapper, excelled when it came to anything technical.

"She's got some pretty hefty security set up," Jake said, his voice sounding distant. "Weird for just a diary."

"Do you think you'll be able to find it still?"

"Please, who do you think…?" Jake said, and didn't bother finishing. His fingers had stopped moving. "I'm in."

"Jake, you are amazing. Just tell me what she's up to over the next few days."

"Wow."

"Wow, what? What, wow?" I said.

"No wonder she didn't want anyone accessing her files. Looks like she has the personal details of some pretty big cheeses. The Prime Minister. The President of America. Even Vladimirovich."

"Who's that?"

Jake broke free from his focus to give me a disappointed glance. "Like the richest man in the world! She's going to a party with him tomorrow." He pointed at the calendar on the screen where under tomorrow's date Frankie had pinned a link to the launch of an art exhibition.

"I think it's about time I brushed up on my culture, don't you Jake?"

"Can I come?" he said,

"I'm sorry, Jake. I get you in trouble, your sister will have my balls for earrings. And it's bad enough having one girl angry with me."

"But things are so boring," he said, spinning around in his chair.

"Boring is good. Boring is safe."

"Rosalie wants me to leave ARES, you know? To go to a normal school. With normal kids." He scrunched his face up, like the idea was revolting him.

"Jake, maybe one day you won't think normal's so bad after all. I tell you, I would do anything for a spot of normal about now. And besides, you live above the coolest club in London. That's hardly normal, is it?"

"I guess. But what's the point in having this power to get myself out of trouble, if I don't go and get *into* some trouble?" He looked at his hands, as if they were the source of his Shifting ability.

"I don't know, Jake. To help out friends when they need it?" I ruffled his hair again.

He pushed my hand away and straightened his fringe. Seemed he was too old for hair ruffles.

"Yeah, I guess," he said.

A chugging sound started and a moment later three sheets of white paper spat out from Jake's printer. I picked up the printout of Frankie's diary, folded it up and slipped it in my pocket.

"Thanks, Jake."

"See ya, Scott."

Jake spun back around and faced his computer. I wanted to stay and talk to him, maybe hang out like we used to, but I didn't have the time.

I left the room and headed back downstairs. The club was starting to fill up, and the music was on full blast.

Rosalie was buzzing around the organising staff. She stopped when she saw me and walked over.

"You done?" Rosalie said.

"Done. Thanks, Rosalie. I appreciate it."

She made a huffing noise that made her nostrils flare.

"Do you have a message for Aubrey, if I happen to see her?" Rosalie said.

Where could I begin? "Tell her I meant everything I said that night. That I'd rather die than hurt her. Tell her it wasn't me; that I'm going to stop the person who did this and I'll put everything right. And tell her that I love her. And that I'll never stop loving her, even if she never speaks to me again."

"I think that last bit will be better coming from you. But I'll tell her the rest."

"OK. And thank you," I said.

"Just don't get yourself killed before you have a chance to tell her, OK?" Rosalie said, picking a bit of loose thread off my sleeve.

"I'll try."

CHAPTER TWENTY-FOUR

The Victoria and Albert Museum shone as if it was on fire in the drizzling rain. A huge projection of an abstract image rippled across the façade, turning the building a deep red, and spotlights illuminated the dark clouds overhead. Large signs outside advertised the exhibition that was opening tonight: *Interference – Quantum Photography.*

Queues of people wearing long coats over their smart clothes walked up the steps and disappeared inside the double doors. I could already hear the chatter of a crowd over the sound of Kensington traffic whizzing past. The party was in full swing. I just had to find a way in.

One of the bouncers on the door looked my way, watching to see what I was up to. I considered just walking in, blagging my way as a guest. But I looked at my ragged jeans and trainers and decided that probably wasn't going to work.

A white van with "Delacroix Catering" painted on it was parked in the side road, and black-aproned waiters were emptying its cargo into the rear doors of the museum. One of them slipped on the wet pavement.

"You drop that bloody tray and I will personally shove these cocktail sticks up your arse," a man I assumed was Delacroix shouted, shaking a handful of wooden sticks at the waiter.

Well, I'd seen it in enough movies. It was worth a go.

"Sorry I'm late," I said. "The agency gave me the wrong address."

Delacroix looked me up and down. "Well, hurry up then. Get your apron. Can't stand around here all night." He threw a black apron in my face. I slipped it over my head and wrapped the strings around my waist. The chef looked at my trainers and sighed. "You're washing up. And bring those glasses." He pointed at a cardboard box. I picked it up and heard a gentle clinking from inside.

"Right, that's the lot. Come on then." He slammed the boot of the van closed and stormed off towards the entrance.

I hefted the box and followed him inside.

The first gallery we passed through was filled with Buddhist sculptures. Golden crossed-legged figures and stone carvings of men on horses lined the walls. I carefully manoeuvred the box of glasses, worried I'd knock something off a plinth. The next room was lined with white marble statues that looked like figures out of Greek or Roman myths: muscular men wrestling snakes and impossible creatures. In the low light they looked as if they were waiting to jump off their stands and go to battle.

This led into the cafe. Huge stained-glass windows let in light from the garden outside and the ceiling was painted with gold flowers and swirling patterns. I'd been in here once with Mum and Katie, when Mum decided we needed educating about something or other. We'd only got as far as having a cup of tea in here and buying a postcard from the shop.

"You going to stand around all night?" Delacroix said.

"Where do you want the glasses?"

"In the kitchen! Seriously, agency staff these days. Oi, you! Where do you think you're going with those oysters?" he shouted at another guy walking towards the party with a white polystyrene box.

I followed the trail of catering staff into the kitchen and placed the box of glasses on the side. Everyone was bustling about, chopping vegetables and placing lumps of meat in steaming copper pans. The kitchen doors swung open and a girl dressed in a black skirt, white shirt and the same black apron as me came in.

"More champagne glasses. These greedy buggers are knocking it back like it's going out of fashion. I've gone through a whole crate already," she said.

"Er, here!" I said, peeling open the lid of the box I'd carried.

I pulled out a couple of glasses and showed them to her.

"Well, come on then. Get them on a tray and fill em up. We don't want them causing a riot if they run out of *Cristal*." She shoved a black rubber tray into my chest.

If this was what a normal job was like, I was starting to regret leaving ARES. I filled the tray with glasses and she did the same, topping each one off with bubbling golden liquid.

"It's Prosecco," she whispered to me. "But they won't know any different."

I laughed like I knew what she meant and picked up the tray. It slipped in my hand and the glasses nearly fell over.

"First time, hey?" she said.

I gave a weary shrug and the glasses rattled. "Yeah."

"Well, don't look so nervous. They don't bite. Much."

She cackled to herself, scooped the tray up onto one hand and carried at shoulder height. I followed her through the swinging doors and towards the reception hall.

I'd only gone a few steps when a red-faced man, wearing a tuxedo that looked at least two sizes too small, stopped me and took two glasses. He knocked the first one back and waved the second in my direction. "Cheers," he slurred.

"That was Lord Cuthbert," the waitress said, as I caught up with her. "He pretty much owns Scotland. Some big oil baron. But watch yourself around him. He's got a thing for cute boys."

I tried not to blush at the compliment as we pushed forward and into the party proper.

The circular entrance hall was even more impressive than the exterior. Hanging from the huge domed ceiling was a massive tangle of blue and green glass. It reminded me of Thomas Jones's rainbow song. Where would her father be now? Watching over Aubrey from afar? Or stalking me, to make sure I finished the job. I looked around for a tall man with shabby hair and piercing eyes. But there's no way he'd have been allowed in here. There were maybe three hundred people, all milling about and dramatically air kissing each other as they drifted from group to group. No one seemed to be actually looking at each other. Instead, they were scanning the room, as if waiting for someone more interesting to turn up. A string quartet was playing in one corner, but I could hardly hear them above the chatter.

The waitress squeezed her way through the people, stopping every now and then to offer a guest another glass. I followed her, scanning the room for any sight of Frankie. I caught a glimpse of a woman with long, sun-kissed hair. But when she turned around to gather a man with long dreadlocks into an embrace, I saw she was nearing eighty, with eyebrows that had been plucked out and drawn back on, and thin, purple lips. I turned away as she popped a large prawn into her mouth. And saw Hamid.

It was strange to see him without his mirror twin. He was standing on his own in the corner looking uncomfortable. I didn't blame him. The guests didn't bother to hide their disgust as they stared at his deformed head. Some even gathered around him and pointed, as if they were looking at a living art exhibition. He shouted at them in angry Arabic before pushing through the group. They gasped in mock shock and laughed as if it was all part of the show.

A man waved me over with two fingers, demanding another glass of champagne, and I shoved the whole tray into his hands. He shouted after me, but I didn't stop to look back. I wasn't going to take my eyes off Hamid because he would lead me to Frankie.

He walked around the edge of the crowd, brushing his hand along the carved walls, keeping his head down and turned away from the partygoers. I stayed as far back as I could without losing sight of him. Not that it was hard. There weren't too many kids at the party, let alone ones who looked quite as distinctive as Hamid. He left a trail of shocked onlookers as he pushed through, many of whom were still staring his way as I caught up. I wanted to shout at them for being so shallow. Only, the truth was, I'd been a lot worse when I'd first seen him and his brother.

Hamid kept glancing up, and I wasn't sure if it was just my paranoia, but it looked as if he was following someone too. Ahead of Hamid, a man was barging his way urgently through the crowd. I couldn't be sure from behind, but he looked like the same man I'd run into earlier, the oil Lord with the wandering hands. He was swaying back and forth in a way that I was pretty sure had nothing to do with the gentle music that was playing. He tripped out of the double doors and into the gardens outside. Hamid followed him. And I followed Hamid.

The garden was illuminated by moving spotlights and strings of lights hung from tree to tree. Small groups of people were huddled together, blowing cigarette smoke into the rain-filled sky.

Hamid looked over his shoulder and I ducked behind a sculpture of a woman holding a vase just in time. I peered out as Hamid turned back to the drunk. The lord plodded through the flowerbeds, crushing daffodils under his clumsy feet, and stopped next to a large tree. With one hand, he steadied himself against its trunk and a moment later, I heard a trickle as he emptied his bladder.

Hamid stepped over the flowers, more careful than the man he was hunting, and stopped just feet behind him. I wondered what on earth he was up to. His twisted face looked even more distorted in the leaping shadows.

The man still hadn't realised he had company: he was too busy whistling and letting out happy sighs. I watched through the arm of the statue as Hamid reached behind his back. When it reappeared he was holding something. A passing light illuminated both Hamid and the thing in his hand: a slim plastic tube with a thin silver needle. A syringe. Hamid clasped it with both hands and raised it above his head. His one eye was closed and he was shaking, fighting against whatever he was about to do.

I tried to call out. Tried to scream – but only a rasping came from my throat. The moment hung there for what felt like an age: the man whistling; Hamid's hands hovering over the man's back. No one else was paying any attention. They were too busy in their own worlds.

Hamid was going to strike at any minute and I seemed incapable of doing anything to stop him. He arched his back, ready to plunge the syringe into the man's neck. There was a high whistle from across the garden. Hamid opened his eye and a relieved smile spread over his face. He lowered his hands, turned around and threw the syringe into the flowerbed.

There was a lightness to his step as he crossed the garden heading back toward the party and toward the direction of the whistle. When he arrived at the doors, Hazid, his brother, was waiting. The two greeted each other by resting their foreheads together, united once more. They straightened up and disappeared back inside the museum.

It was only then I found I could breathe again.

CHAPTER TWENTY-FIVE

That was the final confirmation. Hamid was a good kid. A bit weird, but who wouldn't be if they'd spent the first half of their life in a freak show? And he and his brother loved to annoy each other, but there was no way he'd go around injecting strange men if he hadn't been told to. As for why he hadn't gone ahead and done it, I had no idea. Maybe it's so that Frankie could force him to change his decision later. Or rather force Hazid to change it for him. What would that be like, I wondered, having your choice Shifted by someone else? If it was Hazid who made the Shift, but Hamid who'd done the act, which one of them would be the real killer? The thought was making my head hurt. I didn't know what was going on. All I knew was that I needed to find Frankie and stop her. Fast.

I raced back into the hall, not bothering to sneak anymore. I ignored the complaints from the guests as I pushed them aside, knocking glasses and canapés to the floor, then finally saw her.

She was at the far end of room, dressed in a long

purple gown that fell to the floor. Her hair was bundled up on her head, like a Greek goddess. She was chatting with a man I recognised from the newspapers: a billionaire who owned two football clubs and an energy company. This must be the Vladimirovich Jake mentioned. Frankie threw her head back and laughed at one of his jokes and he smiled, pleased with himself.

I pressed forward and stumbled as a tall lady wearing ridiculous heels tottered and fell against me. I pushed her roughly out of the way, but when I looked back, Frankie was gone. I darted my head around trying to find her again.

Vladimirovich was leading her through the crowd towards the exit. Only then did I see that she wasn't alone. She had some of her kids with her. Hamid and Hazid, walked shoulder to shoulder – standing tall now they were together again, and laughing at the weird looks they were getting. Ella and Kia followed them, chatting amongst themselves. Kia's smile, which could light up a room, was missing. She looked tired and tense. Prestige came last. He was walking bent over, his shoulders hunched, as if he was carrying a heavy load. Gone was the proud, dignified boy I'd met just a few days before, replaced with this twitching, nervous kid.

I had to dodge a large man wearing a black kaftan and lost sight of Frankie and the kids for a moment. I panicked, thinking if I didn't catch up before she made it onto the street I'd have lost her. But instead of heading for the revolving doors, Vladimirovich led the group left and towards a long corridor. A black rope blocked access into the rest of the museum, but as Frankie and Vladimirovich approached, one of the museum guards unhooked the rope from its gold stand and let them pass without a word. The children moved to follow Frankie, but Vladimirovich held up his hand and I could just about make out what he was saying.

"Make yourselves busy, kids."

Frankie pointed at the museum shop. Ella nodded and led the kids off that way.

Even better for me. Apart from the billionaire, Frankie would be alone.

I ignored the man clicking his fingers in my face and sidestepped a tall skeletal woman in a short silver dress.

By the time I made it to the edge of the hall, the security guard had replaced the rope. I saw Frankie and Vladimirovich turn left and out of sight.

"No access," the guard said, holding up his hand to me.

"The caterers told me I have to get something from down there," I pointed at the long room behind him, which was filled with sculptures. As he turned around, to look where I was pointing, I unhooked the rope and slipped past.

"Wait!" he called after me as I started jogging down the corridor.

"I'll only be a second," I shouted back. He seemed to hesitate and then turned back to the crowd.

I slowed as I approached the exit Frankie had taken. I peered into the room. Soft spotlights picked out glass cabinets. I heard the clack of Frankie's heels and the gentle murmur of conversation up ahead. I counted to thirty and then crept into the room. If I got this wrong, I couldn't just Shift my way out of it. I had to be extra careful.

A glass box in the centre of the room contained an enormous red carpet, protected from ever being walked on again. I wondered what its maker would have thought of that. Something made to be used now locked away, unable to fulfil its purpose.

I snuck past the carpet towards an arched doorway that led into the next exhibit. The oriental room, judging by a sign on the wall.

Frankie and Vladimirovich were standing on the other side of yet another display cabinet. I ducked down, hiding behind a suit of Samurai armour, and listened.

"And you can persuade him to take my deal?" I heard Vladimirovich say, his accent East London by way of Moscow.

"I can persuade him to take any deal. Miller has been most malleable. And I am, I have been told, very persuasive."

"I do not doubt that." A pause. A shuffle of feet. "And the coltan supply? Will that be a problem?"

"No, I have taken care of that too."

"My, you have been busy. And what do you want in return?"

"Nothing."

"I don't believe you. No one does anything for nothing," Vladimirovich said.

"Let's just say that I believe in your deal and I think it will be better for everyone if he takes it. If you so happen to owe me a favour in the future, well, that's just a bonus."

I heard her heels on the tiled floor. They sounded as if they were getting closer.

The man laughed. "Remind me never to get on the wrong side of you, Mrs Goodwin."

"That's a good plan," I said, stepping out from behind the cabinet.

"What the...?" Vladimirovich said. "Waiting staff shouldn't be back here."

I looked down at my apron and ripped it off. "I'm no one's staff," I said.

"Scott, how nice to see you," Frankie purred. I swear she didn't look even a little surprised.

"You know this boy?"

"We've met, yes. What are you doing here, Scott?" she said.

"I'm here to stop you."

Frankie pouted her perfectly painted lips. "Come now, Scott. Don't be silly. I thought we were friends."

"No. You made me think we were friends. You made me..."

"But we are friends." Her eyes bored into mine.

I shook my head. "Stop it. It's not going to work this time. I know what you're doing and I... I can do it too."

It was a long shot. Sir Richard and his stupid game with the gun had shown me that I didn't have any control over the power. But the question was, would Frankie know that?"

"I thought as much. I read the files on Greyfield's, you know. Sir Richard gave them to me. It seems you are quite a special boy."

"Will someone tell me what the hell—"

"Shut up!" Frankie said. And Vladimirovich's jaw snapped shut.

"Just go back to the party, Anton," Frankie continued. "We will continue this discussion later."

Vladimirovich glared at me and then Frankie. "No

woman has ever spoken to me like this. You may find your deal is off the table." He pushed past me and wound his way back through the exhibits.

Frankie watched him go and sighed. "It's a shame my power only works on Shifters."

"Is that so?" I said.

"Yes. Something to do with the shape of their unique brain. Or perhaps they are more susceptible to my instructions because they exist in a constant state of uncertainty. As soon as I give them a solid idea to hold onto they grab it, like a drowning man onto driftwood." She mimed holding on to something, wrapping her arms around herself. "No one really wants that much choice, not really. Especially not children. They need absolutes. Boundaries. They want to be told what to do." She sighed. "Dr Lawrence would have known, I'm sure. He would have explained it. Quantified it all and tried to replicate its effects. But then where would we be, Scott? You and I? Ordinary. Not special at all."

"Make it stop," I said. "Take back what you did to me."

"Or what?" She glanced away and looked at a row of tiny statues in one of the displays.

"Or... or I'm going to tell everyone what you're doing!"

"And what exactly am I doing, Scott?" I hesitated and she laughed. "You have no idea, do you? You've come running here, alone, and you think you can... what? Surprise me into revealing all? This isn't a film, Scott. I'm not a villain."

"Yes, you are. You kill people!" I shouted.

"I've never killed anyone."

'Then... then you get your kids to do it for you. Like

Hamid and that fat man earlier. And Kia, did you use her to get close enough to poison Tsing Ken-ze?"

"I wouldn't worry about Ken-ze. He'll be returned once his father agrees to my plans."

I flinched at her words. She was talking about life and death as if it was nothing more than changing what shoes she wore in the morning. "But why? If you bring Ken-ze back, then his father will just forget and whatever you've made him agree to will vanish. The whole thing will have been for nothing."

"Allow me to let you in on a little secret, Scott. There are ways of making people remember. Especially when the event is particularly traumatic. I would have thought that you, of all people, would understand that."

"What are you doing it all for?" I said, confused and desperate to find something to hold on to.

"Oh, Scott, you really have no idea. You are so out of your depth. I feel sorry for you, I really do. We could have been friends, but now... Hurt him."

I saw her look behind me and spun around just in time to block Prestige's foot coming for me. I trapped his boot under my arm and we stood there, frozen, waiting for the other to move. He stared at me, but I don't think he really saw me. It was as if he was looking through me, to whatever horrors he'd been forced to see. Again, I was struck by the change in him. The boy I'd seen a few days ago had been haunted and emotionally scarred. But this boy looked totally broken.

He tried to free his leg, but I pulled, yanking him forward and off his feet. I felt someone jump onto my back, pummelling me with their fists and feet. I reached up to grab a handful of hair and twisted my body. Kia went soaring over my shoulder, crashing into a glass display of kimonos.

I gasped, as the glass shattered beneath her, the patterned silks falling from their stands and crumpling over her head. I hadn't meant to hurt anyone. Kia scrambled to her feet, looked down at the cuts on her arms, and Shifted into Pia.

Prestige took advantage of my shock to land a fist in my stomach. I doubled over, spraying spittle over his dark trousers.

"Please, no!" I heard Ella gasp. I stared up at her. I didn't want her pity. I hated her and everything about her. Hamid and Hazid pushed her aside to better see the fight.

I straightened up in time to dodge a kick from Prestige, but I was too slow to avoid a heavy blow that knocked me off my feet. I looked up to see Pia holding a silver dustbin; his eyes were dark and empty, as if he wasn't in control any more. I just had time to pull myself to my feet before I saw the twins coming for me.

I was a good fighter, but without the ability to Shift I was at a serious disadvantage. And these kids were at the peak of their powers. Every blow I threw at them, they Shifted and were no longer in the way. And there were four of them. Maybe if I was just up against three I'd have stood a chance. But I was losing badly.

After minutes of being punched and kicked, I heard Frankie speak. "Get rid of him," she said.

In my own personal world of hurt, I felt myself being dragged through the dark and empty museum, only half aware of what I was seeing. I was thrown against something solid and felt myself falling through a set of doors.

I landed face down in thick, stinking mud. I couldn't breathe and I pulled myself to my feet. Just in time to receive another punch from one of the twins. I couldn't tell which one it was now.

"This is from me." Pia smacked me in the face with a clenched fist. I staggered back, just about managing to stay upright.

There was a ripple of a Shift and it was Kia standing in front of me. "And this is from me." Her knee jerked upwards and pain exploded in my groin. Waves of agony exploded through my body and I fell to my knees. Hot nausea rose into my stomach and settled there. I crumpled forward and curled into a ball, rocking back and forth, fighting back the bile rising in my throat. I heard a high-pitched laugh and watched Kia's high heels clip clop away through the puddles.

Time passed. It might have been a minute or an hour. I didn't know. I just lay there in the rain, wishing I could die.

I heard more footsteps behind me. They'd come back to finish me off. And I didn't care. Not if it meant the pain would go away.

I heard a small sigh and someone bending down next to me. I summoned up the energy to roll onto my back and looked up, ready to face my attacker.

Through eyes clouded with tears I saw a face illuminated by the red glow of a cigarette. It came closer to me and I really hoped I wasn't dead after all.

"Now you know how I feel," Aubrey said.

CHAPTER TWENTY-SIX

I reached up a hand and went to touch her face. "Aubrey."

"Uh uh," she said, batting my hand away. "We're so not there. I only came because Rosalie said you were babbling mad stuff and looked set to get yourself killed. And how could I still be pissed with you if you were dead?" She took a last drag of her cigarette and stubbed it out on the ground next to my head. I got the feeling I was lucky she wasn't stubbing it out in my face.

I tried to sit up and a wave of nausea hit me again. I pulled my knees into my chest and groaned. "Give me a second."

"You can take all night for all I care," she said.

"Hey, don't be like that, Brey," a second voice said. "You know what they say about kicking a man when he's down."

The last person in the world I wanted to see moved into my view.

"Zac?"

Of course it was Zac. Who else would turn up when I

had just been kicked in the nuts and was lying in a pool of mud, blood and my own vomit? Zac, the man that Aubrey had made me swear never to mention again, after she said he betrayed her and all Shifters by using his powers to set himself up for life. Zac, star player for Chelsea Football Club and my least favourite person in the world.

"Hey, Scott. You're not looking too good there. Want a hand?"

"I don't want anything from you," I said. Or at least that's what I tried to say. It actually came out as more of an "urrghna".

Zac laughed, and patted me on the shoulder. "Come on, Tyler. Let's get you on your feet."

Grudgingly I accepted his hand and let him pull me up. I couldn't straighten, so remained bent over, clutching at my groin. I spat bile and blood on the ground and probed at my back tooth. It felt loose.

"They really gave you a kicking."

"Yeah, thanks, Zac. I hadn't noticed," I said.

"Don't be even more of a prick, Scott. What's going on?" Aubrey said.

I forced myself to stand upright and breathed heavily. "It's Frankie. She's forcing those kids to kill people."

"They didn't look like they were being forced to hurt you. They looked like they were loving it," Zac said.

"That's how it works. She puts ideas into your head and you think they're yours. She controls you. That's what she did to me." I shook off Zac and staggered towards Aubrey. "Don't you see? I would never hurt you, Aubrey. It wasn't me."

Her chin lifted slightly, but she stayed just out of reach.

"OK, so let's say we believe you," Zac said, stepping up to Aubrey's side. "We." I didn't like the sound of that "We." "Who's she killed?"

"The Prime Minister's daughter."

"Not this again!" Aubrey said. "The girl is alive, why can't you just leave it be?"

"It was Ella…"

Aubrey let out a snort of outrage at the mention of her name.

"Ella was with Charlotte Vine on that weekend. Frankie must have sent her to kill the girl, but then she changed her mind and… I don't know. But she was dead. I swear it."

"And you can still remember the reality where she was killed?" Zac said.

I nodded.

Zac let out a whistle. I don't know if he was impressed or what. "Brey said you hold on to the alternatives. Doesn't that send you kind of loopy?"

Aubrey let out a small, mean laugh. "Look at him. Does he look sane?"

I ignored the sting of her words. "Then there's Ken-ze, President Tsing's son. You must have seen that. It was all over the news. He was killed at a charity ball. A charity ball that Frankie and Kia just happened to be at. Don't you see? She's behind it all!"

There was the crash of a bin being hit from a nearby alley followed by drunken singing.

"We need to talk. Can we go back to your flat and–" I started.

"Brey's staying with me at the moment," Zac cut me off.

"Oh, is she now?" I said, rage overcoming the still aching pain deep in my stomach.

"Don't you dare, Scott Tyler. Don't you dare!" Aubrey said.

She was right. I nodded and backed down. It wasn't as if I was in any state to do anything about my anger anyway.

"How about we all head back to mine? Unless you like hanging about on street corners?" Zac gestured to the road with a wave of his hand. "My car's just over there."

Aubrey strode off in the direction he motioned and I limped after them both.

When I saw Zac's car, I almost decided just to give up and go home. It was a matt grey sports car, lying about an inch off the ground. It bleeped as Zac approached it and started to purr like a tame panther happy to see its owner.

"That's your car?"

Zac opened the passenger door and Aubrey slid in. "Sure," he said. "You'll have to squeeze in the back if that's OK. It's technically a two-seater, but I'm sure you'll be fine." He opened the driver's door and pointed at the back seat. I peered into the space at the back. There was probably room for a small child. Or maybe a dog. I poured myself into the space, hitting my head on the roof as I did. I was still trying to find a way to get comfortable when Zac slammed the door and hit the accelerator, pushing my face into the shiny leather upholstery.

After five minutes of being thrown about in the back seat, we arrived. I guess Zac's car should have been an indication of what to expect from his house. Even so, I was speechless.

As the car rumbled up a gravel drive, lights came on, illuminating a three-storey building made of silver wood and glass. A fountain erupted into life next to us as the car rumbled to a stop: jets of water chasing each other like fireflies.

"Here we are," Zac said.

He got out of the car and pulled his seat forward. I crawled out onto the gravel on all fours. I got to my feet and dusted myself off, as Aubrey rolled her eyes at me.

"So, looks like the footballer's life is paying off, Zac," I said bitterly. "Shame you had to cheat your way into it."

Zac laughed and slapped me on the shoulder, harder than I thought necessary. "Come on in. Make yourself at home. Aubrey has."

I made faces behind his back as I followed him up the drive and into his palace of a house. The hallway was bigger than my entire house. He clapped his hands and lights came on, revealing an enormous staircase, spiralling up three flights.

"Through here," he said, turning left into an open plan living room. Another clap of his hands and the lights dimmed and soft music played through invisible speakers. God, I hated Zac.

I collapsed onto a leather sofa, that practically sighed as I sat in it, and pulled one of the soft pillows from behind me and pressed it into my lap. Kia, Pia, whoever it was, had a lot to answer for.

"You want a drink?" Zac said, pushing a panel in the wall. It spun around revealing a drinks cabinet. I *really* hated Zac.

"Water, thanks," Aubrey said. And I mumbled I'd have the same.

I didn't know if it was because I'd swallowed a mouthful of mud and blood, or because Zac had special water shipped in from the Tibetan mountains, or something like that, but it tasted unlike any water I'd had before. I had to admit, it was damn good. Not that I was going to tell Zac that.

"OK," Aubrey said, perching on the arm of a chair opposite me. "Tell us what happened. From the start."

I took another sip of the water and started talking. I began with the evaluation on Frankie and how everything had started to go weird. I told them about how I'd run thirty miles home, simply because she told me to. I told them about the connection between the unidentified Shifts, the deaths and accidents and Frankie's kids. And finally, I told them about confronting her tonight and getting my arse kicked.

"About that," Aubrey said. "You're too good a fighter to let yourself get knocked about like you did. What happened?"

"I can't Shift," I said quietly.

"What?" Aubrey and Zac said together. And their unison grated on my nerves.

"Is it entropy?" Aubrey asked.

"No, that's what I've been saying. It's Frankie. On that morning…" I paused, remembering the broken look on Aubrey's face. "Frankie told me not to change. She made me promise not to change. And well, since then I've not been able to Shift."

"So that's why you didn't undo what you'd done? I've been wondering," Aubrey said. "I guess I'm lucky, otherwise I'd have never known about what you were up to with Ella."

"I wasn't up to anything with Ella. She kissed me and when I tried to stop her I couldn't. I was frozen in place because of a thought Frankie had put in my head. I promise you. I swear on my sister's life, I'm not interested in Ella. She's nothing. Nothing compared to you. Please, Aubrey, what do I have to do to convince you?"

Aubrey picked at her flaking nail varnish and didn't say anything.

"And this Ella girl, she's a murderer?" Zac said.

"I don't know. I don't think so. I think Frankie makes them do it, like she made me run home."

"And does she make them change their minds, so that people can come back to life?" Aubrey said, sounding cynical.

"That's the bit I can't work out. The kids of important people are in near-miss accidents and then they're not. Like tonight. I saw Hamid go to inject this Lord something or other. I thought he was going to kill him, only he didn't. I don't know if he really didn't want to or if it's a decision he can undo later. It's like Frankie's putting her pieces in place for something. Like the President of China."

"Who's still alive," Aubrey said, with a sigh.

"Only I watched him die! A kid, I'm pretty sure it was Kushi, gave him a toy and he started choking to death. But his Little Guards Shifted and saved him. But then, two days later, his son dies of poison at another party where Frankie just so happens to be with one of her kids."

"Have you told Sir Richard?" Aubrey said.

"Yeah, and he told me I wasn't to go near the woman or I would be fired. So I quit."

"You quit ARES?" Aubrey stood up from the chair.

"I told you I would. I said once all the stuff with Project Ganymede was over I'd leave."

"I just never believed you. ARES is your life." She paced back and forth between the chair and the sofa.

"Well, it's not any more. Stopping Frankie is all I care about now. That and you."

I stared at Aubrey, but she looked away. Zac, lounging on a bar stool and sipping a dark drink, looked from me to her and back again. "I'm going to leave you two alone."

Aubrey looked up in protest, but he stopped her with a wave of his hand. "Brey, all you've done for two nights is talk about him. Frankly, I'm bored of it. Sort it out. Or you can both sod off." He slid off his bar stool and wandered out of the room.

Aubrey avoided looking at me as she continued to pace back and forth.

"Tell me what to do. Tell me what I need to do to make this better," I said.

She stopped and looked up at the skylight far above our heads. It had started raining again. "You can't do anything, that's the point. It's done."

I pushed myself up out of the sofa and got unsteadily to my feet. "You're right. I can't change what I did. You have no idea how much I wish I could, but I can't. Even if I could change it, I'd still have to live with knowing I'd hurt you. That's why it's what I do next that has to matter. It has to outweigh what I've done."

"Life doesn't work like that. You can't make the bad

stuff go away just by… by doing lots of good stuff. It's not some great big balancing act. You make mistakes and they're made," she said.

"Unless you can Shift?"

She sighed. "Unless you can Shift."

"And even then, Aubrey, I'm not so sure. That's what's been scaring me so much lately. Even if we can make the bad choices we've made go away, aren't they still there? Somewhere? Some stain on our cosmic balancing sheet," I said.

"No. That old reality collapses. It's gone. Taking your mistake with it."

"Then why can I still remember?" I shouted and Aubrey flinched a little. I wanted to run to her. I wanted to wrap her in my arms and hold her till it all went away.

"I don't know," she said quietly.

"Because somewhere, it is still there. That reality."

"I don't… I don't want to believe that," she said.

"Why not?" I said.

"Because I've made mistakes too, Scott," she snapped. "I've done things that were bad and wrong, I'm sure of it. I can't remember them like you, but I know me. I know I always make the wrong choice first. And if I wasn't a Shifter then… I just don't know. And what's going to happen to me when it all goes away?"

"You'll realise what a truly amazing person you are. Beneath all the power and the make-up–"

"Hey! What's wrong with my make-up?"

"Nothing. I love it. I love you, Aubrey."

She made eye contact with me for the first time that night. Her grey-green eyes wide and uncertain.

"And not because you're a Shifter," I continued. "But

because I know the real you. The one that will make the right choice. First time."

"I don't know about that," she said looking away again.

"Don't you see? It's only because you're a Shifter that you allow yourself to make mistakes. Because you know you can wipe it away. Like… like a rough draft of a story. But pretty soon, we're going to have to learn how write our lives in permanent ink. With no erasers or delete buttons. And we're going to fuck up and make mistakes. That's what real, what normal teenagers are supposed to do. They mess up and they learn from it. But Shifters never do, do they? They just blink and it all goes away. No need for second chances. No need to live with where you went wrong. So, what kind of adults is that going to make us?"

Aubrey bit her bottom lip and swallowed. "Messed-up ones?"

"Probably," I said.

We laughed. And it felt like a shot of anaesthetic for my soul.

"I thought about changing it, you know?" she said, softly. "I knew that I could make a Shift and it would all go away and then I wouldn't hurt so much. I thought about never meeting you. I seriously wondered if it would be worth undoing everything we've been through just to take the pain away." She let out a small, sad laugh. "I didn't know a boy could ever make me hurt this much. So stupid, isn't it? I certainly never thought that you…" she gestured at me almost dismissively, "with your silly hair and too long legs and never knowing what to say, could hurt me *this* much. I thought I was tough. Untouchable.

I promised myself after Dad left I would never let another man hurt me. And ever since my mother killed herself, I've tried to keep everyone away from me. Not let anyone get close. Because if I actually cared about someone, really cared, then…" She let the sentence hang.

Like always, I didn't know what to say. I wanted to tell her I loved her, to promise her I would never hurt her or leave her. But the truth was, I had hurt her. Whether I'd meant to or not. She was hurt because of me. And who knew, maybe I'd hurt her again. Maybe risking getting hurt was part of being in love. I wanted to tell her all of that. But instead, I looked at the rain on the skylight.

"You were right," she said finally. "What you said that night. I do make every decision in my life knowing that if someone or something hurts me, I can just make it go away. But when it came to you, I couldn't." She turned to look at me again. Her head tilted slightly to one side. "Why do you think that is?"

I knew what I hoped was the reason. I hoped it was because she loved me just as much as I loved her. "I don't know," I said. "But I do know that when it comes to you, I'd never change a thing either."

"So, what do we do now?"

"Now? We stop Frankie and then… we take it from there."

"And my father?"

"We find him. We tell him we stopped Frankie and then he won't have to stay away. He can be in your life again."

Aubrey's expression softened. "I think I might like that."

"You two done?" Zac said, coming back into the room.

I looked over at Aubrey. She hesitated for a moment and then nodded. I nodded too.

"Good. There's only so long a guy can pretend not to hear in an open plan house. So, what next?"

I pulled out the copy of Frankie's diary Jake had given me. "She's going to another big party tomorrow night and after that she's booked onto a plane to Texas. So it has to be tomorrow. But…"

"But what?" Aubrey said.

"I can't stop her on my own."

"You're not going to be on your own," Aubrey said.

"You'll help? You'll both help?"

"If it means I get my house back to myself, then yes. I'm in," Zac said.

"Great. But we'll need a Fixer. Until she takes back whatever she's done to me, I'm pretty useless."

"You were always pretty useless."

"Thanks, Zac."

"My pleasure. How about Dick Morgan? He's a Fixer, right?" Zac said.

"We can ask him. I bet he's dying to do something that doesn't involve standing in the rain all night," Aubrey said.

"Rosalie might be persuaded to help," Zac said. "I'm not her favourite person at the moment, but we can ask."

"And I think Ella could be convinced to help," I said.

"You have to be kidding me!" Aubrey said, shoving her fists into her hips. "If I so much as see that girl I'm taking a swing for her."

"And that's fair enough," I said, holding my hands up as if trying to calm a startled horse. "But I think she's starting to lose faith in Frankie. And Prestige. I saw it in his eyes tonight. Whatever she's making him do, he wants out. So, if we can get them on our side, we'll only have the twins and Pia to go up against."

"And Frankie," Aubrey said. "Isn't she a Mapper? What if she sees this all coming?"

"Mapping isn't looking into the future, Brey. It's plotting the past and using it to make an educated guess on what might happen," Zac said. "But you throw up lots of variables and then what the consequences will be are anyone's guess."

"So, we come hard and fast and don't give her time to think," I said.

"Exactly."

"For that, we're going to need as much help as possible," Aubrey said.

"So, let's get it."

CHAPTER TWENTY-SEVEN

"Morgan!" Zac said as we approached Bailey's. "My man!"

"You are barred," Morgan said, pointing at Zac.

"Come on, don't be like that. It's all water under the bridge." Zac made a wave like motion with his arm. "Us Shifters have to stick together, isn't that right, old chap?"

"Don't 'old chap' me. And you can all go and stick together somewhere that isn't here. I don't want to see any of your lot again," he said, and there was a slight catch in his voice.

"What do you mean?" Aubrey said. "Your lot?"

Morgan looked at the queue of people waiting to get into Bailey's. He turned his back on them. "I mean you Shifters."

"But you're a Shifter," I said.

He swallowed hard. "Not anymore."

"But... We only saw you a week ago. Entropy can't have come on that quick," I said.

"It's been coming on for a while," Morgan rubbed at

his eyebrows as if he were trying to massage away a headache.

"And you can't Fix?" I asked, hoping that maybe that power might take longer to fade like Benjo said it had with him.

"What do you think? You can't Shift, you can't Fix. That's it. I'm all washed up, just like Father said."

"You're talking to your Dad again then?" Aubrey said.

"Come on, when are you going to let us in!" someone in the queue shouted.

"Right, back of the queue. I don't care. Now," Morgan said, pointing at a guy who looked totally puzzled. "Don't pretend it wasn't you. I heard you."

"But it wasn't me," the guy he was pointing at said.

"Get out. You're barred. You're all barred!" Morgan shouted.

"Richard, calm down," Aubrey said, as the queue of people started complaining. Rosalie was not going to be happy if they all left. "It's going to be OK."

"Is it? Is it really?" he said.

"Remember the lessons you gave us about adapting to life after entropy. You're better prepared than anyone," Aubrey said, trying to reassure him.

"Oh, they were nonsense. I didn't know what I was on about," he said, throwing his hands in the air.

I had always thought as much. But now didn't seem to be the time to remind him of just how bad a teacher he had been.

"Father even suggested I go travelling, can you imagine? The grand tour, he called it."

"Sir Richard told you to leave the country?" I said.

"Yes, he called me in to see him yesterday and was

quite adamant about it all. He'd even purchased the plane tickets. But I refused them. First class, too. Oh, he said it was for my own good, some nonsense about protecting me, but I knew it was because he's so ashamed of me he can't even bear to be in the same country."

I remembered Sir Richard's white knuckles as he clutched his desk. I'd assumed he was angry, but maybe it was something else. "Did he seem angry? I mean, more angry than usual."

"Of course he did. His son and heir is working as a bloody bouncer!" Morgan said.

"No, I mean, did he look worried?" I asked.

"What's going on Scott?" Aubrey said.

"It's just when Sir Richard warned me off from going anywhere near Frankie he looked, I don't know. Scared? I wasn't paying too much attention at the time as I was all wrapped up in what was happening to me."

"Scared of what?" Aubrey said.

"Scared of losing his only son, maybe?" I said.

We all looked at Morgan. "What are you on about?" he said.

"Have you heard of Frankie Goodwin?"

"The charity woman? Yes, Father mentioned her yesterday, actually. Told me I wasn't to go anywhere near her or any of her children. I didn't know what he meant, as I've never met the woman, so I was hardly going to go looking for her."

"Do you think…?" Aubrey said.

"The woman who controls powerful people by hurting their children?" I said. "Yes, that's exactly what I think. I think Frankie got to Sir Richard. That's why he closed the case and told me to stay clear."

"He was trying to protect his child," a voice from behind us said.

We all turned to see a man, with shaggy black hair, wearing a tatty tweed coat.

Captain Thomas Aubrey Jones, reporting for duty, I thought.

"How many times do I need to tell you to clear off?" Morgan shouted. "Hanging around here…"

I placed my hand on Morgan's arm. "Wait."

The man blinked and twitched. "I shouldn't have… She'll hurt her. Hurt her."

"It's OK," I said, softly. "Aubrey is safe. Frankie isn't going to hurt her, I'm going to make sure of it."

The man's twitches seemed to soften as he gazed at Aubrey.

She was looking at me, wondering what was going on.

"Aubrey," I said, wondering if this was a terrible idea. "Meet Thomas Jones."

"Dad," Aubrey said looking at him, her voice soft and weak, as if she was a little girl. "Dad," she said again, stronger this time.

The man nodded.

Aubrey launched herself into his arms. "Where have you been?" she said, her voice muffled by his large coat.

"Watching over you, my munchkin. My little munchkin."

Zac and Morgan looked to me, as if for instructions. I held up my hand to say everything was OK.

Aubrey stepped back from her dad. "But why? Why didn't you ever speak to me? I was all alone. You left me all alone!" Tears poured down her face, leaving dark trails as her make-up ran. She punched him, but there wasn't much force behind the blow. Just a whole load of pain and anguish.

"I couldn't. She killed you. Gone, just like that. I couldn't lose you again. I was supposed to be the one to have the op," he said, tapping the side of his head. "But she made me step down. She took my place. I was powerless. But I told, I told on her and that's why…"

"That's why she killed Aubrey?" I said.

He nodded. "My last Shift was to bring you back," he said, his hand hovering next to Aubrey's face, as if worried that if he touched her she would vanish.

"Your last Shift?" I said. "But if you're not a Shifter then what did I sense in the alley?"

"Reality being shaped," he said. "I can no longer Shift, but I can still Map. Drop pebbles in the pond and watch them ripple away." He sounded almost gleeful.

"So you sent me on the path to Greene knowing it would lead to Frankie. Knowing she would take control of me?" I said, anger stirring. I was just a pawn in his game to protect Aubrey. A puppet.

"I needed you to see," he said. "See what she's capable of. It was the only way I could keep my baby safe."

"So, you can remember?" I said, my anger softening. I'd give my life to protect Aubrey after all. "You can remember the other version, the one when she died."

"I forced myself," he said. "Forced myself to remember." He pushed up the sleeve of his tatty coat revealing his arm. A word was tattooed in shaky lettering. "Aubrey."

"Holding on to that memory almost undid me. But I had to remember. To keep you safe." He looked back to Aubrey. "But you were so strong, I knew you'd be OK.

After your mother… I called ARES. I told them about you. I knew they'd look after you." He was crying too now. But whereas Aubrey's tears were black from her make-up, his cut a path through the grime. Like mirrors of each other.

"I wasn't OK, Dad," Aubrey said. "I was never OK."

"But you survived. And now look at you." He held her by her shoulders. "So beautiful. So strong. I'm so proud of you." They hugged again, and he rested his chin on her head. "Thank you," he said to me. "You listened. You followed the path."

"I… I didn't. It was Aubrey who made me," I said.

"Either way, you know now. And you'll tell the world, and then she'll never be able to hurt anyone's child again." He lifted Aubrey's chin and wiped away her tears with a thick, callused thumb. "You'll be safe, now. And when it's all done, I'll come and find you."

"But I don't want you to go," Aubrey said.

"For now. Until she's stopped for good, I can't risk it." He tapped her chin with his closed fist. "Stay strong, my little munchkin." He turned to face me. "She's in your hands now," he said.

Aubrey turned to hug me, burying her face in my chest. I closed my eyes, breathing in her scent, trying to pull every last atom of her into me.

When I opened my eyes again, Aubrey's father had gone.

"Alright. Alright," Zac said to the people in the queue, who were leaning around, trying to see what was going on. "Enough gawking. Haven't you ever seen a heart-warming family reunion before?"

"So, that was your dad," Morgan said. "Interesting chap."

"Don't you start," Aubrey said, wiping her eyes with the cuff of her sleeve. "If it wasn't for him, we'd never have known about how Frankie was manipulating your father."

"Wait. Are you saying this woman threatened to hurt me in order to get to Father? That she threatened a Morgan? The very cheek!"

I caught Aubrey's eye. "Are you OK?" I mouthed. She nodded, smiling, the way she did after I'd kissed her. As if a weight had been lifted.

Once this mess was all over, she and her father could start to build a relationship again.

"OK, enough faffing," I said. "Are you going to help us or not?" I asked Morgan.

"He might still be of some use," Zac said, looking Richard up and down. "Even if he can't Fix. He could, I don't know, carry our bags."

"What are you on about now, Black?"

"We're going to stop the woman who did this. And we need help," I said.

"Well, count me in," Morgan said. "No one threatens a Morgan and gets away with it."

"And that's four," I said.

"I've forgiven him, Rosalie. Just about. So you might as well."

Inside the surprisingly empty club, Rosalie stood with her arms folded across her chest. "I'm not pissed at him," she said, pointing at me. "It's him!" She pointed at Zac.

"Hey, what did I do?" Zac said, holding up his hands.

"What did you do? You... you sell-out! All that

bull you fed me about beating the system and then you go and get an approved licence and use your power to get rich!"

"It's not the money, Rosie. It's the love of the game," Zac said.

"Don't give me that. You always hated football."

"OK, it's all about the money. But come on, I've only a couple of years of this power left, I have to think about my future. We all should be making hay while the sun shines, guys."

"You should see his house," I said.

"Really? Is it that nice?" Rosalie said, softening a little.

"It's a veritable haystack," I said.

"Well, it's still… wrong," Rosalie said, although she didn't sound quite so certain.

"You two can argue later. We need your help," Aubrey said.

"What is it this time?" Rosalie said.

"The woman I told you about?" I said.

"The Forcer? What about her?"

"We need to stop her. She's forcing kids to do bad things: killing people kind of things," I said.

"Only we don't have any actual proof," Aubrey said.

"And how am I supposed to help? And why aren't you on the door?" she added, noticing Morgan standing behind us.

"I… er…"

"I think you're going to need to shut up shop for the night," I said. "Because if you're willing, we need you to get your best dress on and come with us."

"My best dress? Why? I'm not going to seduce anyone for you. Those days are over."

"No, of course not," I said. "I just need you and Zac to crash a party and create a distraction."

"What kind of distraction?" Rosalie said, her eyes tight.

"I thought you could start an argument?" I said.

"With him?" Rosalie said, pointing at Zac. "Can I throw things at his head?"

"If you feel you have to," I said.

"Hang on–" But Zac didn't get a chance to finish. "OK, I'm in."

"And that makes five," I said.

"Six!" Jake said, appearing from behind the bar.

"Make that seven!" CP's head appeared next to his. "You're not going anywhere without us."

"CP, what are you doing here?" I asked.

"Jake called me and said you needed help. So here I am."

"No way. You're staying here," Rosalie said, striding over to the bar. "Back upstairs, both of you, now."

"Come on, Sis. What's the point in having a cool power if I never get to use it? You say the word and I Shift back into my bed like a good little boy."

"Yeah, and we spend all day training and training. It's about time we got to put it to some use," CP added.

I looked at their two eager faces. "Well, we could use all the help we can get," I said. "And I promise you, they won't get hurt."

"You said that last time," Rosalie snapped.

"I only broke my arm. It would have been a broken back, if Scott hadn't Shifted and saved me."

"Don't remind me!" Rosalie said, holding up her hand.

"And he saved my life. I owe him," CP said, vaulting

over the bar and landing perfectly on her feet. Jake scrambled after her, looking slightly less graceful.

"Besides, you can't leave a couple of kids on their own. In a bar. Who knows what could happen?" Jake grinned his cheeky grin.

Rosalie took in an angry lungful of air. Then let it out with a long sigh. "OK, you can come. But…" She silenced Jake and CP's victory cheer with a raised finger. "But if there's a sniff of trouble, CP, I'm trusting you to Shift and get the three of us out of there, understood? I can't one hundred percent rely on my power any more. And I certainly can't rely on Jake to make the right decision."

"Hey!" Jake said in protest.

I shook my head at him. "Rosalie is right. What we're about to do is dangerous, maybe really dangerous, and I wouldn't even consider it if I didn't know that she was looking out for you. So, this is the decision, right here and now, you all focus on. Really think about it, so that if the time comes you won't have a problem undoing it." I looked around at the group, glad to see they were taking my words seriously. Their heads were bowed and some had their eyes closed. Morgan looked up at the ceiling, whistling. Only Aubrey stared straight at me.

"And you won't stop us?" Rosalie said.

"I'll be honest, Rose, I can't stop you."

"And neither can I," Morgan said.

"What do you mean? You can't Fix?" Rosalie asked him.

Morgan shook his head.

"Then what good are you to me? Because you suck as a doorman."

"I guess I'll have to hand in my jacket." Morgan stroked the arm of his black bomber jacket, as if it was a pet.

"You'll do no such thing. As soon as this mess is sorted, you'll get your arse behind the bar and serve drinks," Rosalie said.

"Not in a clown outfit?" he said, his eyebrows knitting together.

"Dressed as a monkey, if I say so. Now, I have a dress to pick out and a bar to shut up. So if you don't mind… " She strode off through the door to their flat.

"So, where's this party going to be?" Jake asked, excited.

"The Pyramid," I said. "And there will be security all over that place. We'll need help getting in."

"I can try and hack their systems, but there's only so much I can do with the crappy computer I have here," Jake said, gesturing upstairs. "I asked Rosalie to get me a better system, but she says I have to pay for it myself."

"So, we ask Carl," Aubrey said.

"Yeah, only one problem with that," I said and they turned to look at me. "I'm not a part of ARES anymore."

"True," said Aubrey reaching into the large bag she'd brought with her. She pulled out a crumpled jacket and shrugged her arms into it. She pulled her Bluecoat straight and dusted off the shoulders. "But I still am."

CHAPTER TWENTY-EIGHT

I had expected some comments from the Regulators, as Aubrey and I stepped out onto their floor. Some snide jeering or a "look what the cat dragged in" at the very least. But it was just business as usual: all shouting TV screens, bleeping machinery and angry, serious-looking older teens who just ignored me as I walked past. Great to know what an impact I'd had on this place.

We were going to meet the others at the bottom of Tower Bridge in an hour. Which didn't give us much time to get the information we needed.

The loud rock music pouring from Carl's office grew louder as Aubrey pushed the door open. Carl was standing with one foot up on his chair, knee bent, cradling an invisible guitar. He thrashed his head back and forth in time to the wailing chords, the little that was left of his hair flailing about.

"Excuse me!" I said, trying to be heard above the screeching guitar.

Carl continued to rock out, playing air drums now,

flecks of sweat splattering over his many computer screens. I turned my head away and tried not to laugh.

Aubrey placed two fingers in her mouth and whistled louder than I've ever heard anyone whistle in my life. The shrill note cut over even the energetic drum solo.

Carl stopped and spun around. The pink flush in his cheeks from his stadium performance turned to a scarlet red from embarrassment. He fumbled around, trying to stop the music, only managing to turn the volume up even more before finally silencing it. My ears rang in the sudden quiet.

"Aubrey, I..." Carl started.

Aubrey waved away his shame. "Hey, Zeppelin rock, right?" she said smiling.

Carl sunk back into his chair, a stupidly huge grin on his face. "So, what can I do you for? I mean, what can I do for you?" He stroked his forehead.

"We need information about a target. Francesca Anderson, nee Kingly, now Francesca Goodwin. Also known as Frank and Frankie. She's the head of Pandora Worldwide."

Carl started typing before Aubrey had finished speaking and within seconds Frankie's face was filling the largest screen.

"You carried out an eval on her a couple of days ago, right?" Carl said, fingers dancing across his ergonomic keyboard.

Aubrey gave me her Look, and I felt my heart leap a little inside. I'd missed that look so much – the way her eyebrows disappeared beneath her long fringe and her chin tilted forward. I knew it was supposed to make me feel small and stupid. But right now, it made me feel great. Almost felt like things were getting back to normal.

"Well, numptie here did the eval and missed a few things," Aubrey said, gesturing at me with her thumb. My swelling heart shrunk right back into place. "That's why we need to work out where she is."

"Oh, you," Carl said, noticing me for the first time. "I thought you'd quit? I was just about to remove your name from the system and block your access."

"Sir Richard and I had a little misunderstanding, is all. Don't worry about it. Just focus on Frankie."

Carl tied back his lank, thinning hair, and returned to the screens. "Well, she's high profile. UN advisor and spokesperson. The Angel of England, the press like to call her. Runs an orphanage for messed up Shifters."

"Anything we don't already know, Carl? Anything unusual?" I said.

He punched a few other buttons and we watched as higher security files were crosschecked. "She was a Project Ganymede volunteer?" Carl, said looking at us. "Isn't that the mess you guys got into over summer?"

"Anything else?" Aubrey said.

"No, that's it. She's clean. In fact, she's cleaner than clean. She's got clearance on the highest level, which I've never actually seen before. Higher than anyone at ARES. Straight from the Prime Minister. She must have done something pretty impressive to get that."

"She helped him get into power," I said.

"That would do it. What do you want with her anyway?"

"We want to arrest her for murder," I said.

"Well, not exactly. It's not like we have anything to actually charge her with," Aubrey chipped in.

"You still don't believe me?"

"No, it's just that almost everyone who you say she killed is alive now. So, she's not really responsible for their deaths, is she?" Aubrey said, combing her fringe out of her eyes.

"Not in this reality," I said.

"Or in any reality, Scott. There is only one reality, remember?"

"Not for me."

"Whatever!" Aubrey threw her hands up, her voice getting higher pitched as she became increasingly irritated. "What exactly are we going to charge her with? Killing people in an alternative reality? What court is going to listen to that?"

"Then why are you even here?" I said, exasperated. I thought we'd been through all of this last night at Zac's place.

"To get you back!" Aubrey snapped. And then looked down at her shoes. "I mean, to get you back to normal. To make her undo what she did to you."

Carl's head had been moving back and forth between Aubrey and me as if he was watching a tennis match.

"Oh, right," I said, my shoes also suddenly becoming really interesting.

Carl coughed. "Er, hello! I am still here, you know?"

"Yes, sorry. Right, where were we?" I said.

"Well, I was falling in love," Carl said, gazing up at a headshot of Frankie looking into the middle distance.

"She's not all that," said Aubrey, her nose crinkling. "She has weird lips. They're too big."

"Hmm," Carl said, flicking through more photos of Frankie with a dumb smile on his face. "Why don't you just go back to her place in Sussex and speak to her there?" Carl said, scanning our evaluation visit order. "And if you do, can I come?"

"She's leaving for America tonight. So we're going to a party at the Pyramid to stop her. Which is why we need you."

"The G28 thing?" Carl said, still gazing at Frankie's pictures.

"Er, I don't know. It just says Party at the Pyramid," I said.

"Sure, it's the launch of this big conference about alternative energy and saving the future. You know the kind of thing. Lots of talk, not much action. Anyone who's anyone's going to be at that. Including your Ms Goodwin, by the looks of it. You know I have an idea for an alternative fuel engine. Maybe she would be interested. It runs on–"

"Yes, that's the thing," I said, cutting Carl off.

"Ha!" Carl laughed. He looked from my serious face to Aubrey's then laughed again, only it came out as more of a wheeze. "You're not serious, are you? You're going to walk into the Pyramid, past the mass of security protecting heads of state, not to mention the celebs there to boost their PR, and take down this woman?" He pointed at the screen. "Who from what I can tell here is Mother Teresa and Angelina Jolie rolled into one."

"Yes," Aubrey and I said in tandem.

"Well, good luck to you. I'll send you a card in prison."

"Can you bring up the plans of the Pyramid?" I asked.

"No," Carl said folding his arms. "I'm not going to help you. Not again. You know I very nearly lost my job after helping you last time?"

"Come on, Carl," I said. "It's not like we're asking you to hack into anything."

He shook his head.

"Carl, can you do this tiny little thing. Just for me?" Aubrey said, hitting him with her pouting lips and tilted head. I knew I was powerless against that look. And it seemed that Carl was too.

"OK, I'll pull up the plans, but that's it. I'm not going to help you past the security or anything."

"Oh, of course not. I mean that would be too hard for you anyway," Aubrey said.

"It wouldn't be that hard, not really," Carl said, melting gently.

"Seriously, you can do that? Wow, you're so impressive Carl. But let's start with the plans."

Carl's eyes looked a little dazed as he pulled up details of the Pyramid, including all security exits and entrances. "You know this wasn't the original plan?" he said. "They were going to build this huge tower, the biggest in Europe, but the government vetoed it."

I remembered what Miller had said about his involvement in the planning of the building. How the Pyramid gave out the right message. "Yeah, I remember hearing something about that."

"And of course, our Pyramid was really about sticking up two fingers to the French. Five times higher than their *Pyramide du Louvre* and all that."

"This is all very fascinating," Aubrey said. "But what can you tell us about the security?"

"Pretty high-spec stuff. You'll need someone on the ground to override it. It can't be done remotely. What? What!" Carl said, noticing us both staring at him. "Oh, no. No way. Look around you." He indicated his office with a wave of his hand. He'd certainly made this place his home: it was packed with toys of comic book heroes and posters. "This is my lair."

"Your lair?" I said, with a snort.

"Yes," he snapped. "My lair. My base. My sanctuary. I don't leave it."

"Not even to go home?" Aubrey asked.

"Well, yes to go home."

"And to go to the loo?" I added.

"Yes, OK. I do sometimes leave it. But this is where I'm strongest. Where I'm in control. That's why it's my lair."

"Aren't lairs normally secret? And have sharks and stuff?"

Carl pushed away from the desk and sent his chair wheeling over to the other side of the room. He plucked a toy shark off one of the shelves. "Shark!" he said, as if that were all the explanation that was needed.

"I would be so grateful," Aubrey purred.

"Nope. Don't try it," he said waving the rubber shark around. It squeaked. "You said let you look at the plans and I let you look at the plans. So, if you would please leave?"

"Could you talk someone else through it?" I asked. "Without having to leave your lair?"

"What? I, yes, I suppose I could. If they know their way around a computer. But I'm not going to. I'm not going to get into any more trouble and nothing you can do will make me."

Aubrey bent over and whispered into Carl's ear. I saw it go pink and his mouth dropped open.

She straightened up and winked.

"Um, so, yes. If you take this and these earpieces with you, I can talk you through it from here." He handed me a black, plastic device, which was about the size of a matchbox, and a bunch of wires.

"Thank you, Carl. You won't regret this. I promise," she said, managing to turn the word "promise" into the suggestion of a kiss.

I saw Carl's Adam's apple bounce up and down in his throat like a yo-yo. I looked from him to Aubrey and finally persuaded my legs to work.

As I got to the door, I turned around. "Carl, does 'coltan' mean anything to you?"

"Sure, it's a mineral used to make tantalum capacitors. They're in computers, mobile phones, you name it."

"And where would you get it from?"

He chewed on his cheek. "Most of it is mined in the Congo as far as I know. The Chinese have set up a huge mining operation out there. Why?"

The Congo? And Frankie had said she had the coltan situation under control. I suddenly had a feeling that I knew what had caused the change in Prestige.

"Nothing." I shut the door behind me. "OK," I said, catching up with Aubrey. "What did you say to him?"

"Wouldn't you like to know?" Aubrey said, spinning around and then walking away.

"Yes," I shouted after her. "Yes, I really would."

She waved her hand at me over her shoulder and put an extra sway in her walk.

I wondered how she and I had ever been together. With powers of manipulation like this she could have had any guy she wanted. Just like Frankie.

I shook off the disturbing comparison as I caught up with her at the lift.

"OK, Carl done. Now what?" she said.

"Now," I said, knowing that I was about to wipe the smile off her face. "We need a Fixer."

"But with you and Morgan out of action, there's no one left."

"There's another Fixer. A really powerful one too."

"Oh, god, you're not thinking who I think you're thinking."

"That depends. Are you thinking Benjo Greene?"

CHAPTER TWENTY-NINE

—

The strip lights buzzed and flickered as we stepped out into the basement. I heard a soft sobbing from up ahead and looked at Aubrey.

"I really hope we don't end up down here," I said.

"Oh, I don't know," she said, looking around. "It has a certain charm."

"Yes, can I help you?" I looked up to see a spotty-faced Regulator sitting behind a metal desk. He was huddled over a computer and judging by the frantic movements his hands made on the keyboard he was busy playing a computer game. Quite the difference to the stern-faced NSOs who used to be on guard down here.

"We need to speak to Benjo Greene," Aubrey said.

"No can do. He's designated off limits."

"Yes, I know," I said. "I was the one who designated him that."

The boy sighed heavily and finally looked up from the screen. "Well, bully for you. And?"

"And… now I need to talk to him. Please." I added as an afterthought.

The boy, whose name I could now see on his badge was "Matthew", tutted and punched a few keys on his computer. "OK. Cell 7."

"We might need to take him off site," I said. "We need his assistance in another case."

"Take him off site?" Matthew said. "You mean out of his cell?"

"Yes, that's what off site means," Aubrey said, leaning on his desk with both of her fists.

"I don't know about that. I'll have to check." He reached for the phone on the desk. Aubrey placed a finger on top of the handset before he could pick it up.

"What does this mean?" she said, pointing at the stripes on her arm with her other hand.

"It means you're Third class."

"And what does that mean?" Aubrey said, pointing at his arm. He followed her finger and gazed at his jacket sleeve where there was a single, silver stripe. "It means you're a Regulator working down here. And you know what that says to me? That says to me that you've made some pretty bad decisions in your time, Matthew. Don't make this be another one."

Matthew looked up at her, his face fixed in an expression of defiance. The battle of wills only lasted about ten seconds, before he looked away. Aubrey straightened up and smiled at me.

"OK. Cell 7. Here's the key to let him out." He handed over a white card with a black strip down the side. "But I want it stated that I was following orders of a higher ranked officer, OK?"

"We'll be sure to include it in our report," I said, knowing full well there would never be a report and we were most likely going to get Matthew demoted even more with this little trick.

"Well done. You made the right choice. Keep going and you'll be back with the rest of the Regulators," Aubrey said.

Matthew stood up as we walked away. "Could you put a word in with Sir Richard?"

Aubrey spun on her heels and continued to walk backwards. "I'm sure Sir Richard will be hearing all about you soon enough."

Most of the cells were empty today. But Cell 5 was still occupied. Instead of holding Zac, it was now home to a girl with long, lank hair that fell in front of her eyes.

"I didn't have a choice," she muttered as we walked past. "I tried everything else. Everything."

The sobbing grew louder as we approached room seven. I stopped and took a deep breath, expecting to be confronted by a crying Benjo and my guilt. But as I stepped forward I saw it wasn't Benjo who was crying.

It was a young kid in room eight. He was curled up in a ball in the corner of his cell, while Benjo sat in the next room along, gazing at the shaking boy through the adjoining bars, smiling.

The boy looked up first and ran towards us.

"You have to get me out of here!" he cried, reaching his hand through the bars and trying to grab hold of Aubrey's jacket. "I only tried to get a girl to like me. But he… He's a monster. He keeps licking the bars and looking at me."

There was a small snickering from Benjo, followed by coughing. He spat on the floor: dark brown spittle.

"Good to see you again, Scott. And you too, Aubrey. I love what you've done with your hair."

Aubrey flinched and stroked her fringe back down over her forehead to hide the thin scar Benjo had given her. "I like what you've done with your face," she said.

Benjo smiled – that terrible smile which haunted my dreams. "Are you here to kill me? That's what you said, isn't it Scott? That if you ever saw me again you'd kill me." Benjo examined his cracked fingernails and started to dig out some dirt from beneath one. He looked as if he was sitting on a park bench, rather than in a prison cell.

"No. I need your help."

Benjo looked up, an amused expression on his sagging face. "*You* need *my* help. Well, well. Isn't that interesting?"

"I don't have time for your little games, Benjo. So, what's it going to take?" I said.

He stood up slowly, pushing himself up out of the bed. It looked as if the movement caused him pain. The sobbing boy scuttled away from the bars and back into his corner.

"That depends on what kind of help you are after," he said, a dark grin playing around his twisted mouth.

"I need you to come with us and stop people from Shifting," I said.

"And why can't you do that?"

"I need backup," I said, quickly, not liking the way Benjo's black eyes twinkled.

"And who do you need backup against? No, let me guess," he said, holding up a bony finger. "You met Frankie, didn't you? And she got into your head, just like I said she would." He tapped his temple.

When I didn't answer, Benjo clapped his hands together.

"Forget this, Scott. We don't need this… this freak," Aubrey spat.

"Oh, but you do. Especially if I'm right. Tell me Scott, done any interesting Shifts lately?"

"I don't know what you mean," I muttered.

"Come now, we're all friends here. You can tell Uncle Benjo. She's stopped you from Shifting, hasn't she?"

"You've seen this before?" I asked, ignoring Aubrey's pleading look.

"She tried it on me once. But she couldn't get her claws into my flesh."

"Surprising, considering how much there is of it," Aubrey said.

"How did you stop her?" I said.

"Get me out of here and I will tell you," Benjo replied.

"And can you make it go away?"

He sighed. "Get me out of here and I will tell you."

"Yes, yes!" shouted the boy in the cell. "Get him out of here."

"There are some conditions," I said, staring at him. Wanting him to know that I was the one in charge.

"I wouldn't expect anything less of you, Scott."

"You'll do absolutely everything I say, or I will kill you."

He nodded.

"And you won't try and run away, or I will kill you."

"Crystal," Benjo said.

"And you so much as breathe in Aubrey's direction, I'll let her kill you."

Benjo placed two fingers to his blackened lips. "I won't so much as breathe on her," he whispered between them.

"And…" I looked at Aubrey. I wasn't sure about this next bit. But she'd insisted. "You have to swallow this."

Aubrey reached into her jacket pocket and pulled out a small, silver ball about the size of a cherry.

Benjo looked at it. "And what is that?"

"It's a bomb." She tossed it in her hand and caught it again. "We pulled it out of a Ganymede member's head. And…" With her free hand she pulled out a phone. "I have the trigger."

The bombs that had been placed in the men's heads by Dr Lawrence could be activated by a mobile phone. It's how Abbott had killed Sergeant Cain. A single press of his finger and Cain had dropped down dead. Aubrey had loaded the app on her phone in case any of the men from Ganymede gave us trouble. And now she wanted Benjo to swallow the bomb so she could kill him if we needed. I had no idea if it would still work.

Benjo looked from the ball in Aubrey's hand and then to me. "And how do I know you won't set it off as soon as I swallow it?"

I took the phone from Aubrey's hand. "Because you have my word."

"And once I've helped you?"

"The bomb will be out of your system in a day or two. Sure, it might be a little uncomfortable, but that's the least you deserve. And consider yourself lucky, because I wanted to cut you open and shove it in your gut," Aubrey said.

Benjo licked his lips, considering the offer. Then he reached his hand out through the bars so quickly I thought he was going to go for Aubrey. Instead, he snatched the bomb out of her hand and shoved it in his mouth.

We watched as he struggled to swallow, his face contorting in pain. He then opened his lips, showing his empty, pit-like mouth. I turned away from the stench.

"Now, will you let me out?" he said.

I still wasn't sure this was a good idea. But he *had* warned me about Frankie; I just hadn't realised it at the time. And if he really knew how to take whatever she'd done to me away, then it was worth putting up with him for a little while at least. And it wasn't as if he could go anywhere. The guy could hardly run away from us.

"OK," I said finally, slotting the card into the lock.

Aubrey's hand stopped mine before I could press the green button that would open the cell. "Are you sure about this?" she asked.

"No. Not at all. But what choice do I have?"

"We could just leave. Go away and forget all about Frankie and him."

"But I'd never be able to Shift again," I said.

"A couple of years and you won't be able to anyway. What difference does it make? Really?"

I moved my hand from the lock and placed it on her face. She didn't flinch.

She was right. In the end, my power to Shift would fade anyway. But if I was honest that wasn't really what this was all about. It was about Frankie.

"I have to stop her, Aubrey. I have to know what she's really been up to. And this is the only way I can think of."

As an answer, Aubrey pushed the button herself. The bars swung open and Benjo stepped forward. Then stopped and turned to the whimpering boy in the next cell. "See you later," he said, wiggling his fingers in a teasing goodbye. He turned back to us, took a deep breath and smiled, showing off his stumps of rotting teeth.

"Where to now?"

CHAPTER THIRTY

It was probably the most unlikely team ever put together. Aubrey, with her dyed hair, oversized boots and a cigarette trailing out of the corner of her mouth. Zac, wearing a tailored tuxedo, looking like a male model or James Bond, the git. Rosalie, in a midnight blue strapless ball gown that trailed to the floor, with her hand on Jake's shoulder. He was wearing an old ARES jumpsuit with the name badge torn off the back. CP had her long blonde hair wrapped up in plaited bunches and wore her cadet uniform. Behind them came Morgan still wearing his black bomber jacket. Then there was Benjo, who stood out most of all, his burnt face and sagging flesh barely hidden by a tent-like shirt, shovelling down a bag of marshmallows I'd given him. And me. Scott Tyler, former Shifter and now just your average teenage loser wearing my least favourite jeans and a hoodie.

We didn't have a chance in hell and I knew it. We all knew it. And yet we were willing to try.

The others had nothing to lose, not really. They each

had their Shifts planned if things went wrong. I'd made sure they'd thought long and hard about joining me and each one knew they could escape with a thought. If one of them Shifted, the chances were that none of us would be here. I didn't really know if I was mad enough to try this alone. Probably. I'd likely have dragged Benjo into it as well just because I could have. The thought of a reality with just me and Benjo going up against Frankie while all my friends disappeared was so disturbing I had to shake my head to get rid of it.

But he had told us how to stop Frankie taking control of us.

"And you're absolutely sure that will stop her?" I asked Benjo for the third time.

"Absolutely. Firstly, the delightful Frankie's power only works so long as you are unaware that she is trying to control you. When it is done covertly. If you are aware and focus hard enough, you can simply resist it." He popped the last pink marshmallow in his mouth and licked his blackened lips.

"Like hypnotism!" Jake said. "Remember Grampa George and his Mysterio act?"

"The one where he made people act like chickens?" Rosalie said.

"Yeah, he said it was really hard if the person didn't want to be hypnotised."

"Hard, but not impossible?" Aubrey said, sounding nervous.

"Trust me," Benjo said, with a terrible smile.

We all looked at him and a shudder passed through the group.

"You said firstly. What else?" I asked.

"Frankie is more able to control people who want to be controlled. Weak-willed people."

"What are you suggesting?" I said, anger and insult making my face burn.

"I am suggesting, Scott Tyler, that you start believing in yourself. Rather than expecting everyone else to do that for you."

We stared at each other. His tiny, black eyes boring into mine. And as much as I hated to admit it, he was right. It's why Frankie hadn't been able to control Aubrey, and why I'd fallen under her spell so easily. Self-belief. Now was the time for me to man up.

"Shall we get this ridiculous plan over and done with then?" Zac said, straightening his bow tie.

We were huddled under a disused railway bridge, around the corner from the Pyramid. I consulted my watch. 8.31pm. The party officially started at 7pm, but Zac assured us that no one turns up early.

"OK," I said. "Are everyone's mics working?"

We all fiddled about with the lumps of beige plastic we'd shoved in our ears and started speaking into our lapels, where we'd placed the microphones.

"Testing, testing," Rosalie said, half-heartedly. "Yes, it works, now can we go? Because I'm freezing my exquisite tits off in this dress."

"Yes, get going," I said.

"The slightest hint of trouble and you Shift your arse out of here, OK, Jakey?"

"Yeah, yeah. I know the drill," Jake said.

I looked back to the rest of the group. "Let's do this."

Zac lifted his elbow for Rosalie to take. She considered it and him for a moment, before slipping her hand

under his arm. They headed towards the row of flaming
torches that were guiding all the guests into the Pyramid. Zac had wrangled an invite without much effort.
"Perks of the job," he'd said.

Morgan pulled off his jacket to reveal a policeman's
uniform. I decided not to ask how he'd managed to get
hold of it on such short notice.

"Any police turn up and you're to tell them it's a false
alarm because there's been a malfunction. If Carl's done
his job, there will be."

"Are you sure I won't be more use inside?"

"I'm sorry, Richard. We can't risk having a non-
Shifter in there." Not another one, I added to myself.
Morgan looked sad and useless and I felt sorry for the
guy. "And I need you to keep an eye on CP."

"Hang on," CP said. "You didn't say anything about me
staying here with him. Why aren't I coming with you?"

"Because I need you to create a diversion."

"What kind of diversion?"

"Use your imagination."

"Can I cause a fracas?" She smiled with such mis-
chief, I wondered if I was making a huge mistake. But I
didn't have time to worry about that.

"Sure, not that I know what a fracas is," I said.

Morgan still didn't look too happy. He was muttering
about being useless. I knew how he felt.

Aubrey stepped forward and squeezed his arm.
"Richard, the one thing you'll never lose is the power to
tell people what to do. So, go do it."

He smiled, bowed slightly. Then nodded to CP and
the two of them walked away. On the way, Morgan
shouted at someone for dropping litter. Whatever else

happened, I reckoned Morgan was going to enjoy his part in all of this.

As for Aubrey, Jake, Benjo and I, we were going to have a less swanky way of crashing the party.

We all looked down at the metal sewer cover.

"Is Carl absolutely certain that this is the only way in?" Aubrey asked.

"I most certainly am," Carl's voice crackled in our ears. I'd forgotten he would be listening in. "Unless you want to get arrested before you've made it past the front doors."

"Nope. Thanks, Carl," Aubrey said.

She squatted down and dragged a crowbar from behind her and placed the edge against the cover. With a small grunt she pushed down and levered it open.

"Oh, my god, it reeks," Jake said, reeling away from the open hole, his face covered with his sleeve.

Aubrey turned her head away as well, her tiny nose wrinkling in disgust.

"It's not that bad," I said, leaning in and taking a small sniff.

"Are you kidding me?" Jake said. "It's like the bog of eternal stench in there."

"You should smell Scott's bedroom," Aubrey said, peering into the depths below. She threw her cigarette in and we watched as the glowing ember was swallowed up in the shadows.

"Ladies first," I said grinning.

Aubrey rolled her eyes. "You got us into this mess, literally," she said pointing at the sewer below. "You get to go first."

I bent over and reached into the hole with my foot,

trying to find the first rung. Then slowly lowered myself
into the dark.

The rungs were slippery and a couple of times my feet
slid off. My first instinct was to Shift, as I still hadn't got
used to the power being gone. By the time I'd made it
down into the tunnel I was cursing Frankie's name.

Aubrey slid down after me, her boots splashing in the
low stream of water running along the bottom of the
tunnel.

"Lucky the rain held off," I said.

"For now," she said. "Let's get a move on."

We looked back up at the hole where we could see
Benjo's face peering down at us.

"I'm not sure he's going to fit," Jake shouted down.

"Try," Aubrey said, without much sympathy.

The light breaking through the opening went black as
Benjo started to lower himself in. There was a lot of
huffing and muttering, and a sound like someone peeling
off a rubber glove, and then he was through. He climbed
down the ladder rung by rung, then stood blinking in
the gloom.

Jake followed quickly. When he reached the last rung,
his leg dangled down, not able to reach the floor. I
helped him down. He wiped his hands on the jumpsuit
and smiled his lopsided smile. I went to ruffle his hair,
and then seeing the dark stain on my hand thought better of it.

I turned on my torch, and then regretted it instantly.
Seeing what we were standing in just made it worse.

"Which way?" I said.

"Straight ahead and left," Carl's voice crackled over
the headsets.

Our feet splashed in the shallow water and I tried not to think about it too much when I felt something heavy brush against my ankle. Aubrey had one arm up, covering her nose, and the other holding a torch. Jake was wearing a pair of yellow glasses with torches on either side of his head, which in the darkness made him look like a robot. Benjo looked down into his torch and banged it till it turned on. When it did, it lit up his multiple chins, making him look even more like a horror movie villain. He pointed it ahead. The circles of light bounced off the black slimy walls and did almost nothing to light the way.

I took the first left as instructed. It looked pretty much like the last tunnel, only the floor slanted upward slightly, so after one hundred yards we were walking on dry ground.

"Not much farther," Carl said. "The maintenance hatch is just up ahead."

"If you say so," mumbled Aubrey. "I can't see a thing. What was that?" she screeched suddenly, grabbing hold of me and practically trying to jump into my arms to escape whatever it was she thought she'd just seen.

"It was nothing," I said, trying not to laugh. "Just some rubbish."

"Nah," said Jake. "It was a rat. Most definitely a rat. Look, there's more over there." He shone his lights on a pile of squirming cardboard. Pink tails and slick grey bodies lay curled up against each other.

I grabbed Aubrey as she turned and started to head back the way we'd come. "Come on, we're almost there." I pointed at the hatch up ahead.

She looked again at the rat's nest and closed her eyes in disgust. "I hate you, Scott Tyler. Have I ever told you that?"

"Quite a lot recently. Now come on."

She ran forward, trying to stay as far away from the nest as possible, without actually touching the sides of the tunnel walls.

"What are you doing?" I asked Benjo, who had crouched down next to the pile of cardboard. He plucked a tiny, hairless baby rat out of the nest and luckily I turned away before seeing anything. But the sucking sound was enough.

When I turned back, he was sucking a pink tail through his lips like it was spaghetti.

"Oh, I will regret that later," he said patting his stomach. "But I just couldn't resist."

"If you've quite finished snacking, Benjo, can we go?"

The hatch resisted at first and then opened with a heavy shove of my shoulder. Aubrey pushed past me and was out of the tunnel first. She shook her arms and legs as if trying to rid herself of invisible rats.

We were in a basement. Service pipes crisscrossed each other overhead and there was a low rumbling of air-conditioning units and the hum of electricity.

"The service lifts are in the right-hand corner," Carl said. "Oh, and one of them appears to be on its way down there. I suggest you find somewhere to hide."

We heard the lift doors *ping* and we all dived behind a broken fridge. With Benjo, the three of us were hardly hidden at all.

"Find somewhere else to hide," Jake hissed.

But it was too late. A security guard entered the basement. He was whistling and his heavy black boots squeaked as he walked.

"Anyone here?" he called out and I felt my heart freeze. Then I suddenly wondered what the hell I was doing. Hiding from one overweight security guard when I was planning on going head to head with a Shifter and her team of teen assassins.

I started to straighten up when I heard his boots spin around and walk away from us, back to the lift. "Of course not," the guard muttered to himself. "Just me down here on my own while everyone else has fun. Just like always." He sighed loud enough to be heard from our hiding place. Punched the lift button and was swallowed up by the doors once more.

"OK. No more hiding," I said, stepping out from behind the fridge. "We go up there, find Frankie, expose her in front of everyone, and go home. I'm sick of creeping around."

"We don't creep around, we get chucked out. Let's just stick to the plan." Aubrey laid a hand on my chest and I felt my pounding heart soothe instantly.

"The lift's free now. I don't know about you, but I'd like to go home some time tonight," Carl said.

"I thought you never went home, Carl. I thought you never left your lair," I said.

"Yes, well. Even a mastermind has to do his laundry sometimes," Carl said. "Jake, you'll have to plug me into the pass lock so I can override it. Clip it onto the black wire."

"Sure thing," Jake said, pulling a tab out of his bag. He slotted in the device Carl had given us and plugged that into the cables. Then he unscrewed the panel on the front of the lift control unit, exposing a tangle of black wires. "Um, Carl. They're all black wires."

"Oh, right. Well clip it to the one running from the far left of the circuit board."

Jake did as he was told. There was a fizzing noise and sparks.

"OK, not that one then. Try the far right."

"Do you know what you're doing?" Jake said, shaking his hand in pain.

"Of course I do. Clip it onto the right wire."

More hesitantly this time, Jake clipped the device onto the right wire and pulled his hand away instantly. There were no fizzes or bangs and the tab started glowing blue. Numbers whizzed across the screen.

"You're in," Carl said, the sound of him rubbing his hands together loud enough to be heard over the microphones.

Jake pushed the lift call button. "Which floor?" he said as we entered, giving us a mock doorman salute.

"All the way to the top, please."

Jake punched the black button reading sixty-five and we were on our way.

CHAPTER THIRTY-ONE

The weird whooshing in my stomach as the lift hurtled upwards reminded me of the feeling when I Shifted: that unsettling sense of being in two places at once. And it made me hungry to have the power back.

"All clear," Carl said, as the lift juddered to a halt.

The corridor was empty as we stepped out. Soft beige carpets lined the floor and gold mirrors lined each wall. We were in the corridor that led to the penthouse flat, in the very tip of the Pyramid, occupied by the owner himself. Although he would be busy at the party on the floor below us.

The door to his flat was painted gold with a large number one. None of the apartments had regular keys, just keypads for extra security. Shame whoever designed it had never heard of Shifters.

"Jake, if you would do the honours?"

Jake pulled back the sleeves of his jumpsuit and started punching buttons. His fingers were a blur of motion as he kept Shifting the numbers he tried. There was a sudden clunk and the door swung open. "Ta da!" he said, pushing the door open.

The apartment inside was like nothing I'd ever seen. I'd thought Zac's place was showy, but it was nothing compared to this. Everything in here appeared to be made of gold. Gold sofa, gold rug on the floor.

"All this gold could probably pay off the third world debt and they wouldn't even need this stupid G-whatever thing," Aubrey said, the venom in her tone reflecting my own disgust at the display of wealth.

"I think it's all rather tasteful."

"You would," Aubrey said, glaring at Benjo who was picking something out from between his back teeth with his fingernail.

I looked at my watch. 8.50pm. The arranged distractions were going to begin in ten minutes. We didn't have long.

"Jake, you keep watch outside and tell us if anyone comes."

"No way!" moaned Jake. "I'm coming with you."

"I promised your sister that you wouldn't be put in harm's way."

"What? You weren't lying? Oh, come on guys. I want to help!"

"And you will help. By staying here," Aubrey said, laying a hand on his shoulder. She lowered her voice. "Besides, someone has to make sure he doesn't run off." She gestured to Benjo with a nod of her head. "Take this." She pressed a yellow taser gun into Jake's hand.

"Those don't work on me," Benjo said.

"Maybe not. But the shock will set off the bomb in your stomach," Aubrey said, returning Benjo's grin.

Benjo laughed and shrugged. Aubrey had won this round.

Jake took the taser and he sucked back in his sulky lip. "OK. But I hear even a tiny scream, I'm so coming after you."

"I wouldn't expect anything less." She turned back to me and nodded.

I gave Jake a playful punch on the shoulder and headed for the glass doors that led to the balcony. As soon as I opened them I could hear the noise from the party below. High-pitched laughter mixed with donkey-like braying.

After the balmy temperature of the apartment it felt bracingly cold on the balcony. Even here every last detail had been thought of. The floor was covered in golden tiles and the guardrails were gold. There was even a plant in a gold pot. I plucked one of the leaves. It too was gold and warm to the touch. Could it be real gold? I threw away the leaf before I got too angry.

I looked out at the city around us. The Gherkin shimmered in the darkness and I could see the steeple of St Paul's Cathedral lit up by the lights below.

"Nearly time," Carl said.

Aubrey and I checked the equipment we'd stolen from the Regulators. One remaining Taser, which I took, although I didn't really know how to use it. We also had two pairs of mute cuffs. Plan A was to slap a pair on Frankie and just bring her in. Straightforward operation. Minimum fuss.

I didn't believe for a second that it was going to happen like that.

At the bottom of the bag was an item I didn't recognise. "What's that?"

Aubrey pulled out an old-fashioned pistol. "I liberated this from Sir Richard's desk," she said, holding the gun up.

"Fair enough, just don't point it at me."

We walked towards the edge of the balcony and Aubrey and I lay down on our stomachs. Benjo plonked himself down next to us and it took him three attempts to lie down, huffing and groaning the whole time.

"Do you have to be so loud?" Aubrey asked.

"Ask your boyfriend," Benjo snapped. "He's the one who broke me."

I shuffled forward a bit more and craned my head over the edge.

There was a second balcony below us. The road below was just a series of glowing lights as ant-sized cars moved up and down. My head swam with the dizzying distance to the safety of the ground.

A small voice in my head said: jump. Jump. Compelling me to throw myself into the void.

Only it wasn't a small voice in my head. It was Benjo whispering in my ear. His hot breath making the hairs on my neck itch.

"Get off me," I said, wiping my ear clean.

He chuckled and spat over the edge of the building. I watched the phlegm wobble as it fell down and down and didn't envy the person who would have to clean the windows where it landed on the side of the pyramid.

"Thirty seconds." Carl's voice snapped me out of it.

I pulled out a flexible snake scope camera, plugged in into the tablet, and angled the camera so we could see what was going on without being seen ourselves.

I saw hundreds of people dressed in ball gowns and tuxedos milling around, drinking golden liquid from gold-stemmed glasses and eating nibbles from golden cocktail sticks. It was like watching the party on a TV screen. I zoomed the picture in on a woman standing in the middle of the room. She seemed to be telling a very dramatic story, while everyone around her hung on her every word. Frankie Goodwin. Frank Anderson. Whatever her name was. Soon enough they'd see her for who she really was. And her kids too. They were all here, as I had expected. I zoomed the camera in even more on Ella. Her face looked red and blotchy, like she'd been crying.

Aubrey made a small cough, and I pulled the picture back out to see the whole party.

Zac and Rosalie drifted into view. They were ready to do their thing.

"You… you…!" Rosalie's voice drifted up from the floor below. She threw her glass of champagne into Zac's face.

"What's that for?" he shouted back, wiping his face clean.

"You know what for," Rosalie screeched. "You made me believe your lies. I would have done anything for you." I wondered how much of this was for show, and how much was true.

An explosion stopped their argument in its tracks. I looked down onto the streets below to see a car in flames.

"CP's bang on time," I said.

Seconds later I heard a crash from beneath us. I looked back to the screen to see Rosalie hurl a glass toward Zac's head, hitting the wall behind him.

"You bastard," she bellowed. "You cheating bastard."

"Can you blame me? You stuck-up bitch," Zac roared in return.

All of the party guests had stopped to look at them. In the background, I could just about see men I assumed were security guards moving around the edges and heading for the lifts.

"And so the games begin."

I put down the tablet and pulled a rope out of my rucksack. I went to wrap it around my waist.

"I'll go first," Aubrey said, taking the rope off me. "Then you can lower me down. Him, I don't trust."

Benjo had picked up the tablet and was angling the camera so it focused on the buffet table. "Good idea," I said.

I wrapped the rope around her waist, taking the chance to breathe in her vanilla smell. There was nothing more I wanted than to bury my head in her hair. Before I had a chance, she clambered onto the rails of the balcony and leaped off the edge. A second later, the rope went taut and she hung just a few feet off the floor of the balcony below. I guided the rope through my hands and lowered her the rest of the way.

I leaned over to see her untie the rope and squat down by the doorway.

"Are you sure you can Fix her from up here?" I asked Benjo, pulling the rope back up and wrapping it around myself. "You don't need to have eye contact?"

"I just need to be able to see her. So, keep her on this side of the room."

"And you're sure you won't Fix us all. Only Frankie and her kids?"

"Scott, the difference between us is that I've had years to hone my skills. I am like a surgeon."

That brought back unwanted images of Benjo cutting into brains. I shuddered. "And remember, I still have the phone. One button and that bomb will tear a hole in your stomach."

"What, this bomb?" he said, holding out his palm. On it sat the silver cortex bomb.

"But… You swallowed it."

"Oh, Scott," he sighed. "You really are a stupid boy who believes far too easily."

I stood there, unsure of what to do. This whole time, I thought I had Benjo on a leash, that he was following after us because I could kill him on command. But now, it turned out he'd been free the whole time. He could have done anything he wanted. So why hadn't he?

"Don't look so worried, Scott. I will still hold up my end of the bargain. And it's not like you'd have ever been able to push that button anyway. You're not a killer. I know." He leant forward so his nose was only inches away from mine. "It takes one to know one."

Only problem was, I needed him. I handed him the rope. "OK."

He looked at it in his hands, considering it for a moment. Then his sagging fists clenched around it and he pulled it tight. "You know I would love to wrap this around your neck and snap!"

"You could. And then what? You escape and spend your last days hiding in damp buildings eating rats?"

"After spending a day in one of ARES' cells, I'm not sure that would be such a bad fate after all."

"You help me get out of this alive, and I'll make sure you get buried like I promised. Not chopped up into little pieces and experimented on. Because I promise you, if you cross me, that is what will happen to you. I'll make sure of it. Carl?"

"I'm here," Carl's voice said in my ear.

"You picking up the tracker OK?"

"Yep, it's beeping away quite nicely."

"What tracker?" Benjo asked.

"The one I hid in a marshmallow. I'm not that stupid, Benjo. So, if you do anything but be helpful tonight, Carl's going to send every member of ARES after you with the precise instructions of handing you over to the docs to use you as a lab rat. They won't even bother waiting till you're dead before they start drilling into your skull. Do we understand each other?"

The rope in his hands went loose. "Come on then. I'm hungry."

I slowly lowered myself over the edge of the balcony until I was hanging in the air, reliant on Benjo seeing me safely down. When my feet landed on the slippery surface of the balcony below I looked up and saw Benjo's drooping face gazing down at me. I gave him one last warning look and then joined Aubrey over by a large potted plant.

"Rosalie is really going for it," she said.

Inside, Rosalie was throwing golden cocktail sticks at Zac's head, while waiting staff tried to calm her down. One of them pulled her arm aside and she spun around and gave him a slap so loud the whole room of people gasped.

"Someone get security," a woman yelled.

Just then there was a second explosion from below, louder this time and all the guests flinched as they heard it.

"CP sure knows a thing or two about making a fracas," I said.

Panic swept through the room like a wave, touching each person in turn and soon they were running towards the exits.

As they clambered to get over each other, staff looked on stunned, trying to tell them all to calm down. But no one was being calm.

Even the few politicians I recognised in the crowd were walking very quickly to the doors while trying to make it look as if they weren't utterly terrified. I saw James Miller, his golden hair blending into the surroundings. He wasn't smiling now.

And there was Frankie. She hadn't moved from the middle of the room. She was watching all the people rush around her like she was standing in a train station. Curious, rather than worried. She looked faintly amused by all the fuss.

Kushi edged forward and reached up to take Frankie's hand, while holding her headless doll in the other. Frankie smiled down and patted the girl on the head, reassuring her.

Prestige stepped forward to stand on the other side of Frankie, his eyes wary and tight, hand twitching at his belt. Had he really been able to sneak a weapon in here, or was it just a nervous twitch? Kia was flapping her arms around and trying to drag Frankie away to the lifts. Frankie whispered something in her ear and she calmed down. Suddenly Pia was standing there in a sharp grey suit. He went to sit in the corner, looking miserable.

Only Hamid and Hazid looked relaxed. They were taking the opportunity to raid the buffet bar, making each other eat weird-looking things.

Ella was the first to see me as I walked into the room. She stiffened and then quickly stepped in front of Frankie to block me from her view and shook her head. Warning me to stay away? Well, it was too late now.

The rest of the guests were trying to squeeze into the lifts, but security guards had blocked the way, stopping anyone from leaving. They were trying to tell everyone to calm down and stay put. But no one was listening. They were screaming and crying, helped along by Rosalie shouting, "Oh no, oh no, we're all going to die" a lot while looking at her nails.

Frankie saw me at last and smiled. This time she looked genuinely surprised.

"Scott, I didn't think I'd be seeing you so soon."

I felt Aubrey's hand on my shoulder and saw Rosalie and Zac walk over to stand next to me. "Ah, and you're not alone this time, I see. Are all your friends Shifters then?" She smiled as I clenched my jaw, worried. "Good."

She rolled her head in small circles, as if she was getting ready for a workout. Then she centred her head and glared at Zac.

"You will take your girlfriend here and go home and make mad passionate love to her. A much better way to spend the evening, I think you'll agree?"

There was a moment where we all looked at Zac, waiting for a reaction. Had Benjo been telling us the truth? It seemed so. Nothing happened.

"I couldn't agree more. But I'm afraid I'm not going anywhere," Zac said.

Frankie looked momentarily taken aback. Then she turned her attention to Rosalie. "That's a very pretty dress, my dear. You wouldn't want to get it dirty. Why not go home now?"

Rosalie laughed, a loud clear "Ha!"

Frankie tried again, "Ah, Aubrey. How nice to see you again. I must say, I'm rather surprised to see you supporting Scott. After what he did to you. A strong woman like you should never allow yourself to be..."

"Shut it, bitch," Aubrey snapped.

"Oh, so brave," Frankie said, holding her hands together. "Just like your father. Oh, yes, I know you, Aubrey. I had you killed when you were just a tiny thing. It broke your father. And I can do the same to you."

"No you can't," Aubrey said, her voice cracking slightly, as if she was having to fight to keep her rage in check. "Not any more. And whatever you made Scott do, you're going to undo it."

"Or else?" Frankie said. But I could see we had her rattled. Her power wasn't working on any of us. I allowed myself to breathe and stepped forward.

"Or else I tell everyone here at this fancy party exactly what you and your broken children do."

The crowd had mostly vanished through the lifts; celebrities and VIPs hustled away by security. The few people left stopped to stare at Frankie and us.

Frankie threw her head back and laughed. Then spun around, arms outstretched to the huddles of terrified guests. "These people are my friends, Scott." She turned back to me. "Do you really think they're going to believe an unhinged boy? Look at yourself, Scott. I feel for you, I really do. And I could have helped you–"

"I have proof," I shouted.

"No, you don't." She said it without a flicker of concern. Not a single doubt.

She was right. A photo of Ella and the PM's daughter on holiday together wouldn't be enough. Even all the incidents I'd gathered showing that one of her children had been around when accidents happened would be written off as nothing but coincidence. The only death she'd yet to undo was that of Tsing Ken-ze. And from what she'd said, that could be any moment.

How exactly did you trap someone who could undo every mistake and leave no mark? Even if I managed to link Ella to an event, Frankie would just cut her off and walk away. The only way I could do this was to make her confess in front of hundreds of people, pinning the confession in place. And for that, I needed leverage.

"Tell them, Ella. Tell them what she made you do."

"I just want it all to stop," Ella screeched, holding her hands to her ears. "I just want it to all go away. I never wanted to do those things."

"Ella," Frankie snapped. "Be quiet now. Go home."

"No one is going anywhere," I said.

Frankie ignored me. She shook Ella by the shoulders. "Go home."

Ella seemed to come to her senses. She wiped a tear from her cheek and her body sagged as she let the other choices come into her mind. She closed her eyes, expecting any minute to be back home, never having come to the party. Maybe she'd be in bed. Or watching a bad movie. Anything but here.

I counted slowly in my head, waiting for the realisation to strike.

Ella's eyes snapped open. "I can't Shift."

Frankie looked around. "Kushi, go home," she said.

The little girl did as Ella had done, only she scrunched her eyes up really tight when the change wouldn't come and then started to wail.

"How are you doing this?"

"We all have our little secrets, Frankie."

I circled her, cautious not to block the view of the camera so Benjo could keep his button eyes on Frankie. I was trusting everything to him now. "No one is going anywhere until we finish this," I said.

"Well, well, well," Frankie said. "So it's come to this. You and your family against me and mine. And what for, Scott? So you can have your power back?"

"It's your power that should be taken from you. Look what you've done with it. You've used it to destroy people," I said.

"I have used it to save everyone! You have no idea what I have done for this country, for the world! I have used this power to control fate itself. And yes, I have manipulated and cheated, but it was all for the greater good, Scott. For your good. For everyone's good. Do you have any idea what chaos these petty politicians and men with their money would have called down on us if it wasn't for me, guiding them. Showing them the way to go. Do you have any idea what they'd do to this planet? They'd rape it of all its reserves and then turn on each other, if I wasn't there to stop them. And I'm so tired. So very tired. But I don't have a choice. Isn't that ironic? That I, of all people, don't have any choice?

Once I started down this path, I knew there was no way back."

I resented the empathy I felt for her. I knew what it was to have a job to do, to sacrifice everything in the pursuit of it.

"There's always a way back," I said, because I had to believe that.

She let out a high-pitched laugh that echoed around the silent room. "You want to finish this? Then let's finish this," Frankie snapped, the first time I'd seen the angelic mask drop. "Prestige, kill them. Kill them all."

Prestige looked at Frankie, his eyes sad and questioning. And then he sighed and reached into his belt. He had got a gun in here after all.

Aubrey reached into her jacket and pulled out Sir Richard's gun and directed it at the boy. I could see that he had the steadier hand.

"Wait!" I shouted, reaching out to Prestige. "You don't have to do what she says. None of you do." I looked at all the kids. "I know you don't want to do the things she makes you. Even after you've undone it it's still there, isn't it? Like a bad dream, haunting you. Eating away at you. Believe me, I know. Ella, tell them. Tell them all the things they've done. That she's made them do. You remember, I know you do."

"No," Ella said, tears now flowing freely. "It's bad enough that I remember."

"Nonsense," shouted Frankie. "I don't make you kids do anything. I'm here to protect you. I'm here to protect you all."

"And that's just it. You think you've been put on earth to protect everyone. To make the world a better

place. So you play your games with politicians, manipulating them into doing what you want. And you use
these kids as your pawns. Your foot soldiers. Because
you're too much of a coward to do it yourself."

"I don't like the shouting," Kushi said, pulling her
doll to her chest.

"Kushi, even you. That bunny she gave you. The one
you were meant to give to the old Chinese man. Did you
know it was poisoned?" I said.

"It's just a game," Kushi said, her huge eyes wobbling.
"Frankie said it was just a game."

"Because it is a game for her. And Pia, you know why
you can't settle? Because you're running from yourself
and the things she's made you do. And here's the thing.
She made you do them. They weren't your choices. She
planted them in your head like a weed so you're grateful
to her when she takes them away. Grateful. When it was
her all along. You're just tools to her. Playthings. Nothing more than empty dolls."

"Prestige..." Frankie prompted.

I stepped forward. "What do you think she's going to
do with you when you're no use to her? Do you see any
of her old children around, all grown up and living
happy lives? No, because as soon as entropy sets in
she'll throw you away and you'll be stuck, forced to live
with the things you did." I locked my eyes on Ella now.
Hoping that I could get through to her. "See how she's
already pulling away from you."

"Maybe he's right?" Ella said, stepping next to Prestige
and laying a hand on his outstretched arm. "She promised
me I'd find peace. But I don't feel it. She gave me a home
and I thank her for that. But a home is not enough."

"She's right, Prestige," I said. "You've seen enough death. You don't have to listen to anyone any more. You can be free."

"Aim for his heart," Frankie said, sneering.

Prestige looked down at Ella, then back at me. "I'll never be free," he said. The first words I'd ever heard him speak.

Then he fired his gun.

CHAPTER THIRTY-TWO

———

I heard shouts and screams along with the crack of the bullet. I closed my eyes, waiting to feel its impact, waiting to feel the bullet tear through me.

But nothing came. He missed, I thought.

I slowly opened my eyes, a relieved smile playing about my lips. Then I saw Aubrey was standing in front of me, holding something to her chest. Something red and wet.

Prestige hadn't missed. He'd aimed for my heart after all.

Aubrey must have jumped in front of me, to stop the bullet.

"Scott," Aubrey said in a small voice. Not her voice at all. It was too scared, too lost to be Aubrey's.

She started to crumple and I caught her before she hit the floor. Wet hands held my face and I didn't dare to look down to see where the wetness was coming from.

"It's OK, Aubrey," I said, more to myself than to her. "It's all going to be OK. You just Shift and get out of here. Like we planned."

She shook her head only a fraction. "Not coming with you was never an option."

It took me a while to understand what she meant. That joining me had been her only choice. So she couldn't Shift her decision not to come. But that was fine, there had to be other ones. There had to be. Her eyes started to roll back in her head.

"Stay with me, Aubrey," I shouted, shaking her. "Find another way out. You're good at this. Just don't be here. Stay away from me, like you said you should. Don't come looking for me at the museum. Whatever it takes, find a way out." I was shouting now.

"Since the day I met you, Scott Tyler, there was no way out."

She was smiling, her grey-green eyes locked on mine.

"So, don't meet me," I said, my voice croaking as I knew what that meant. It meant that with a single thought I'd be back in my old life, never having known Aubrey or any of this.

She tried to laugh and red bubbles formed around her lips. "And miss out on all of…" Her eyes went still and the sparkle in them faded away.

I tried not to panic. It was going to be OK. The hypnic jerk, the brain's reboot trick. It would happen any second as her dying mind searched for ways to save itself. The way I'd rebooted myself after Benjo had killed me. Any second and she wouldn't be here.

Only it didn't come.

"I don't understand," I said, looking up at Zac who had come to stand over us. "Why won't she Shift?"

He didn't have an answer.

I looked down into Aubrey's pale face. There was a

smudge of black on her cheek. Dirt from the tunnel or from her make up, I didn't know. I thumbed it away.

Whoever said that dead bodies look as if they are sleeping must never have seen one. Aubrey looked dead. Cold. Absent. Whatever had been Aubrey was gone. I held up one of her hands, and pressed it against my face. But I felt nothing. Only the press of cooling flesh against my skin. Something glinted around her neck. I reached down to pull out the necklace I'd given her. My lucky penny. She was still wearing it.

I laid her to the floor and stood up.

Agony and rage and hatred rushed through my body like a fever taking over me. I wasn't Scott Tyler any more. I was revenge incarnate. I was a focused ball of pure hate. It wasn't even a thought. It was rawer than that. Primal. Like an energy flowing through my very bones. A single, overpowering drive to destroy.

The rage pushed out all other thoughts, unlocking something in me.

I focused first on Prestige, who was still standing with his arm outstretched, gun in hand. Ella was begging with him to put it down.

"Die!" I roared at him. And watched with nothing but delight as he turned the gun and pointed it at his own head.

There was a second bang and Prestige fell to the floor. Ella screeched and held her hands up to her blood-splattered face. She turned to look at me, horror and hatred pulling her lips up into a snarl.

"Go home," I said. And she was gone. I looked in turn to each of Frankie's children. Kushi, Pia and the twins.

With a thought each of them vanished. But Frankie was still there.

The calm, relaxed expression was gone and she was looking panicked as I took another step forward. "So, you can Shift again? Good. Well, just Shift and save your little girlfriend. And none of this needs to have happened," she said.

"I'm not going to change anything," I said, the words escaping between my clenched teeth like gas.

Frankie's eyes tightened in suspicion.

"You are," I said.

I started to run, heading straight for her. And with every pounding step, things became clearer. Clearer than they had been for days.

She'd only been able to control me because I was weak. Because I wanted to be told what to do. But not anymore. I was the one in control now. And she was going to bend to my will.

Everything moved in slow speed. I saw every object in the room in crystal-sharp focus. Brighter colour. Sharper detail. The faces of the crowd, caught in horror and shock, unable to move out of fear or morbid curiosity. The food, on the buffet table, left abandoned and already going dry. Zac and Rosalie, my friends, who were both bent over Aubrey's body, sobbing.

I had Sir Richard's gun in my hand. I must have taken it from Aubrey. It felt cold and surprisingly heavy. I raised it, and Frankie flinched, lifting both hands, not in surrender, but as if trying to calm a spooked animal. I couldn't be calmed.

I pulled the trigger three times. Three sharp bangs. The golden window behind Frankie's head shattered into a spider's web of cracks. I threw the gun down, scooped up a small stool and hurled it straight ahead of me. Frankie ducked as the stool flew over her head and through the window behind. The wind sucked it and the splinters of glass out into the black night.

She uncovered her head and started to get to her feet, to run or to fight, it didn't matter. I put on an extra burst of speed and tackled her, picking her up and carrying us both towards the open window.

She stretched out her arms and managed to cling onto the metal frame with her nails, pinning us both in place like flies trapped in a web. She twisted her head around to look behind her at the golden glass sloping away to the ground five hundred feet below. Then she looked back to me and smiled, realising even if I pushed her out she'd be safe. The angle of the Pyramid meant we would slide all the way to the ground.

Words and images came back to me, crystal sharp.

"Not the original plan."

I returned her smile and heaved us both out through the open window.

We flew through the air for a moment before crashing onto the sloping glass. It cracked beneath the combined weight of our bodies and then we began to skid downwards on the glass slick with rain.

"You're crazy!" Frankie shouted, almost laughing as we spun in circles, sliding ever downward.

But I wasn't. I was totally in control.

The last time I'd felt this kind of power I'd been able to make people do what I wanted. Helped them make the decision I wanted them to make. But that was just the beginning of what I knew I was capable of doing. Abbott had been right. Sir Richard had been right. Even Benjo had known more than me. Changing your own decisions is only the beginning. With the right focus you could change the decisions of anyone you wanted.

Like starlight bending around a planet. Like an architect's plans.

I closed my eyes and roared, pushing all my rage and loss into the single thought. I imagined the Shard as it had been, jutting out of the ground to puncture the sky. I saw it rising above the city like a blade of glass.

When I opened my eyes again, I had Frankie in my arms and we were freefalling through the air, dark glass walls whipping past my eyes. With the slightest effort the golden Pyramid was gone and the Shard was there once more. We were falling one thousand feet.

Frankie's screeching blended with the roar of the wind against my ears. "We're going to die!"

"Just you," I said so softly into her ear as if I was whispering a secret.

Her eyes widened as she realised what I was asking her. No, forcing her to do. I was making her unravel her life, stitch by stitch, starting with coming to the party and going all the way back to her decisions to start Pandora. Every move she'd made in her great political game to save the world, I was forcing her to take back. Every life she'd toyed with, every politician and CEO she'd caught in her web, would be free to make their own choices without her interference. It was either undo every choice in her life from entering the Ganymede project or die within in the next few seconds.

The cars and street below were growing clearer, ever closer. We were just feet away from the concrete when I heard her let out a broken sob.

And the world flipped.

CHAPTER THIRTY-THREE

Consciousness came slowly. Fragments of images flashing before my eyes punctuated by a pounding blackness. *Aubrey laughing*. Darkness. *Aubrey dead*. Darkness. *My sister crying*. Darkness. *Frankie falling*. *Me falling*. Darkness again.

I inhaled a wet breath through my aching lungs and it felt like my very first gasp of air. The air smelt damp and musky, like concrete after the rain.

I dared to open my eyes and saw a lump of flattened chewing gum an inch from my face. OK, so I knew this much; I was lying face down on a pavement, my head pressed against my right hand. I moved a finger and waited for the pain. It was inevitable. You didn't fall one thousand feet without incurring some kind of injury. I imagined shattered shinbones, ruptured organs, broken spine. Only there was no pain. My hand was covered in dirt and small cuts, but otherwise, just fine. I moved my focus down my body, checking each limb in turn. Arms. Check. Chest. Check. Legs. Check. Everything was still where it was supposed to be and miraculously unhurt. I rolled over onto my back and looked up into a black sky.

I was alive. And judging by the silhouetted skyline I could see peeking over the wall next to me, I was still in London.

I peeled myself up off the pavement, sat up and looked around. I was in an alley, which was covered in a graffiti mural showing London on fire.

"That was a close one, sir," a familiar voice said from behind me. I twisted my aching body to see Zac striding toward me with three figures behind him. Regulators, judging by their black jumpsuits and visored helmets. I guess Morgan had called them in after all.

"You can say that again," I said, trying to get to my feet. My head spun again and I slumped back on the ground.

Zac held out his hand to help me up and reluctantly I took it. I hadn't seen the guy in months and now twice he'd been the one to find me while on my arse.

"That Shift registered a sixteen on the Lawrence scale," one of the Regulators said, making an impressed sucking sound. I couldn't place his voice so maybe he was one of the civilian recruits. His uniform was different to most Regulators; he was wearing light body armour and there was a string of tools hanging around his waist. I looked to the other two standing next to him. They too were in the same tricked-out gear.

"What are you on about?" I asked finally, rubbing my palm against my pounding temple.

"Your Shift, sir. It was the strongest we've ever seen."

"Why do you keep calling me 'sir'?" I asked, irritated. This was hardly the time to be taking the piss.

"Er, should I call you commandant?" he asked.

I blinked, trying to clear the glittering spots of light from in from in front of my eyes.

"Zac, what's going on?" I turned to Zac again and realised he was wearing the same uniform as the others. The black jump suit and body armour with ARES written in white type across the chest and three golden stripes on the arm. He was holding a helmet in his hand. Why wasn't he still wearing his tux? How long had I been unconscious for?

"Is that a Taser?" I said, pointing at the yellow gun on his belt.

He raised his arm and looked at it. "Sure, standard issue, sir."

"Stop calling me 'sir'!"

I ran my hand through my hair, expecting to find my shabby curls and found only stubble. My hair was cropped in a close shave. I looked down at what I was wearing and realised it was similar gear to Zac and the others. Only whereas they had three gold stripes, I had five.

I spun around, worried now, trying to work out what was going on and where I was really. I started to run down the alleyway, ignoring Zac's protests and the confused gestures of the three Regulators. I needed to get out of here. The walls were pressing down on me, crushing me. I burst out onto the street and saw I was just feet away from the Thames. Only something was wrong. There were no lights along the Embankment. No boats moving their way up and down.

I ran up a set of stairs and onto what I knew was Tower Bridge. Only when I looked ahead to where St

Paul's Cathedral should be, there stood something that looked like a broken egg.

"What… what happened?" I said, pointing at the shell of the cathedral.

"It was hit in the first strike, sir," Zac said, catching up with me. "Look, I think we should get back to HQ. You might be having a reality attack. Not surprising given the force of your last Shift, sir."

"Stop it! Stop it! Stop it!" I shouted, spinning around in circles trying to make sense of everything. When I finally came to a stop I was facing the river again. As well as the wreck of St Paul's I saw the shells of other buildings, crushed and crumbling.

A loud, clear gong rang out. Big Ben declaiming the time. I turned to my right, grateful that something hadn't changed, and reeled. Vomit rose into my mouth and I doubled over, choking. The Houses of Parliament were gone. In its place was a black crater.

"Big Ben…" I managed to say, once I'd stopped being sick. "Big Ben."

"They broadcast the gongs," Zac said, looking up into the sky. "It's supposed to give a sense of continuity. But sir, we really need to get you back to base." He placed a gloved hand on my back and tried to get me to stand up.

"Back? No, I don't want to go back. I need to…" I struggled to remember what it was that I needed to do. And then it came to me, clearer than the gongs ringing across London.

"Aubrey! I need to find Aubrey," I shouted.

Frankie had Shifted as I'd forced her to. She'd undone her decision to ever start Pandora. Which meant none of the children would have ever been used. None of those people manipulated and robbed of their loved ones. And Aubrey would still be alive. I just had to find her.

"Do you mean Captain Jones?" Zac said, stepping away from me, looking worried now.

"Yes, Jones. Aubrey Jones. Stop messing about."

"She's right here, sir." Zac stepped aside.

The three people I assumed were Regulators had joined us on the empty bridge. One of them pulled off their helmet revealing a shock of messy blonde hair.

"Aubrey," I said, my heart swelling.

She tucked her hair behind her ear, and I saw she wore a black eye patch over one eye.

"Um, yes, Captain Jones, sir. Reporting for duty." She executed a sharp salute. "I'm glad to finally meet the legendary Commandant Tyler," she said and there was absolutely no irony in her voice.

"Meet?" I said, struggling to speak at all.

"I've been transferred to the London branch after Brighton got wiped out in the last attack. I, er, I thought you'd got my paperwork?"

"Attack? What attack? Aubrey, what are you on about? What is everyone on about?"

"War, sir," Aubrey said. "The country is at war."

ACKNOWLEDGMENTS

First off, thanks to my husband, Chris, who put up with more than his fair share of crazy during the writing of this book. You never need to read it again now!

Never-ending gratitude to my early readers: James Smythe, Victoria Morely, Regan Warner, Sandie & Sam Dent, Adam Christopher and Lou Morgan. Without you this book would be decidedly more shoddy.

Much love to my band of cheerleaders: Tanya Byrne, James Dawson, Gwenda Bond, Miranda Dickinson and Katie Marsh who supplied me with endless support, wisdom and cups of tea.

But most of all, to everyone who read *Shift* – bought it, wrote about it, tweeted, blogged or reviewed it – a colossal thank you. I hope you like *Control* as much.

EXPERIMENTING WITH YOUR IMAGINATION

"Wonderfully vivid writing."
Teri Terry, author of Slated

EXPERIMENTING WITH YOUR IMAGINATION

"An enjoying, compelling read
with a strong and competent
narrator ... a highly satisfying
adventure."
SFX Magazine

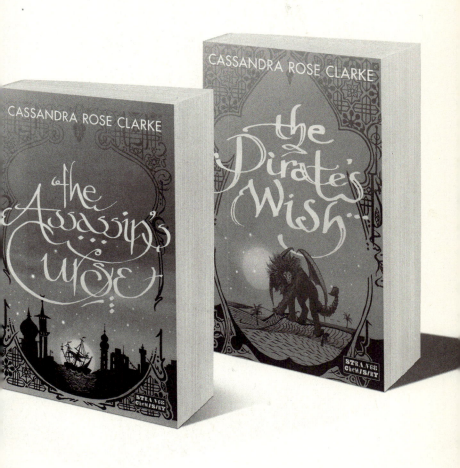

EXPERIMENTING WITH YOUR IMAGINATION

"One part Real Genius and one part War Games... Costa is on my auto-buy list from this day forward!"
A.G. Howard, author of Splintered

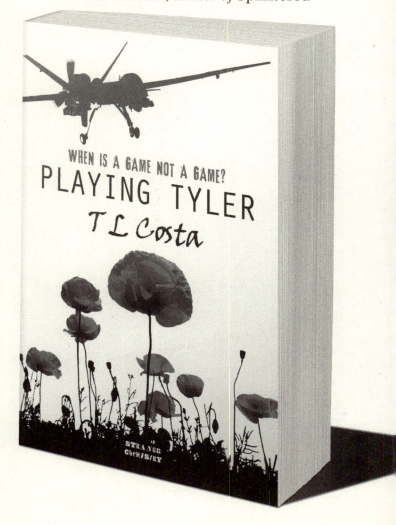

WHEN IS A GAME NOT A GAME?
PLAYING TYLER
T L Costa

STRANGE CheMIS/RY

EXPERIMENTING WITH YOUR IMAGINATION

"A rollicking adventure yarn with plenty
of heart – *Emilie & the Hollow World*
shouldn't be missed."
Ann Aguirre, USA Today *bestselling author
of the* Razorland *and* Beauty books.

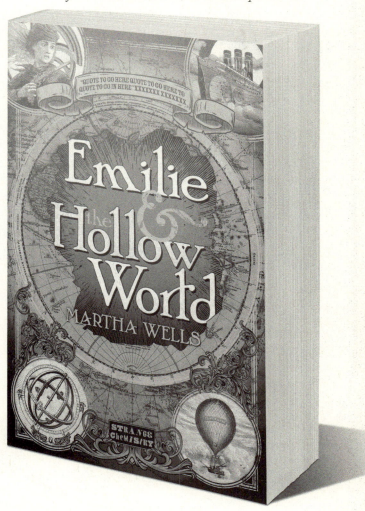

The home of BBC Audiobooks

If you liked reading this book, you'll love listening to it as an audiobook, and the rest of the AudioGO range too!

AudioGO has over 10,000 titles available as CDs and downloads including Young Adults, Sci-Fi and Fantasy and more.

Use this **£5 free voucher** on anything from the AudioGO range.

Simply use discount code **OSPREY14** at **www.audiogo.com/uk** by December 2013.